# MARIKA'S BEST LAID PLAN

## JUDY STANIGAR

ALL THINGS
THAT MATTER
PRESS

Marika's Best Laid Plan
Copyright © 2021 by Judy Stanigar

This is a work of fiction.  While actual places referenced may in fact
exist,  all events are the product of the author's imagination.   Any
resemblance to actual persons, living or deceased, is purely
coincidental.

ISBN: 978-1-7377671-3-8
Library of Congress Control Number:2021947659

Cover  ©All Things That Matter Press

# Acknowledgments

While writing may essentially be a solo and personal journey, many are owed thanks in helping me bring this novel to its fruition.

My first special thanks goes to my publisher All Things That Matter Press for their belief in my book. To my editor Deb Harris and her unerring eye and astute edits which raised the level of my writing, as well as brainstorming the title with me until it finally "clicked."

To my entire writing class and especially our teacher, Laurie, for reading many of the chapters and giving me encouragements and feedback in equal measure.

The list of supportive friends is long, but special thanks go to my friend Dvora who read my first draft and still encouraged me to go on; and to my friend Michelle who did likewise. To my sister Lea, who always believed in me.

And most of all, a giant hug and thanks goes to my husband for his unconditional love, support, and encouragement throughout the years.

*Hope is the thing with feathers*
*That perches in the soul,*
*And sings the tune with the words,*
*And never stops at all...*

~Emily Dickinson (1830-1886)

# ~CHAPTER ONE~

Monday. There was nothing unusual about this particular Monday; it was just like any other day. I forced myself to get dressed and trudge to work, after a weekend spent mostly in bed with my books and movies. The only person I socialized with was Mr. Saperstein, my downstairs neighbor, the elderly gentleman I had adopted as my grandfather, mostly because he was alone and had no family and I understood only too well his plight. Besides, I'd never had grandparents, so why not adopt one? I figured people adopt children, why not grandparents.

Otherwise, on most weekends there was nothing grounding me. I often felt like a leaf dislodged from its branch, disconnected, drifting. Mondays were the days I started growing roots again as I got jostled inside the jammed subway car on my way to work. That I felt a certain comfort by the bodies around me seemed awfully counterintuitive. All my life, I'd craved connection and I found a strange solace in being alone together. A shared solidarity with perfect strangers. We're all together for a moment in our joint mission of going where we're needed—or are at least made useful.

It had been a particularly crappy weekend; it was the tenth anniversary of my mother's suicide. This morning in the shower, while letting the water rinse off the weekend's dreariness, I took stock of my life. In six months, I'd turn thirty and I was losing hope that my empty so-called life would change for me. All my attempts to get a mate have been miserable failures. And the thought of chugging along like this for years was untenable. Suddenly I saw Mom's suicide in a different, more positive light. She made a choice, and who was I to criticize her? I turned off the water and shivered as I reached for a towel. I shivered with fear and excitement. I wasn't ready to make that same choice today. I'd give myself until my birthday, six months, and then I'd join Mom.

\*\*\*

At last, the subway doors opened and I was heaved out onto the platform by the throngs. It was then I caught a glimpse of Cecil's unmistakable leonine head. I was momentarily frozen, memories flooding me. Heart pounding, I sprinted after him. My heel got wedged in a groove and I went sprawling on the ground, headfirst. Luckily, I'd worn pants so didn't lose total dignity. I jerked my foot and my heel detached from its shoe, which went flying. I picked up the unmoored heel and limped in search of the shoe. An elderly woman approached and handed it to me, shaking her head as if to say "That's what you get for running after a man."

She couldn't have been more mistaken. I've never been one to run after men. I was taught better by my mom, may she rest in peace. If anything, I shy away from love altogether. Love means nothing but loss, pain, and misery, and contributes to more unhappiness in the world than possibly even hate. Despite what everyone wants to believe, it was security, not love, that was necessary. Why else are there so many gorgeous young women on the arms of old, ugly, rich men? Not that I'm a gold digger ready for that kind of compromise. I just don't want to always be worried about money. So security is a necessity.

I pressed my fingers against my eyes and tried to focus, to still my racing thoughts about Cecil. The first year after our breakup, I had mistaken strange men for Cecil all the time. I imagined I saw him everywhere. Then, after a year had gone by, I stopped searching for him in every man with a blond mane. I had finally accepted he was out of my life. My dream had been shattered, but not my heart. I had loved Cecil in my way but was never in love with him. He was a trust fund baby, someone my mom would rate "a good catch." So, of course, now, after all that time, I saw him. Unfortunately, I'd lost him again. I limped up the subway stairs in my one good shoe.

I was late for work at the methadone clinic, and if there's anything I hate, it's being late for anything. I inherited my father's penchant for punctuality. Also, having a job where my boss, Phoebe, thinks I'm an ineffective clinical supervisor, I work hard to toe the line. I hurried up the stairs of the 92nd Street station, dodging the crowd, hobbling along as best I could, holding on my severed heel in my hand. I stepped on a discarded paper cup, picked it up, and dumped it into an overflowing trashcan. Mayor Koch had promised to clean up the city. But it's 1985 already, and so far, his success is negligible. Still, I was rooting for him.

For a split second I thought of running across the street to the shoemaker. I looked at the broken shoe and wondered if I should even bother to have it fixed. Such preposterous stilettos. A long-legged model pranced around me like some exotic gazelle, her lean, lithe body making me feel like a midget, which I practically was at five feet and zero inches. I tended to add an inch if anyone asked my height.

The private methadone clinic where I worked was in the dank basement of a venerable brownstone on the Upper East Side. People lived here in their gracious refinement, without a care in the world, not suspecting that the patients streaming in and out of the Care Health Institute were a bunch of heroin addicts coming in for their daily methadone fix. Having a drug rehab clinic in their midst would not be acceptable, so we did our best to disguise our small, ragtag clinic as some sort of unspecified medical facility; hence the ambiguous name.

Our patients slunk furtively in and out. They didn't loiter nearby for fear they'd be sent packing, without so much as a three-day detox, by Phoebe Drysdale, our executive director. She wouldn't hesitate to toss anyone out. Phoebe had the ability to make people feel insignificant.

I arrived out of breath and, despite the still mild June weather, rivulets of sweat trickled down my back. My curly hair, which was no longer quite so blonde without the aid of Clairol Number 8, and which no amount of product could tame, was matted and stuck to my neck. I adjusted my dark sunglasses, hiding my eyes, red rimmed from lack of sleep. Taking a deep breath, I pressed the doorbell, and Theresa, the nurse and my only current friend, buzzed me in.

There was no side entrance to my office, so I endured the daily ritual of walking through the dingy waiting room. The windowless lobby was gloomy, with its garish green walls long since faded into a drab nondescript color. The dirty beige linoleum floor was pockmarked with cigarette burns, even though smoking was prohibited.

Keeping my head low, I rushed through the room. It was crowded, as was typical on a Monday. A few people were sitting on the hard-plastic chairs; others were standing in line waiting restlessly to be medicated. To see a true melting pot, come to a methadone clinic. Addiction knows no color, race, or even economic boundaries. It's an equal opportunity disease and one quick glance at our waiting room attests to that.

Overlooking the waiting room was the nurses' station. Theresa sat, medicating patients through a sliding glass window, like a queen bestowing alms to our one hundred, give or take, patients. She passed out little paper cups with the liquid methadone the patients referred to as The Juice because the bitter drug was mixed with a sweet red sugary drink. Another door, always locked, led from the waiting room to the offices beyond. Before I could make my escape into the inner sanctum, a husky voice stopped me in my tracks.

"Marika, ju late." Carmen's irrefutable gravelly voice and rolling R's accosted my ears. She was a difficult client, though I tried my best not to play favorites. "Rosie's number's up and Theresa don't give her the medication because she can't pee-pee."

I gritted my teeth and reminded myself of the hard life Carmen had led.

"Good morning, Carmen," I said, modulating my tone and forcing a bright smile.

"Ju late, so don't good morning to me," she said, nodding her head and mimicking my overly jovial smile. Fair enough.

I turned to Rosie and, using my best 'therapeutic' voice, said, "Could you give me a few minutes? I'll drop my things in my office and then take your urine. Hold your waters," I added, in a weak attempt at levity.

Rosie, propped up by Carmen, didn't laugh. Her facial muscles were definitely slack, her eyelids at half-mast. I averted my eyes and nodded to Theresa, who finally buzzed me into the inner offices. Theresa, with her no-nonsense, unsentimental ways, kept me sane.

I poked my head into her office. "Goodness, Rosie looks horrible this morning."

Theresa let out a robust laugh. "She sure does. It's been a madhouse all morning; had to do a lot of breathalyzers. 'Cause remember, assistance checks came on Friday."

Yep, I knew that.

"And there's a bunch of patients wantin' to see ya." She nodded her head. "What happened to your shoe?"

"Ugh, the price of vanity." I rolled my eyes. "So, why aren't Kumar and Dinesh seeing their patients?" The two counselors sometimes didn't rise to the occasion, but they were my staff, and we took care of one another. They toiled here by day and went to medical school at night. It couldn't have been easy for them.

"Seriously?" Theresa cracked up again. "They couldn't keep up with the demand today. And Phoebe called, she wants to see you, *toot sweet*."

"Now what?" I moaned.

Theresa tugged at her short spiky dark hair and shrugged. "Don't let the old bat get to you. Anyway, maybe she just wants to tell you about our new shrink? Or about Doctor B's retirement party Friday?" Theresa, unlike me, was an optimist, eternally upbeat.

"More likely Phoebe wants to chew me out about something or other."

"Stop that," she scolded. "Anyway, don't forget to get Doctor B to write you a script for those sleeping pills you've been hankering for before he's gone. You never know what the next doc's gonna be like, so get them while the getting's good. Today!" The irony of using sleeping pills while rebuking our patients when they asked for them may have escaped her.

Theresa called for the next patient to get his medication and I went into my office without stopping to talk to my two counselors. Kumar and Dinesh came to work at six in the morning, and if at times they took a little nap or studied for their upcoming medical exams, I couldn't fault them. In a pinch, I knew they had my back, and I had theirs. It was the Cecil sighting and my fall that had shaken me up and I was in no mood to banter with Kumar today. There was Rosie to deal with, and, worse yet, Phoebe-the-old-battleax.

I dropped my purse and broken heel on the desk, took off my shoes and put on the pair of flats I kept under my desk for days when my feet rebelled from the discomfort of heels. I turned on the light and looked out the window facing north into the back garden. In the afternoon, the office would get a bit of sun, but it was still shady at this hour. I dumped the yogurt, my daily breakfast, into the trash. The Cecil sighting had put me off food. My little fern was woefully droopy; it looked like I felt.

Rosie stuck her head through my open office door. She was the patient I had great hopes for because she'd fallen from greater heights than most, having been a math teacher once upon a time. However, I was mindful not to get too emotional over any patient, for they lived a risky lifestyle and were especially vulnerable now that AIDS had crept into our midst. When I'd just started working here, I'd often stay awake at night worrying about my patients, but it's been over six years now, and I guess I've hardened. Now whenever I feel weepy over a patient, I visualize a pretty Caribbean beach, or some other beautiful scene, to be transported to, like in the Calgon commercial. Take me away.

"Ready for the cup?" I asked, trying to lighten the mood.

Rosie gave me a slack smile. She wobbled and I held her arm as we walked to the bathroom.

Despite having lived a hard life, at forty-one, Rosie was still an attractive, chiseled-cheeked, ebony-skinned woman. From pictures she'd shown me, I knew she was once a great beauty, with almond eyes and a glowing complexion. However, in the decade since she'd lost her last job, the drugs and prostitution had taken their inevitable toll. She could still pull herself together some days, but this was not one of those days. Her eyes were bloodshot, her hair matted, and her skin blotchy. There was a noticeable reddish stain on her blouse, perhaps from a cocaine nosebleed.

I looked aside as she pulled down her jeans and tattered red thong and perched on the toilet. The first time I'd had to take a supervised urine, I was mortified at the idea of watching someone in this private act. Even now I stood away from the toilet, casting sidelong glances at her as she spread her thin thighs and put the paper cup between them. After much wincing and writhing, she produced a few drops of dark liquid. It was probably not enough for a conclusive test.

"Come on, squeeze out a few more drops," I said.

5

"Can I start getting take home meds for the weekends? I'm tired of coming in on Saturdays," Rosie said, enunciating her words slowly.

Everyone starts asking for weekend take homes on Mondays. I'm used to it, and I admire their perseverance, even when they know they haven't been clean for the three months necessary to qualify for them.

"Gimme a break, Rosie. If I gave you a breathalyzer test right now you wouldn't pass it, and I doubt this drug test will come out clean."

"But—"

"*And* you failed the last drug test just a couple of weeks ago."

"It was a fucking lab error."

I'd been waiting for that old excuse. "I can't bend the rules, not even for you. Maybe if you stop hanging out with Carmen—" Right after the words escaped my lips, I wished I'd bitten my tongue. I knew better.

"Fuck you, Marika, and fuck your urine tests." Rosie sprang up from the toilet seat, suddenly agile as a cat, and pulled up her thong. "Here, keep your fucking take homes." She shoved the urine bottle, now full, into my gloved hands and stormed out. A drop spilled on my hand and I winced, despite being gloved.

I stayed behind in the bathroom, trying to stop my hands from shaking. I hated these angry outbursts, a reminder of Mom and her fits of rage. On Mom's bad days, my sister and I would tiptoe around the house. I tried to shrug off the patients' anger, not take it personally, and reminded myself that they were all in some ways broken people. But Rosie was different. She tugged at my heartstrings for some reason. I stood in the bathroom holding the urine bottle, the yellow liquid warming my hand. A knot formed at the pit of my stomach, and I held my breath, then exhaled slowly. It was going to be a long, long day. And I still had to deal with Phoebe.

***

Trudging upstairs to her office, flashes of my interview popped into my mind. When Phoebe'd asked me why I wanted the promotion, I hemmed and hawed about improvements I'd make. She asked me how I saw myself in ten years, and I blurted that I wanted her job. I didn't, not really, but I wanted to impress her with my ambition. She'd scrutinized me and muttered that I reminded her of herself at that age, hungry. *Ha*, I'd thought, *in fact, I have a very poor appetite.*

"Come in," Phoebe's gruff voice came from inside her office.

I tilted my chin upward and swallowed hard, stilling my roiling stomach, as I marched in. My eyes stung upon entering the smoke-filled room and the stench of tobacco assaulted my nostrils. It took a second to find her through the haze, but there she sat, a regal figure behind her desk. Her coarse short hair reminding me of a hedgehog. No makeup, except for blood-red lipstick, a smudge on her thin lips, with their corners pulled downward, making her appear dyspeptic. Rumor had it that Phoebe was in her seventies, but she was one of those people who grew into their age and she'd probably looked the same in her youth.

"Sit." Phoebe pointed to the stiff-backed chair across her desk with her knobby index finger. It was piled high with folders.

I picked up the mess of papers and looked around for a place to put it down.

"Here, give them to me," she said. She dumped them on her desk on top of another pile. "There." She exhaled so forcefully I could feel her breath on my face. I flinched.

My throat was bone dry, as if I had grit in it. I inhaled a short little breath as I fingered the buttons on my blouse.

"You asked to see me." My voice was reedy. I loathed myself for it. I straightened my shoulders and wedged my hands under my thighs to stop their fidgeting.

"You were late this morning. But no need to look as if you're going up to the gallows. Buck up." She gave a short bark-like laugh, which quickly disintegrated into a coughing spasm. I waited while she lit another cigarette, even though the stub of the last one was still smoldering in the overflowing ashtray.

"It's come to my attention ...." Phoebe always started with that line. Somehow everything came to her attention, and it was never a good thing. "It has come to my attention that you went to get a haircut from Pam, *your* patient."

I swallowed hard. That had been three months ago, and I had my hair washed and blow dried, not cut. I fidgeted in my seat, even though I didn't do anything wrong. "Let me explain—"

"Nothing to explain." Phoebe raised her hand. "It's simple enough. We do *not* accept *any* favors from patients. That's a dual relationship and I've fired people for that. There are boundaries, and there are *no exceptions.*"

"It wasn't like that," I started again. "I paid fully for the service. I was trying to show support to Pam for finally accomplishing her goal, for completing hairdressing school."

It took Pam three years to get the courage to go to school; I had walked her to her first day like a parent walks their child to Kindergarten. She'd been so proud of her accomplishment and I had promised her that when she graduated, I'd let her blow-dry my hair. But there was no point telling Phoebe any of this; she'd scoff and tell me I was overly and unhealthily attached to my patients.

Phoebe let out a little snort followed by another short coughing fit.

"I don't need to hear any of your therapeutic reasons." She drew out ther-a-peutic so it sounded like a dirty word. "You crossed a boundary you shouldn't have. It has the *appearance* of impropriety, and that's what matters."

My stomach clenched and I recoiled at the rebuke. "I get your point, but again I merely thought—"

"Yes, I know." The matter was officially closed. "Now, as you know, Doctor Bird is retiring and our new psychiatrist, Doctor Scott, will start next week. And, unlike Doctor Bird, he won't be so … so easygoing. I expect he'll be much more involved in every aspect of the clinic, not just medical matters." She glared at me with her steely grey eyes. A little smile pulled the corners of her mouth further downward.

My armpits were damp. This new shrink would probably be her spy downstairs, a new obstacle to be reckoned with. I knew I was good at my job, even though Phoebe was the ever-present thorn in my side. Now I'd have a second thorn. "I'm *really* looking forward to working with Dr. Scott," I said.

"Well, things will have to change downstairs. I'm disappointed in you; you've been too lax." Phoebe stabbed her cigarette into the ashtray, and I understood that my audience was over.

My throat itched and my eyes stung. I couldn't wait to get out of the suffocating, smoke-filled room. I scrambled to my feet but held myself back from leaping for the door. I'd escaped the harridan relatively unscathed this time. But, damn, I'd let her get the better of me yet again.

\*\*\*

The morning wore on with similar tussles to the first of the day with Rosie, leaving me spent, but it kept me from obsessing about my Cecil sighting. By eleven, Theresa had finished dispensing methadone and the clinic closed for medication.

At lunchtime, Theresa and I went out, as we sometimes did, to the corner deli. I had my usual salad, without dressing, and listened to her go on and on about my being too skinny and not eating enough as she tucked into her mayo-oozing club sandwich. She was what people euphemistically called voluptuous. Like my sister Daphne. No thanks. My sister had the perfect life with a husband and two adorable kids and a house in the suburbs with a picket fence. But I had the slim body.

"Guess who I saw this morning," I said, jabbing my fork into the salad. Although Theresa was only a couple of years older than me, she had a ton more experience in the men department, having already been once divorced and twice engaged.

"Seriously? Out with it, kiddo," she said, her eyes open wide.

"Okay, you'd probably never guess anyway. Cecil, in all his glorious glory."

"What's the big deal?" She shrugged, disappointed in my news. "You both live in Manhattan."

I didn't explain that it'd been three years since we broke up and I haven't once run into him. "For all I knew, he could have moved all the way to Brooklyn, or, worse, Queens." I took a dig at her borough. "Anyway, it got me thinking." I paused for effect. "Maybe it's an omen."

Theresa let out a yelp. "An omen? Gimme a break. Since when d'you believe in omens?"

She was right. I didn't. "I just mean what are the chances of randomly running into someone in this city? Maybe it means something."

"Like what? Don't even think it! If you two belonged together, you wouldn't have broken up in the first place. How's that for an omen?" She slurped the last of her Diet Coke.

"Lots of couples break up and get back together. It happens all the time. People change, mature." That had been Cecil's main complaint about me, my lack of maturity.

Theresa rolled her eyes.

She had a point.

I left my salad half uneaten, and we returned to the clinic.

***

The afternoon, without patients, dragged on. Sitting at my desk with all my paperwork strewn messily around, I became sleepy. At some point, I even closed my eyes and drifted off until Theresa buzzed to let me know she was leaving. It was two o'clock. Shortly thereafter our two counselors, Kumar and Dinesh left, too, although not before we had our daily skirmish about their need to catch up in their chart work. I was at last alone in the clinic with images of Cecil floating in my head. Cecil, my handsome, vapid, trust fund ex-fiancé.

I had just gotten my Master's in Social Work from New York University and was excited at the prospect of becoming a full-fledged working adult, leaving the confines of dormitory life for an apartment in the city. In college, I'd only had one boyfriend, a quiet bookish boy, like me, but he dumped me shortly before graduation because he was going to medical school and had decided he wouldn't have the time for a relationship. We'd never gone all the way, because Mom had brought me up strict. Sex for the sake of sex was whorish. But at twenty-three, my virginity was an embarrassment, an appendage I needed to free myself of. I was advised by my roommate to just have my first hideous one-night stand and get rid of it, be done with it. Still I couldn't do it. To be naked with a total stranger? Have him touch my private parts and me touch his? Mom told me—a lot—that men didn't marry if they got it for free. I was conflicted. I wasn't looking for love, but I *was* looking for marriage.

Then I met Cecil. My first impression of him was that he was confident, debonair, and fun. That proved to be not totally true.

As the memories flooded me, a lump lodged in my throat. I might have given way to a flood of tears had the doorbell not rung at that moment. Startled, I picked up the intercom and peered into the video monitor.

I'd never gotten completely used to being alone in the clinic in the late afternoons, and harbored irrational fears that some disgruntled patient might attack me. The face staring at the camera was unfamiliar and I wasn't about to open the door to a stranger, even in an upscale neighborhood in Manhattan.

# CHAPTER TWO

"We're closed now. How can I help you?" I asked through the intercom.

His response was garbled. *We need to fix that intercom*, I thought for the umpteenth time. But Phoebe was cheap, and I had to pick my battles with her. The last time I'd brought it up, she harrumphed something, but nothing came of it.

The distorted face peered at the fish-eye camera lens. Yellow-flecked green eyes darted around; he couldn't see me. I opened the door a crack. Before me stood a caramel complexioned man of medium height, with a chiseled chin like I'd seen in magazines. Unfortunately, his face was half covered by a mop of medium length dreadlocks falling in multiple angles. He was in his early thirties, I guessed, wearing scruffy jeans and carrying a battered backpack on his shoulder. A little black and white Beagle yapped at his heels and I retreated further behind the door. I'm not used to dogs; we never had pets growing up, although secretly I yearned for one.

Peeking through the half open door, I said, "If you're interested in getting into our program, you'll have to come back in the morning." *Why don't these patients call first before showing up at our doorsteps demanding treatment?* "It's best you leave your dog at home when you come back for your intake. They're not allowed inside." I might as well let him know our rules sooner rather than later.

His eyes narrowed and he looked at me with a strange expression, twisting his full lips. "No mon, me wan see someone now," he said in a heavy Caribbean accent.

He didn't look high, but perhaps he was, so I enunciated my words slowly. "We close for medication by eleven. For an intake, you must come in at nine." I raised both my hands and showed nine with outstretched fingers.

His cat-like green eyes narrowed. He looked at his dog. "Bruce, I think I've been mistaken for a patient," he said, his accent less pronounced now. Still Caribbean, but with an added British lilt. Seeing my baffled expression, he went on, "This is my dog, Bruce. Say hi, Bruce." He pulled lightly at his dog's collar. "And I'm the new psychiatrist, Doctor Bird's replacement. Derrick Scott." He offered his hand.

I wasn't sure I liked his sarcastic tone, and I certainly didn't like to be made a fool of. "Excuse me for mistaking you for a patient," I said. My eyes went to his torn jeans. He chuckled, producing an astonishing dimple in his left cheek. Ridiculously, I wished I'd put on mascara that morning.

We shook hands. His felt a little damp, but I fought the urge to wipe mine after his touch. "We were expecting you next week. I'm Marika Rosen, the clinical director," I introduced myself properly. I've been taught manners. Good manners and etiquette were very important to my parents, especially Mom.

"I came to fill out some forms. I thought the office was open until five" He glanced at his watch. "It's not four yet."

"You want the administrative offices. Second floor up."

He waved his hand. "Sorry I yanked your chain. See you Friday then, at Doctor Bird's farewell lunch. And not to worry, Bruce will stay home," he said and winked. "By the way, I'm looking forward to our working together. Phoebe told me about you." He switched his backpack to his other shoulder, picked up his dog, and bounded up the stairs, his body supple. Leopard like.

I remained rooted to my spot for a moment. This Dr. Scott was not quite the replacement for old Dr. Bird that I'd expected. I was wary. The old doc was docile and mild and didn't get too involved in clinical matters. As long as he could have his little snooze during the course of the day, he was happy to let me do as I pleased. Phoebe's warning about how things were going to change with the new doctor had me worried. I wondered what she'd told him about me. Whatever it was, I expected it wasn't complimentary. She thought I was incompetent. Dr. Scott might pose a much greater danger than his casual dress and friendly manner suggested.

***

I locked up and set the alarm before heading home. The day, which started out on a misstep, ended on a similarly unsettling note. I thought again of my new resolve and a little prickle went up my spine.

I pushed myself onto the crowded subway car. It was packed with the usual rush hour traffic, and I stood the entire ride, struggling not to collide with the tide of people surging in and out. I no longer felt the communal sense that I did in the morning. Someone stepped heavily on my foot and yanked on the strap of my shoulder bag. I was grateful to be heaved out at my stop in the semi-seedy part of Chelsea, way too west and near the river to be fashionable. Truthfully, I could barely afford Manhattan and should have chosen one of the outer boroughs to live in. That I emulated Mom by choosing to live somewhere I couldn't afford was something that didn't escape me.

I'd bought the fourth-floor walk-up with my modest inheritance, shortly after Cecil and I broke up, three years ago. I loved my little apartment. It was my haven. But today, thoughts of Cecil plagued me with an oppressive force. My empty life. I didn't even stop to check on Mr. Saperstein, my elderly neighbor, to drop off the crossword puzzle as I usually did after work. I dragged myself up the stairs, dumped my bag on the kitchen counter, and flung my ruined red shoes across the living room.

Why some people felt better after throwing things was beyond me. Right after my little impulsive act, I picked up my bag and shoes and put them in their rightful place. I'm not normally the type to hurl things or carry on in any way. Then I did something just as uncharacteristic: I went into my tiny kitchen and poured myself a glass of red wine from an opened bottle which had been lingering in the cabinet for at least two weeks. I rarely drank because I figured I could have a slice of rye with a little peanut butter for the same hundred and twenty-five calories as a glass of wine. However, I did on occasion make exceptions to my dietary rules. I do not have an eating disorder, or anything remotely like it, despite what Theresa may have thought.

I took a sip and flinched. The wine had gone bad. Cecil would have admonished me for keeping an opened bottle for so long. He considered himself a connoisseur, and when we were together his wine rack was filled with rare and expensive bottles, although I would remonstrate about the expense. Now my tiny rack stood empty on top of the refrigerator, symbolic of my life.

I tossed the vinegary wine into the sink and ate yesterday's leftover sushi while sitting on my living room couch as I surveyed my apartment. The place was meticulously clean and tidy, as Mom would have liked, even if it was haphazardly furnished with mismatched consignment store finds. I still had Mom's print of Van Gogh's *Potato Eaters* on my living room wall, flanked by two of his sunflower prints on either side. The prints looked off together, but they made sense to me. Light and dark belonged together, like in life.

My parents would have been proud that I bought a place and reestablished the roots that had been yanked out when they died. They were great believers in owning your home so that you wouldn't end up homeless at the mercy of a landlord. Buying a home was security; it was the second-best thing to getting married, preferably to a man who'd take care of you.

I rubbed my forehead; a headache threatened merely from thinking about them and the devastating blow I'd received early on in my second semester freshman year college. That day remained etched in my mind. It had been a typical lazy afternoon, which I spent, as usual, playing cards with my roommates. That dead time after the last class and before dinner. Mr. Wilson, my college advisor, whom I'd seen only twice, called and asked me to come to his office. His voice was kind, but urgent. I could think of nothing I'd done to warrant the summons. I'd been an exemplary co-ed who hadn't even tried pot or snuck boys into my room at night.

The door to his office was shut and I wondered if I should wait outside, but, after a moment's hesitation, I knocked softly. Mr. Wilson opened the door. He put his arm on my shoulder and led me inside. My stomach clenched when I saw my older sister Daphne there. Her eyes were red, and her face crumbled when she saw me. My legs shook as I fought the urge to run out of the room. Instead, I sat in the chair next to her.

I stared at her. "Daph, what're you doing here?"

She was a newlywed, and pregnant. Daphne, the classic older sister, the high achiever who got her law degree from one of the top schools. I was the dreamy kid sister who didn't always have her head screwed on right, who fantasized about becoming an actress. A flighty profession, according to Dad. Dad died after a short bout with cancer in my senior year. And, although I was devastated, his death freed me to choose whatever career I wanted.

"There's been—" Daphne started, and stopped. The tip of her nose reddened, and her forehead wrinkled. She pursed her lips together and her whole face contorted. Her hand shot up to her mouth.

I looked from Daphne to Mr. Wilson and back to her again.

Mr. Wilson cleared his throat a few times. "There is no easy way to say this. There has been an accident." His words floated in the air, hovering before they reached me. "Your mom. She's dead."

"Dead?" I asked.

"Sleeping pills. Accidental, I think." Daphne spoke so softly I could barely hear her.

The air grew heavy and I found it hard to breathe. I sat in stunned silence. I heard the ticking of the large clock on Mr. Wilson's wall. I heard students' laughter in the hallway. The hum of office noise. Finally, Daphne's dark, haunted eyes, brought meaning to the words. Bile filled my mouth. I bent down and retched. At that moment, I felt worse about puking in Mr. Wilson's office than about my mom being dead. The fact that I would never see Mom again did not register. It simply did not compute in my brain that I would never ever, as long as I'd live, see my volatile, fierce, and loving Mom. Not ever.

***

In keeping with Jewish custom, we bury our dead within twenty-four hours when possible. The next day at the funeral, faces swirled around me, like the snowflakes that were whirling around us, blanketing the cemetery ground. Faces talking, crying, watching me with concern, all blurred in front of my eyes, becoming an out of focus silent film. I lowered my gaze so no one, especially Daphne, who was crying wretchedly, would see my dry eyes. My throat constricted, but I couldn't cry. I felt cold, as if I were one of the headstones in the cemetery.

Aunty Sara, a neighbor we called aunty despite Mom's dislike for her, came over to me, wailing. She hugged me to her huge bosom and moaned, "You poor, poor thing. You are now an orphan. They both died before their time. So tragic."

I wanted to shove her away. Instead I just stood there and let her go on and spill her grief. Mine was buried so deep inside me I couldn't even fathom it.

The rabbi must have brought some of the male mourners with him because Mom didn't have many friends; we needed ten men to say the Kaddish. They began the mourner's prayer, praising God. The Aramaic words wafted in and out of my consciousness with little meaning. I didn't find them compelling or consoling. I had nothing to praise God for.

Then came the seven days of mourning, the Shiva, where Daphne and I were supposed to do nothing but sit and talk about our mom. Daily life and rituals were put on hold so we could focus on our loss. We sat in Daphne's house and endured the procession of the few friends and acquaintances who dropped by to pay their respects. It had been a mild winter up until then, except for the day of the funeral, and most visitors commented on the balmy weather. For us, the week felt like one long, drawn out, cold, dreary day.

Finally, it was the last evening of Shiva, everyone had gone home, and we were free to do as we pleased. Daphne, pregnant but not yet showing, went upstairs to her husband Gerald's loving arms. A few days later, she would lose her baby, but we didn't know that then. I remained downstairs alone. My stomach cramped and my throat ached as I sat in the kitchen, cradling my legs and rocking back and forth. A scream bubbled up from deep inside me. I ran to the bathroom to stuff a towel in my mouth so the sound wouldn't escape. When I was sure I had buried the scream deep down in my belly, I got out and went to the guest room. From then on, I would be a guest in someone else's home.

For the next week, I didn't get out of bed, not even to shower. It was only after Daphne threatened to kick me out that I got dressed. That evening as we sat at the dinner table, after Daphne reprimanded me for not touching my food, Gerald brought up the fact that we should sell our parents' house and better sooner rather than later. I thought I saw Daphne kick him under the table, but maybe I just wanted to see her do it and it never happened. There was no point, he had said, in maintaining the house with all the upkeep it required. Anyhow, as he pointed out, Mom had been thinking of selling it since Dad died.

I felt a seismic eruption shake the earth beneath me. I no longer would have a home. Where would I live during school vacations? You think you have some control of things, some security, and then, boom.

Back at school, I changed my major. Three things had dawned on me. First was that there was nobody standing between me and death anymore. I was next in line with no protective layer. Second, that life happens, and we have little control over any of it. And, finally, that I needed to find a profession to support myself. Theater studies now seemed frivolous. That dream was over.

I switched my major from Drama to Social Work. My dad would have approved. And, if I managed to nab a good provider for a husband, Mom would have approved as well.

***

I finished the leftover sushi. It was only nine o'clock, yet I was so tired my bones ached. It was too early to call it a day, and I didn't want to face my empty cavernous bed. Since Cecil's departure, I hadn't shared it with another man, although I sometimes made up a story to Theresa about someone I'd met and had a tryst with.

There was Mr. Saperstein, or Gramps, as I'd taken to calling him, to check up on. Except for a neglectful nephew who lived in Pennsylvania, my neighbor had no immediate family, and I had made it my project to take care of him. Besides, he helped keep loneliness at bay.

I put on my raggedy jeans and T-shirt and dragged myself downstairs. Mindful of the hour, I knocked softly. There was scurrying, clanking of several door latches, and finally the door opened. He was in his slippers and dressing gown. Downy white tufts of hair framed his gaunt face.

"Hope I didn't wake you, Gramps." I liked the way Gramps rolled out of my mouth, and he didn't seem to mind.

"Wake me? Who sleeps anyway?" He grinned. When he smiled, he looked like Yoda. "I was wondering what happened to my crossword today. I said to myself, 'Sam, why should a beautiful *meydele* bring you the crossword every day?'"

16

"I'm no young girl." I said, though it warmed my insides when he called me that. "Sorry about the paper. It was one of those days." I managed a wan smile.

His bushy white eyebrows furrowed. "Is it too late for a cup of tea now?" he asked.

"Decaf?"

"Decaf, of course. What would two insomniacs be doing drinking caffeine at this hour? Ach, when I was your age," he continued with a wave of his hand, "nothing stood in the way of me and sleep."

"When you were my age, you were in a concentration camp, so I don't know how you slept at all." Mom had talked now and then about those camps. I heard enough.

"Bone weary we were. Slept like the dead. Which we were even when we were awake. The walking dead." He chuckled grimly.

I sat down at his plastic tablecloth-covered kitchen table while he put the kettle on. He seemed deep in thought, and I wished I hadn't brought up the war. I'd always been irresistibly drawn to that topic. Mom was a Holocaust survivor, and I was used to the sadness that would permeate all corners of our house, smother us in its perfume. On the other hand, Mom taught me priceless lessons because of her experiences. The most important ones being that life was cruel, trust no one, and your loved ones die.

"No Holocaust talk today," I said, tapping my fingers on the table.

He made like he locked his mouth with his fingers. "Right. Vat should ve talk about?" he said as he poured the boiling water into two mugs. He dunked the tea bag into one mug a couple of times quickly, then took it out and dunked it into the second mug. Finally, he put the bag in a saucer and would probably reuse it in his morning tea. That had been my dad's routine, I knew it well.

I squinted at the weak tea in my mug. "I ran into my old fiancé today. Well, not exactly ran into him, but I did see him."

"That *shmendrick*, the fool who broke up with you?" Mr. S sat down on the plastic-covered chair next to me. He smelled of talcum powder.

"Ha-ha. Call him what you will, but Cecil is no fool. He went to Yale, for goodness' sake." I could hold my head up at the pedigree of the man I had been engaged to.

"Anyone who'd break up with you is a fool in my book." He blew on his tea and slurped loudly. "Crackers. We need crackers." He got up and rummaged in his cupboard for a pack of greasy Wheat Thins. I declined.

"You're very charitable. But I can't really blame Cecil totally. He said I had too much baggage and he couldn't stick around while I figured things out. Matured. Besides, he needed to focus on his career, and it wouldn't be fair to me. I deserved someone who'd be there for me, he said."

"Pshaw." Mr. S waved his hand dismissively. "He threw you that old chestnut? Feh! If you ask me, your Cecil was right about one thing. He didn't deserve you."

"But you don't even know him," I protested. "Besides, by your reasoning, if he loved me once than he couldn't be all bad, right?"

"Don't be a wisenheimer. Maybe he does have some good qualities, but it didn't work out. Lots of fish in the sea."

Right. But obviously I lacked fishing skills. "I've tried, but meeting a decent man in this city is like looking for … for," I searched for a metaphor, "for gold in California. What am I going to do, Gramps? I'll turn thirty in six months. Then it's all over."

"Thirty? And it's all over?" His eyebrows shot up. "You're so young. Why, you can do whatever you want to do. The world is your oyster."

"Ha!" I rolled my eyes. I didn't even think that *he* believed such hogwash. It was just something people said to make you feel better.

"You can roll your eyes at me all you want. But even in the worst of the war—"

"I thought we weren't going to talk about that."

"Yes, yes, but even then there were choices of how we were going to cope with our lot. There's always a choice." He drained the last of his tea and smacked his lips with satisfaction.

"Okay, so what are my choices?" I wasn't being sarcastic; I really wanted to know. Mr. S *was* my Yoda. Old and wise.

"Simple. Figure out what you want, and then go for it. Don't let anything or anyone stand in your way. *Make* the world be your oyster. And if I was, eh, maybe ten years younger, I'd marry you myself." He gave my cheek a tweak, just like I imagined a grandfather, if I'd ever had one, would have done.

Later that night, in my darkened bedroom, I thought of what Mr. S had said. Of course, compared to what he or my parents had endured, a broken engagement was not a tragedy, and I ought to have moved on. Mom used to pooh-pooh all my little troubles. Nothing measured up to her frame of reference. What's the big deal about not being asked to the prom? It was not a tragedy. And she was right. But she would have been horribly disappointed at my still being single. I thought of all my college friends and of how many weddings I'd gone to the summer after graduation. I stopped going to college reunions, for what had I accomplished? I didn't have a brilliant career. And worse, I hadn't married. That was really it. It was the ring on the finger that people at reunions looked for.

I couldn't fall asleep, so I turned on the TV. Johnny Carson was boring and my mind drifted as I looked at Mom's old sewing machine stand over in the corner. It was a painful reminder of what I'd lost. I could see her sitting, hunched over, sewing our clothes to stretch every dollar, because you never knew what catastrophe life had in store for you. All that scrimping and saving so that my sister and I would have what we wanted. Go to good schools; find superior husbands.

My eyes drifted to the floor and the old Navajo, the one thing I'd bought on a trip with Cecil to Santa Fe. If only I had been able to keep Cecil instead of the rug.

Somewhere between sleep and wakefulness, it hit me. Mr. S was right. The world *could* be my oyster. There was no reason I couldn't have what I wanted, and what I wanted was Cecil. And why shouldn't I have him? Cecil had loved me once; at least I thought so. It stood to reason that it would be easier to rekindle an old flame than make a new man fall in love with me. That I hadn't been *in* love with him was totally irrelevant to me. It was a husband I wanted, security, a family. It seemed a much easier task getting Cecil back than finding a man in this city. This project was a no brainer. First, I had to find out if he had married, though I doubted it, for I had scrutinized the New York Times wedding announcements religiously for the past three years. Still, I had to be sure.

Yes, I knew what I had to do. It was time to name this endeavor: The Cecil Project. Mom would have been *kvelling,* bursting with pride, at my new resolution. And if I failed, well there was always a choice, as Mr. S said. Mine would be to exit.

# ~CHAPTER THREE~

On Friday the mood at work was buzzing, as it was every Friday. But on this particular day, adding to the giddiness, was Dr. Bird's farewell luncheon. Everyone loved a free lunch. However, I hadn't been looking forward to the old doctor's departure. Since my promotion, he'd been mostly letting me run the clinic, while he stuck to writing prescriptions or changing doses, between naps.

I walked into Dr. Bird's office where we assembled for our last staff meeting and surveyed my unconventional staff. Dinesh and Kumar were sitting on the tattered couch, chatting in their native Hindi. Phoebe had a penchant for hiring doctors from India who were trying to get their licenses to practice medicine in the U.S. and meanwhile were willing to work cheaply as counselors.

Even though Kumar got under my skin sometimes with his slapdash attitude towards his paperwork, I had to admit he was a handsome man. He was saddled with five kids and an angry wife who hadn't wanted to be uprooted from her homeland. Dinesh, a decade younger and single, left his parents behind in India, but his natural sweet disposition was not dampened by his hard circumstances. Both of them were doctors in India and were studying to pass their American medical exams so they could work as doctors again. Dinesh waited patiently, in his one-room apartment, for the day his parents would find him the right bride back in India; I envied him that. Instead of running around looking for a mate in what amounted to a meat market, it would have been so much easier to let a professional find me a suitable mate. That idea was quite civilized and appealing. Whenever we talked of love and marriage, Dinesh agreed with me that romantic love wasn't important. A deeper more lasting love would come, he told me, and most of the loveless  marriages he knew were happier than American love matches.

Dinesh took care to maintain a professional appearance, no matter how threadbare his shirt collars, while Kumar's clothes were shrunken and sometimes not altogether clean. He often scoffed that he couldn't wear his good clothes to work. I wondered what company was deemed good enough for his better clothes.

"Goodness me, who's getting married?" Kumar chuckled as he

fingered Dinesh's lapel, an impish look on his face. "This is a very good suit. Did you win the lotto?"

"No, no. I am just showing my respect for Doctor Bird," Dinesh said bobbing his head.

Just then Theresa walked in. Her raven hair spiked wildly in all directions; her attire made me think of a colorful porcupine. Her purple dress hugged her voluptuous curves. I made a mental note to talk to her about wearing such revealing, clingy clothes at work, but I knew that I'd never do it. That if I did, she'd just laugh me off.

She eyed me up and down disapprovingly. "Wouldn't hurt you to put some pizzazz into your clothes. You look like a colorless moth."

I tugged at my black and white dress. Given what little cleavage I had, I doubted tight clothes would be of much use. I had taken the time that morning to put on mascara and gone rather heavy with the eye shadow, giving my eyes the odd appearance of two huge blue pools in the midst of a pale, small face.

The meeting was, as usual, long and tedious. It was memorable for two reasons: it was Dr. Bird's last meeting and Dinesh asked me to take his most difficult patient, Carmen, off his caseload. I rubbed my neck and looked from Kumar to Dinesh to Theresa. Trying to unload a troublesome patient caused friction, bickering, and was usually a struggle as we haggled like market people. We each carried a caseload of between twenty to twenty-five patients, depending on our census, with Theresa having only ten, since she had her morning nursing duties. The burden of tough patients was wearing.

"Maybe you'd do better with her, Kumar, since you're so ... so effective with the difficult ones," I said. More bees with honey.

"But I have the most difficult patients already," Kumar said. "Besides, Carmen should have a female counselor."

"It's not a gender issue," I said.

I didn't have the energy to bicker with him. Luckily, Theresa came to my rescue and offered to take her on. She then moved on to call the next patient's name, Rosie, and clucked her tongue. "Positive for cocaine. Again." My heart sank. Obviously, I wasn't as effective a therapist as I thought. Perhaps none of us were very effective.

"Rosie? Are we changing Rosie's dose?" Dr. Bird asked, having just woken up from a quick and apparently refreshing nap.

"No Dr. B, we're not," I said. "And just think, after today, no more worries about the patients and their doses." Theresa stifled a giggle, and I shot her a look.

The meeting went on in that manner and I gave myself momentarily over to fantasizing about what I'd do if I didn't work here. If instead I'd have become a famous actress. When I drifted back, the meeting had deteriorated into chatter about Dr. Bird's retirement. It was time to end it even though many items on the agenda had not been addressed. That was nothing new. They all tromped upstairs for the farewell luncheon, while I lingered, putting away some charts.

When I arrived at the celebration, Phoebe was in the midst of her speech. She was briskly hurtling her words, heaping praise on Dr. Bird, whom she'd criticized vociferously in the past. Unintentionally, our eyes made contact. She gave me a withering look for arriving late. It reminded me of my protracted promotion and how she dangled it before me. I'd been working here for five years past my internship, but when the clinical supervisor position became available, she didn't rush to promote me. It was only after the other candidates turned her down, probably due to the paltry salary, that she offered me the promotion. She was taking a chance on my relative inexperience, she had said at the time, which was why I had to accept only the barest raise in salary.

"It is certain," she concluded, her smoker's voice rising to the occasion, "that Doctor Bird will continue to be productive in his retirement, inspiring us all."

An uneasy silence descended before someone started clapping, and a more rousing applause followed.

"Speech, speech," someone called. Dr. Bird began to talk, speaking of himself in that embarrassing self-deprecating way. He rambled on about the years that had slipped away, and finally introduced his young successor, Dr. Derrick Scott. There was another round of applause, more spontaneous, perhaps given Derrick's virile presence in sharp contrast to the older doctor's stooped shoulders and haggard face. Finally, speeches over, people clamored around the buffet.

Distaste crept up my throat at the sight of the rich food on the table. Copious amounts of fried chicken glistening with fat and mounds of potato salad swimming in mayo were displayed in tin foiled containers, alongside various unhealthy casseroles. I piled my plate with cut vegetables and salad greens, feeling virtuous, as I always did when I could control what I ate. I scoured the room for a place to sit. I spotted my ragtag staff and scootched over to them. Kumar, digging into the overflowing plate resting on his knees, was nestled in between Theresa and Dr. Scott on a couch. Dinesh was crouched on a rickety stool facing them. I perched on the sofa's armrest, next to Theresa.

"Doctor Scott, this is our fearless leader, Marika. She makes sure we don't neglect our charts," Kumar said by way of introduction. He grinned at me and I narrowed my eyes.

Dr. Scott looked up and smiled. "Please call me Derrick. We've had the pleasure," he said and winked at me as if we had some shared secret. His green-flecked eyes bore into me, like he was trying to figure me out.

"Welcome aboard, if I didn't say it before." I offered a thin smile.

"I'm sure you are an excellent psychiatrist. We've been looking forward to your coming," Dinesh said. I have a soft spot for Dinesh, but sometimes he could be fawning.

"Have your wife and children settled yet?" Theresa asked. I'd wondered how long it would take her to get to the essentials.

The dimple reappeared on Derrick's cheek. "No wife and no kids, thank you very much."

Dinesh's eyes and mouth rounded to an O. "Doctor Derrick, you do not want a wife? I'm also not married, but I hope to be soon."

"And best of luck to you, but marriage is not for me," Derrick said.

My ears perked up. Why was marriage not for him? I wondered if he was gay. Not that it mattered to me. I had my Cecil Project.

Just then my nemesis, Phoebe, joined us. "Derrick, you cannot imagine how desperately we have been looking forward to your joining us," she said, raising her wine glass and puffing on her ever-present cigarette.

"Yes, we've all been waiting with bated breath," I muttered under my breath.

She raised her eyebrows and cast me a sidelong glance. "Someone needs to steer the ship right. I think we've been floundering lately. Lost at sea." She paused, turned,, and looked at me meaningfully.

There was some nervous tittering and glances; all eyes were upon me. My face grew warm and I wished I didn't blush so easily. I looked around and saw Kumar's tiny smirk and Derrick's eyebrows raised up. I joined in the joke and smiled as if I, too, found Phoebe funny. But she was wrong about me. I was doing a good job with the very limited resources we had. Having Derrick here to make my life more difficult was something I'd best be ready for.

\*\*\*

Later in the afternoon, I sat at my desk staring at the overflowing in-box. I hadn't made any weekend plans and had nothing to do this evening except visit Mr. S. For me, unlike most of my co-workers, Fridays were not particularly welcomed days precisely because they ushered in the weekend. My weekends before I met Cecil, or B.C. as I referred to my pre-Cecil life, were spent mostly at the movies. On the rare occasions, when I felt could afford it, I'd splurge and go see a play. But those outings were infrequent, for I was raised not to be wasteful where money was concerned. I had other rules, too, when I'd first arrived in New York City, one being that I could go alone to the movies but only matinees. To be seen out alone on date nights was to be avoided at all cost. Instead, I spent Friday, and Saturday nights holed up in my apartment watching old movies.

After our breakup, I'd sometimes talk myself into going out to the clubs with Theresa or one of my other single girlfriends, but those outings were dismal affairs. I'd pretend I was having a ball while Theresa hooked up with a guy. I'd stay as long as I possibly could before feeling like a wallflower, then I'd slink home. Flirting was an acquired skill I was deficient in, as if I hadn't unlocked a secret code. On the few occasions when I allowed myself a drink or two, I had either ended up in the toilet, face down, or, worse, humiliating myself like the time I met Roger.

That night, we hadn't been at the club for very long when Theresa struck up a conversation with a guy. The club was packed. I stood there in my skimpy black dress, swaying and pretending to be loving David Bowie's "All Night Long", mouthing the words I knew, as if I was having a blast watching others dancing. Finally, a short buff man in very tight jeans approached me and introduced himself. I had to ask his name twice to hear him above the din.

"Roger," he shouted. "You're cute. I like short girls." His brown eyes ogled me. "What's your poison?" He pointed to my empty glass.

"White wine," I said, and he ordered me a glass. I took a sip even though I didn't want to drink anymore.

I could tell he wasn't my type, what with the tight pants and mullet. Not what I'd call marriageable material. But that was beside the point. I was tired of being the shrinking violet. And it had been a long time since anyone held me, a year since Cecil's departure. I missed that human contact. When Roger asked if I wanted to go to his place to listen to more Bowie, who apparently he was a great fan of, my pulse quickened. It had turned cool, and we walked fast and purposefully, making no conversation. I tried to tune out Mom's warning about men not buying what they could get for free. This was the 1980s after all.

"Sorry for the mess," Roger said, opening the door to his East Village apartment. There were leftovers from a dinner consumed an unknown time ago on the coffee table. He saw my face and quickly added, "I'll clean it later."

"Well, if you leave it long enough, maybe the rats will clean it up for you." I chuckled. That's what happens when I drink, loose lips.

But he laughed, showing his crooked teeth, and pulled me close to him. "Oh, you're the funny one. Wanna beer?" he asked. I made a face. He took out a Budweiser and opened the cap. It sizzled and he chugged it down.

He yanked me to his chest again. I smelled his beery breath. He bent slightly down and kissed me hard on the mouth, his tongue protruding and wet. I tried to wiggle out of his grip.

"What's up?" he said.

"Nothing. I just thought we'd chat a bit. Listen to Bowie." I smiled, my cheeks trembling slightly. My temples pulsed as my eyes darted around the room. A tiny, scruffy looking cat came slinking in from the bedroom. The cat eyed me with indifference, its tail and back curled.

"Come on, forget Bowie," he said as he put his arm around my shoulders. The other hand rummaged under my dress, found and squeezed my breast as if it was a grapefruit. I felt an urgent need to pee and asked to use the bathroom. He pointed towards it. "Don't be too long."

The bathroom was littered with cat hair. I gingerly inspected the toilet seat cover as I yanked a wad of toilet paper and placed it over the seat. My heart beat faster. I needed to get out of there.

"You okay in there?" he called.

I came out, my mind racing. I was totally sober. My insides screamed *get out*. This was not the man I wanted to hold me. He would not cure whatever ailed me.

Roger took his top off, displaying his hairy chest. "Relax. Why don't you have a drink?" He was obviously not into small talk.

"I … I need to go," I stammered. "I've got my period. Sorry." I shrugged.

"That's okay, we can do other things. How about a blowjob?" He said it as if it was going to be a treat for me. He pulled me close again, my breasts smooshed against his hairy chest. The pendant on my chain bore into me.

My breath grew shallow and I swallowed hard. My mouth felt like sand. "I … I really have to go."

I pushed and he let go of me and laughed an ugly laugh. "It's been a hoot. Maybe we can do it again," he mocked. I could hear his laughter all the way back to my apartment.

That experience just about summed up my last three years of being single in New York.

# ~CHAPTER FOUR~

I locked up the office and ambled unenthusiastically to the subway station. The Cecil Project, which I had yet to do anything about even though it'd been almost week since I'd conceived of it, unsettled my mind. I had no clue where to start, but there was no time to waste. I'd given myself six months. That didn't leave much time to get him back and nab that ring. But somehow my pact with myself felt freeing. I had nothing to lose.

A quick search in the phone book earlier in the week revealed he had an unlisted number and address. If there was a way I could accidentally bump into him, it would remind him of my existence, get his attention. But there were millions of people in Manhattan, and it had taken three years for my first sighting of him. Leaving it to fate, it would take three more years. Fate clearly needed a helping hand. There were lots of Goldsteins in the phonebook, but only three with first name initial C. I had my start.

At the 59th Street stop I made a quick decision, switched trains and took one to Gramercy Park, where one of the Goldsteins lived. It stood to reason that Cecil would live there. It was an upscale neighborhood, yet not as stodgy as the Upper East Side, and it would be a place where he'd fit in. Projecting the right image had always been important to him, trying as he was to break into the rarefied art world. It was interesting the way people chose where they lived; it reflected on who they were.

My heart raced when I emerged from the subway station, and I reminded myself that this would be just a reconnaissance mission. I just needed Cecil to see me. Jog his memory. It wasn't that same childish impulse I had in college when I'd walk by my ex-boyfriend's dorm, the quick glance up at the window, the hope or fear that his form would appear. Or, worse yet, when I'd call him to hear his voice and hang up. There'd been no point to it, but I'd get a momentary thrill, keeping the connection, however tenuous. This time around it was more the idea of inserting myself back into Cecil's consciousness.

There was no reason why I shouldn't be walking past his building, I told myself as I circled the park several times watching the joggers. But no leonine head of hair appeared anywhere. I didn't expect to see him jogging as he wasn't the athletic type, but maybe walking around the park. I wracked my brain for some excuse to go to his apartment building but came up empty. I crossed the street and walked over to the address I had. Like most of the buildings in this neighborhood, it had a secure front door with buzzers on the outside. At least there wasn't a white-gloved doorman to stop me. I examined all the names by the doorbells and there it was, a neatly handwritten Cecil Goldstein, all in capital letters, with his extra curly C. Oddly, my heart raced a little faster, as if I was on some adventure. This was a discovery of some sort. Now I knew where he lived. What gave me an extra warm jolt was that there wasn't another name next to his. He lived alone. No live-in lover. Even my toes were tingling at this find.

This was some start, and I congratulated myself before heading home, excitement brimming inside me. I was ready to face the weekend.

On the way home, I stopped by a video rental store to load up on movies to get me through the next couple of days. A few people milled around, and I perused the romantic comedies section. I liked movies where I could fantasize that I was the heroine. Problem was that I've seen most of them. I came across *The Way We Were*. How fortuitous. It was at that movie that Cecil and I met.

That day, I'd gone to the Quad, a rather decrepit cheap movie theater in the Village, where they showed the classics. It was a dingy old theater, the sort of place misfits and lonely city dwellers ended up. A rainy Sunday afternoon was perfect for the Quad. I'd seen *The Way We Were* before, but it still had the power to move me to tears. It was a schmaltzy love story that hammered home the point of love being a source of pain rather than happiness, as it ended badly for the lovers. I was drying my eyes when the lights came on and I noticed a gorgeous young man sitting in my row, a couple of seats down. He also was wiping tears. Our eyes met. He smiled sheepishly, probably embarrassed, and I found that endearing.

"When you love somebody, you go deaf, dumb, and blind," he said, quoting a line from the movie.

I wanted to tell him that was precisely why *I* wasn't going to fall in love, but I was dumbstruck. He was gorgeous, tall and thin with a slightly feminine nose. His blond hair was his crowning glory.

"Yeah, better than 'love is never having to say you're sorry,'" I said, quoting the insipid line and the inane movie it came from. I mean, what does it mean, 'love is never having to say you're sorry'? I thought love meant you *had* to say sorry. A lot.

"That was the most romantic movie ever," he said. We got up and moved down the aisle.

"Yeah, who wouldn't like *Love Story*," I said, keeping my voice devoid of sarcasm.

By the time we left the theater, we were quoting and laughing at other movie lines. We went out into the warm summer evening; the rain had ceased, and the sun's rays shimmered and reflected off some of the buildings lending them a pinkish hue. We meandered into one of those cafes with tiny outside tables and chairs that seemed too small for real people. We sat at one of those tables in a row facing the sidewalk. I ordered a sangria and noticed Cecil wrinkle his nose. He asked to peruse the wine list and after a few minutes ordered one he deemed "decent enough." I knew nothing about wines and drank very little on account of the caloric content. But exceptions needed to be made. And by the time I had my second glass of sangria I found myself laughing easily at his jokes and even made a few myself.

He told me all about being an only child and about his wealthy and demanding parents in New Jersey. His father was a successful surgeon and his mother the socialite in their small town. I told him a little about my dead parents and, in the process, promoted my dad from a salesman, and a not too successful one at that, to a manager of his sales team. I suppose I wanted to impress him. He said he had a calling to be in the art world and his ambition was one day to open his own gallery, even though his parents didn't approve. He was working at the prestigious Sotheby's, a job he got via some family connections, but soon he'd come into his trust fund and then he'd open his own gallery. Become a famous impresario.

I'm not sure how much he loved art, but he sure loved the idea of being a promoter.

Cecil was a perfect gentleman on our first date; he didn't even try to kiss me, which was a little disappointing. I'd already made up my mind that I was ready to do it with Cecil, and not just because he was gorgeous. I'd started to fear that if I didn't get rid of my virginity soon, I might stay a virgin forever, a fate worse than death. He took my phone number and called a week or so later and took me to the ballet. It was on our third date, which my roommate assured me was quite respectable, that I finally lost my virginity. The whole experience was over in a flash, and it wasn't exactly pleasurable. But I didn't know any more about sex than I did about art, so when Cecil assured me that it was "amazing," I believed him.

\*\*\*

Walking along the street across from my apartment, I spotted a sinewy-figured man with dreadlocks a short distance down the block. He turned and walked up the stairs of one of the recently renovated brownstones. His hands were full of bags and a little black and white beagle yapped at his heels. I could hardly believe it. You'd think in a city the size of New York this kind of thing couldn't happen. I mean, look at how I tried to run into Cecil, without success, but here was Derrick living practically across the street from me.

This was annoying to no end. It was enough that I had to worry about him at work, spying for Phoebe. One of the things I like about living in a big city is that sense of anonymity. Of not bumping into people when I didn't want them to see me, like when I ran out to the store without make-up, unkempt in my sweats. It was the complete opposite with small towns like the one I grew up in, up the Hudson Valley. There, the problem was people always wanted to know your business. Such busybodies, Mom had railed. Whoever thought that people in small towns were friendly didn't live in ours.

As I got closer, Derrick fumbled with his keys, and something fell out of a plastic bag. It tumbled down the stairs. Normally, I would have snuck across the street and into my building before he could see me. I avoid the need of making unnecessary small talk, something I'm quite horrid at. But, feeling buoyed by my new project, I decided to be friendly and walked over. I picked up the fallen object. It was a round case for a toilet plunger.

He looked down at me and groaned, although he didn't seem embarrassed in the least. I handed him the discomforting object and said something about being his neighbor, pointing to the building across the street.

"Fancy that. Well, if you're ever in need of a plunger, or anything else, of course, just pop on over." He waved the case in the air as if it was some sort of trophy.

"How kind of you. I'll keep that in mind, but hopefully the need won't arise." I smiled and rolled my eyes.

"Needs must." He shrugged.

He didn't behave like a doctor. Too informal or relaxed or something. And then there was the way he looked, like a Reggae musician. Waving a toilet plunger in the street while alluding to my possible need of one, was unsettling. Perhaps I'd been brought up a bit on the formal side, but there was something to be said for proper manners.

I said my goodbye, hoped never to need his assistance in anything, then dashed across the street, leaving him fiddling with his keys. On my way up the stairs, I stopped to give Mr. S his crossword, promised to see a matinee with him tomorrow, and then trudged on up to make scrambled eggs for my dinner. It was amazing how much money I saved with my egg dinners; luckily, I was a small eater. Tonight, I had something to look forward to: planning my next move in the Cecil

Project. My mood was upbeat.

The phone rang as I opened my door. I lunged at it. It's not that I'm delusional; I didn't *expect* it to be Cecil, but what if we had some sort of mental telepathy and my presence this afternoon outside his building triggered him to think about me? These things do happen. I tell my patients all the time about the power of visualization.

It was my sister Daphne. "Hey, Rika, how're you doing?"

We're not that close, but she sometimes called me by my childhood nickname and that felt good, that there was someone alive who knew me as a child.

Poor Daphne, she was eight years older than me and since our parents' demise she must have felt that she had to take over where they left off, parenting me or something. If not for her, I probably wouldn't have made it through college. But there was also something maddening about her. She was a reminder, a consistent pinprick of all that I hadn't achieved and that she had. The perfect marriage, to a doctor no less; the law degree; the two kids; the picket fence. And here I was, the unmarried lowly social worker eking out a measly living, with no prospect of marriage in sight. I could almost hear her clucking to Gerald, "Poor Marika, we need to do something for her."

When Cecil threw me over, I became melodramatic and hysterical, threatening to jump off a bridge. It didn't matter which bridge, but I did think of the Brooklyn Bridge. I mean, if I was going to make such a dramatic exit why not pick the most magnificent and iconic of bridges? But I lacked the courage and didn't jump. Daphne was there to help me pick up the broken dreams and glue my shattered ego back together.

"I'm good," I said. "In fact, I'm just fine." I wasn't ready to confide in her about my Cecil Project. Not until I was further along. I suspected Daphne would not be an enthusiastic supporter. If I had a sardonic view of love and the world, Daph was the unapologetic romantic, and she didn't approve of my somewhat calculating relationship with Cecil. She believed in the love conquers all pablum. She'd met Gerald in undergrad, and they'd been together ever since their freshman year. Of course.

"Sounds like you're in a chipper mood. Good. And I have something that may make you feel even better," she said.

"Can't wait to hear." I figured she was going to line up some doctor date for me. She'd been on a mission in the past year, wanting me to find true love.

"Gerald asked a new, eh, co-worker over for a barbecue, Saturday after next. And he promised that we'd introduce him to a gorgeous blonde. Enter you, ta-da."

"Oh, goodie, a doctor. But I'm not sure." I wondered uncharitably if

Daphne's desire to marry me off was a need to be rid of me. I wanted to focus on my Cecil Project. Still I couldn't decline the prospect of a doctor. Mom would have been besides herself.

"Actually, he's a nurse. An ER nurse," she said. "And I won't take no for an answer. You're coming and that's that."

Once Daphne makes up her mind, you can't budge her. I think that's why she made a good lawyer. It was easier to just give in. Besides, I now had something on the calendar to look forward to in two weeks. We hung up and I went to the kitchen. I opened the cupboards. There were the rows of canned goods: sardines, tuna fish, baked beans, everything I'd need should a war befall. My parents taught me to be prepared. In war, they had said, food is the most precious commodity. As a matter of fact, some of the tins were probably past their due date and I should go through them and toss them out. I wouldn't want to get botulism should war come. But for now, I decided to leave the tins undisturbed. I scrambled some eggs while I watched *The Way We Were*.

Afterwards, I went to plot my next move in the Cecil Project. I drew a bath, despite the warm evening, and sat luxuriating in the sudsy water. First things first. Theresa was right, I needed a makeover, a new wardrobe, perhaps branch into color. I saw the way Derrick had ogled Theresa's curves. And while I can't change my body, I *can* change what I wrap it in. I examined my bitten nails; they, too, needed help. And, of course, there was my curly, messy hair. That was hopeless. However, I needed to be ready for when I ran into Cecil. A new image was essential for my success.

# ~CHAPTER FIVE~

On Saturday a week later, I got up bright and early, energized by my new venture: my reinvention. A healthy yet figure-friendly breakfast was a must. No point in acquiring a new wardrobe if I turned into a pudgy little thing. Being short meant that there was nowhere to hide extra poundage. Speaking of which, it was time to join a gym. I was slim but I could visualize cellulite like cottage cheese, taking over my thighs. A truly horrific prospect. Breakfast was a challenge, though, because I'd been having my eggs at dinner and too many eggs could cause cholesterol build-up. One had to be vigilant. I grabbed a fat free yogurt and sprinkled it with a few nuts and refused to count the calories because it was all good fat. I showered, dampened down my mop of hair with tons of product, and off I went.

Mom exhorted, even in her sad periods when she stayed home days on end in her bathrobe, that one must not scrimp when it came to clothes. Clothes and shoes make the woman. Mom's wardrobe was lean, but she always looked elegant. She'd made her clothes herself from the finest fabric she could afford. Unfortunately, my budget made me a fixture at the discount stores, with occasional forays into Macy's on sale days. I, too, stuck to simple, unfussy clothes. Elegant was the operative word. That day, I set my sights on Saks Fifth Avenue. Desperate times called for desperate measures. Nothing less would do for my metamorphosis.

I entered the posh store looking around furtively, an interloper who didn't belong in this glamorous place. The ground level, with its cool marble flooring, was festooned with over-the-top flower bouquets reaching the ceiling, and I was immediately accosted by the exotic smells emanating from the perfume counters. Perhaps it would be a good idea to start with a new fragrance to go with the new me, for I couldn't remember a time when Cecil complimented me on the way I smelled. Perfume was an indulgence, but I shoved down parsimonious thoughts. I stopped by the Chanel counter. The saleslady at first ignored me. I waved to her. She came over and spritzed from one of the bottles onto a tiny strip of paper, waved it in the air, and then offered it to me.

"Always wait a few seconds before smelling," she instructed. "There is nothing like Chanel Number Five; a classic," she added with some satisfaction, as if she had created the scent herself.

I inhaled. It smelled like Mom. For a moment I saw her spritzing herself whenever she and Dad went out, which wasn't very often. I was loyal to Mom, but her smell would be a constant reminder of my loss. I thanked the woman and moved on to the next counter. A young man with an odd hairstyle, a cross between a mullet and a shag, handed me another strip of paper.

"Try our new Poison, by Dior. Forbidden fruit is always the best," he said with a conspiratorial wink. "Very sexy."

A strong spicy, oriental scent assaulted my senses. Yes, it was definitely not me. "I'll take it," I said, although I wasn't sure how a scent could be sexy. I gave him my credit card, my hands shaking a little.

Armed with my pretty new perfume bottle, tucked into its tiny shopping bag, I took the escalator up to the second floor. It was quiet as a morgue and I swiftly discovered that it would take a good chunk of my yearly salary to buy just a couple of things, let alone a whole new wardrobe. The saleswoman took one look at me in my jeans, T-shirt, and espadrilles and suggested I ought to check out the sixth floor where I'd find more youthful merchandise. I wondered what made her so sure that I couldn't afford the designer floor, even though I was fondly carrying my snazzy new shopping bag sheltering my "forbidden fruit."

The upper floor was livelier, positively bustling with shoppers and I was left to my own devices, the sales force being busy with giraffe-necked gorgeous women who looked like they belonged there. The rich all seem to be tall and beautiful, like some super race. I wasn't envious of their looks, for they, too, would grow old and lose them one day. I imagined that the more gorgeous you were, the harder getting old would be. Age, the great equalizer.

I meandered amongst the colorful racks, furtively looking at the price tags. Even on this floor the items were outrageously expensive. Double or triple what I'd pay at Gimbles. Finally, a young woman approached me with a friendly smile and asked if there was something she could help me with.

"I'm just browsing … not sure what I'm looking for … a kind of makeover," I finally confessed.

That perked her up. Her eyes sparkled. "Of course, something to freshen you up for summer. And you're so petite; we've got just what you need. Come with me."

I followed her obediently as she picked up one colorful outfit after another, each time pointing out the merit of an item and how it would set off my blue eyes or enhance my pallid skin. She kept popping into the dressing room, admiring at how perfectly the clothes fit me.

I was transported momentarily to a day long ago. Mom had taken me shopping before sending me off to college. She wasn't going to let her daughter dress like those teenagers with their ratty T-shirts and sloppy jeans. No. College was a place of higher learning, the *intelligentsia*, she had said, and one must dress accordingly. We'd taken the train to Manhattan for the occasion, and she led me straight to Bloomingdale's. She seemed so happy that day, picking outfits and taking pride at how cute I looked. We picked several dresses and skirts and tops and spent more on me than she'd ever done on herself. I never had the heart to tell her I hardly wore those clothes. That I'd wanted to blend in with scruffy jeans and T-shirts.

"Wow, you look amazing in that. You're so cute," the salesgirl said, elongating the word with delight when she came to check up on me. She scrutinized me up and down as I stood displayed in a tubular, neon green dress, cinched at the waist with a wide purple belt. The exaggerated shoulder pads and short hemline made me look like an inverted triangle. Mom, a firm believer in *not* following trends, and certainly in not showing too much skin, would not have approved, but the svelte salesgirl assured me that I looked amazing and it was all the rage. I was torn.

My face must have registered doubt for she asked, "What kinda work do you do?" I told her. "Stay right where you are. I've got just the thing for you."

I eyed myself in the mirror. A colorless moth Theresa had called me. Now encased by mounds of iridescent hues, perhaps I was turning into a butterfly. My new fashion consultant returned with a bunch of suits on hangers. Did she think I was made of money? I wondered if she heard my heart's fast drumbeat.

"The power suit," she said, displaying a pantsuit on the hanger. "This one in particular is perfect." She pulled one out from the bunch.

The blazer with its wide shoulders was at least in black, and when I put it on, I felt like I grew a few inches, at least in the shoulders.

"I'll take it," I said. "And I'll take the dress and the little black skirt, too," I added breathlessly.

"Wonderful," she cheered me on. "What about this top? It emphasizes your slender waist and gorgeous blue eyes. It'd be a shame not to take it," she said sadly, as if the thought of the top languishing on the rack instead of showcasing my lissome body was tragic.

My palms sweated as I added in my head the cost of all these items. It was more than I spent in a year. But I remembered that if my project failed, I wouldn't need any money, so why worry about it now. Besides, it takes spending money to make money. "Yes," I blurted out impetuously. "I'll take the top, too."

Her eyes shone with delight. "You ought to get large hoop costume earrings to go with that dress," she said. "And stop by the make-up department and check out the new eye shadow colors. If you smooth out your curls with a new hairstyle, you'll look just like Krystal from *Dynasty*." I did have high cheekbones like Krystal, that much was true.

By the time I offered my credit card and signed the bill, I started regretting my profligate way. I practically ran down the escalators and didn't stop by the makeup counters, or the custom jewelry. I didn't stop until I was outside the store, my heart still racing.

I decided to take the bus home instead of the subway. It would be a treat, and I felt no rush. It was nice to relax and watch Fifth Avenue with its tourists and Saturday shoppers carrying their bags, perhaps like I did, with guilty pleasure. I was still agitated by my afternoon extravagance but yet by the time I got off the bus I fairly skipped home. Down the block from my apartment I saw Derrick walking his dog. Would I always be running into him now? I bowed my head and quickened my steps. But his dog with the odd name, Brian or Bruce, must have recognized me and came running towards me, wagging his tail.

I flinched and stepped aside. Derrick held him back. "Not everyone is a dog person, Brucie," he said.

"I like dogs," I said. Dad had taught us that dogs were unclean animals and never to let them lick us because you never knew where their tongues had been. He squashed any childish request of getting one. I switched my bags to one hand and bent down to pet Bruce. He yelped and I jumped back.

Derrick chuckled. "Dogs can tell when people are afraid of them. But really Bruce is a very gentle dog."

"I'm sure he is and I'm not afraid." I chafed. That's all I needed, for him to analyze me as some neurotic, dog fearing nut job. "As a matter of fact, I'm quite fond of dogs." I straightened up and re-shifted my bags.

"You've been shopping," he said, nodding at my Saks's Fifth Avenue bags. "High end."

That was rather cheeky of him. "I stole these bags. I shop at discount stores and put my stuff in expensive bags. So there."

He snorted. "And here I feared you lacked a sense of humor."

"I crack myself up all the time," I said, and flicked my mop of curls out of my face.

"Don't we all. Don't we all," he said.

I could think of nothing else to say and finally I mumbled, "Well, have a nice weekend."

"See ya Monday," he said, producing his dimple. "Week two."

"Hope you like it so far. We all love the place," I said as I crossed the street. I figured he'd find out how dysfunctional Phoebe's clinic was soon enough, so why spoil it for him? He'd been pretty innocuous in his first week, hardly making himself noticeable and I started to relax, just a little.

I didn't let my encounter with Derrick distract me. It had been a productive day. I was making headway in my makeover goal, the first step in the Cecil Project.

On my way up to my floor, I popped in for a quick visit with Mr. S. He was nursing a cold, but he wanted to see everything I got. He made me take out every item of clothing.

"Wow," he said when I waved my green dress in the air. "That's what they call a statement piece, right?"

"Listen to you," I marveled. "A statement piece."

"I may be old but I'm not dead yet. You learn lots of useful things watching daytime T.V. This week I was told that age is just a number. Feh." He waved his hand dismissively.

"Isn't it? I hear it all the time."

"Don't you believe it, Maritchka. It's a number all right, one that tells you how soon your number will be up."

He was right but I didn't like to hear it. "Stop it, Gramps. You're gonna be around a long time. Tomorrow, the Sunday crossword. The week's crown jewel."

"Aha, something to look forward to. And pastry. Don't forget, the Sunday pastry. Can't do the Sunday puzzle without it," he said before I went upstairs.

There was still Saturday night to get through. But my heart continued skipping excitedly from my morning shopping spree. I made myself a salad and ate it without dressing or bread. I cleaned up and started thinking of the next step of my Project, but I came up empty. I didn't feel like watching a movie and looked at the pile of library books on my shelf. None were appealing. Instead, I buried my head in a Jane Austen novel. My current favorite is *Persuasion*, because it's about a second chance at marriage. Anne, a heroine closer to my own age than Austen's usual heroines, and Captain Wentworth had broken off their engagement due to a misunderstanding. Just like Cecil and I did. Perhaps Jane would show me the way, for my own plan still lacked clarity or imagination.

# ~CHAPTER SIX~

The following Monday, I ran a little late as I had been up half the night trying to figure out how to proceed with my Cecil Project. The red digits on my alarm clock flashed 2:00 a.m. before a wisp of an idea came to me and I finally dozed off to a dreamless sleep.

I dumped my things on my office desk and hurried over to Derrick's office, hoping he hadn't noticed that it was a bit past nine. I had to watch it now that Phoebe had her spy in my midst probably snitching on my every move. His door was wide open and, to my annoyance, I found Theresa in his office. She was standing with her back to me, actually leaning on his desk, while he sat reclined in his chair, his feet propped on his desk. They seemed so chummy. Theresa's easygoing manner with men set off my own awkward ineptitude.

"Don't mind her. She can get snippy. She's just uptight, a bit insecure. It's best—" Theresa stopped in mid-sentence when Derrick coughed. She turned around. "Marika! I was just briefing Derrick on Charles; he's asking for a dose increase."

My earlobes tingled from what I'd overheard but I pretended not to mind. "Sorry I'm late. I forgot to tell you I had a dental appointment this morning," I lied. I pasted a wide grin on my face. "As for Charles, maybe if he didn't do so much cocaine, he wouldn't need an increase in methadone. He's speed-balling."

Derrick took his feet off his desk and sat upright. "He wants to know his dose. Most clinics don't medicate in the blind the way you do here. That's a bit unusual. I'm surprised the patients don't rebel."

"I suppose they would if they could. But we've been through the blind medication dilemma many times and concluded that patients not knowing their dose kept them from fixating and obsessing and arguing about it," I explained patiently, though I didn't appreciate his questioning our policy; he's only been with us, what, five minutes.

Derrick cleared his throat. "I'm sure there're pros and cons. Maybe we'll discuss it some other time, perhaps bring it up at our next treatment team meeting."

"You're the medical director, it's really your call," Theresa chimed in. "Besides, our meetings, as you'll see, go on and on and on, and often end with nothing resolved. Doctor Bird used to doze off. Right?" She looked at me for verification.

I'd noticed that she'd taken extra care with her appearance since Derrick's arrival. Her eyes were adorned with heavy false lashes. I had on my new power suit that day, although as yet I didn't feel very empowered.

Derricks' eyes darted between the two of us. He sat straight in his chair, while his hand rubbed his chin, like *The Thinker*, but with dreadlocks.

"We'll talk more later," he finally said as he got to his feet. He stretched his lithe body, then pulled at his dreadlocks. "I have a meeting with Phoebe in a few. I'll meet with Charles tomorrow to discuss his dose."

"Maybe after lunch we can talk some more. Unless you'd rather we do a working lunch," Theresa called after him.

A working lunch. I nearly rolled my eyes. Theresa never worked through a meal. Subtlety was not her strong suit, either. Obviously, she'd already set her eyes on Derrick for the role of hubby number two, and she was welcome to him. Although I wanted to remind her he'd said he wasn't the marrying kind.

I approached my weekly woman's support group with little enthusiasm. I wanted the morning over with so I could focus on my Cecil Project. On my way to the group room, I heard a commotion coming from the waiting room and darted out to see what was going on. Rosie and Carmen stood glaring at each other as a few lingering patients were egging them on. Neither Kumar nor Dinesh were around; they were probably holed up in their offices having sessions, or studying. Theresa had gone to the bathroom and Derrick was on his way to see Phoebe.

"You think I don't know you been fucking that bitch, you motherfucker," Carmen screamed, her face purple.

"Who you callin' motherfucker, bitch," Rosie bellowed. Arms stretched, she shoved Carmen.

Carmen lunged at Rosie, scratching her face with her long nails.

"Hey, you two stop it. Stop it right now!" I wished my voice was more sonorous, instead of so wispy. They ignored me. Blood rushed to my face. I shoved myself between them. "You can't do that here. Stop, or I'll call the police," I shouted.

The two women disengaged momentarily and stood glaring at me before Carmen said, "She been using me, pimping—"

"I—" Rosie started.

"Hey, what's going on?" Derrick's voice boomed. The three of us jumped. He stood looking at us, his green eyes blazing.

"We just been waiting for group and talking. That's all," Carmen said, an innocent grin on her face, showing the gap where her two front teeth once were.

"A little family squabble," Rosie agreed. "Marika knows us with our spats." Rosie put her arm on my shoulder in an affectionate gesture. They were such good actors; I had to give them that.

"Didn't sound like a little family spat to me. You okay?" He turned to me.

"Fine … of course I'm fine," I said, moving away from Rosie's arm. A chaotic clinic with an ineffective leadership was not the impression I'd hoped to convey. Now he'd have something to report to Phoebe: that the patients were treating me more like a friend than a professional, and the clinic was in disarray. My new power suit had failed me.

I spoke up. "Okay, everyone, if you've been medicated and are not waiting to see your counselor, please leave. The show's over." I turned to the two women. "And you two go to group. I'll be there shortly." I followed Derrick to the nurses' station.

"Does this … this kind of thing happen often?" he asked.

"Of course not. We have a strict no violence policy. But they come here daily and sometimes tempers flare." I shrugged. "It was a family squabble."

"More like a free-for-all. What are the consequences?" he asked.

"We're *supposed* to remove their take home privileges, or put them on a probationary status," said Theresa who just walked into her office. "But we rarely enforce the rules." She looked at me with pursed lips.

"Our clients have had plenty of negative consequences in their lives. I believe in positive consequences," I said, shooting her a withering glance.

"Hmm. In Jamaica we believe in 'spare the rod, spoil the child.'" He looked down at his sneakers. "Not that I believe it's the best way to bring up kids, of course. But …."

I laughed. "You're not suggesting that we *spank* our patients?"

He looked at me oddly. "I was only suggesting that maybe we should follow up with consequences. Rules are rules, or why bother having them."

"They really didn't threaten anyone, and it *was* a family fracas. Really. We can't be *that* strict; they respond better to positive rewards," I said. He might be a psychiatrist, but he'd have to learn to adapt, get his head out of his ivory tower. "This is the world we have to deal with. You'll soon get it."

He looked at me as if something had dawned on him, smiled, and raised his hands, palms up, in what I took to be surrender. "It's a slippery slope, is all I'm saying. But it's your call."

As if. "Thanks," I said and turned on my heels. On my way to the group room, I stopped by my office and popped a couple of Tums to sooth my roiling stomach before I entered the lion's den, aka my women's support group.

The group I'd started a few months ago was depressing as all hell. It had taken me months of cajoling and prodding to get the six women to join. And so far, the group hadn't gelled. They were tough customers.

We met in the small, antiseptic, colorless exam room used by the internist who came in twice a month to perform physicals. I had intended to bring in posters and plants to make the space more welcoming ,but hadn't gotten around to it, and I made myself a yet another mental note. It was a long, windowless, narrow room, and some women shoved their chairs further out of the circle while others sat at an angle only partly facing the circle. On this day, Carmen had pushed her chair completely out of the circle. I'd had misgivings about putting Carmen and Rosie, the on again/off again lovers, in the same group. But in this, the real world, I often had to do things that would be considered unorthodox in the books.

"Sorry 'bout this morning," Rosie began. She sniffed. "We shouldn't have gotten into it in the clinic."

I assumed everyone in the group already knew what had happened, and I also knew the story'd undoubtedly gotten embellished in the re-telling.

"You don't want Marika to know you a cheatin' bitch," Carmen said. "But everybody here know you."

"Now we gotta listen to this shit," said Cindy, a rail-thin, harsh looking woman in her thirties. She raised her two hands and pointed her fingers. "You two been knowin' and cheatin' on each other a long time. Tell us something we don't know."

The women burst out laughing and talking all at the same time. I raised my voice and clapped my hands to gain control. "Now, ladies, let's try to be supportive of each other. Yes, relationships are difficult—"

Carmen interrupted. "I ain't never cheated on her."

"Gimme a break. You were with different men every night," Rosie said.

"That's different. They was johns. Business is business."

This comment was followed by another round of raucous laughter.

"You'd think two dikes in love would behave better than men do. But it don't matter. We're all the same. Everybody cheats," said Anne, a morose woman who seldom had anything positive to say. "Ain't that right, Marika?"

As if I was an expert on relationships. My mind drifted to my father, who had been devoted to my mother, and yet they weren't very happy, either. I thought of them and of Rosie and Carmen and of how people in love hurt each other all the time no matter how much in love they were. What was the point? Why did everyone rush to fall in love? It clearly was not the cure for unhappiness.

I said something inane about relationships and made other generalizations, and the conversation drifted aimlessly on. I was relieved when the group was over. On the way back to my office, I waylaid Rosie and chided her for the morning's fracas.

"And must you always dummy yourself down? The way you talk around here, as if you don't know any better," I rebuked her. Rosie, who was undeniably intelligent, and had a master's degree, talked like a street person when around her peers.

Rosie let out a hoot. "Man, Marika, what you think, that out on the street I talked like the teacher I was? You have to fit into your environment to survive. Love ya, Marika, but, man, you're naive." She blew me a kiss and walked off, laughing her infectious laugh. I was astounded at how different she was when she wasn't high, although I suppose the same could be said about everyone.

First thing I saw when I opened my office door were the tons of charts covering my desk. I looked at them with distaste. Writing notes was the least favorite part of my job; I had that in common with Kumar and Dinesh. And I was in no mood to write up group notes. The whole morning had left me feeling spent. Then I remembered my Cecil Project and leaped up from my desk. It was time for Step Two.

I grabbed the phonebook and called Sotheby's. "No," the snooty receptionist informed me, Cecil no longer worked there; he'd left a few months ago. The receptionist was all too eager to share that, as a matter of fact, he was now a partner at a new art gallery somewhere on the Upper East Side. But she couldn't or wouldn't give me the name. No biggie. How many art galleries could there possibly be? Most, I thought, were on Madison Avenue, so I'd start there. This was exciting. I felt like some detective on T.V. as I scanned the yellow pages. As it happened, there were quite a few galleries in the area, with names like La Maison d'Art or Urban Art and some with the owners' names. Cecil Goldstein was not one of those. However, they were all within a few blocks from one another, so how hard would it be?

The next step in my Cecil Project was about to get launched.

# ~CHAPTER SEVEN~

I emerged from the dank building and luxuriated in the sun's warm rays caressing my face. Soon enough it would get sweltering hot and oppressive, wet blanket humidity would descend on the city. Summers in New York could be hellish if you didn't have your country house to escape to, and I didn't. But for now, it was one of those perfect June days. Armed with the list of galleries, I started walking south in the direction of Madison Avenue.

Tiny café tables filled the sidewalks outside the restaurants, and people were sitting reveling in the warmth of the day. Waiters hurried back and forth with their trays of salads and steaming soups. I was engulfed by aromas tickling my senses. My stomach rumbled, and I remembered that I hadn't eaten anything except for my fat-free plain yogurt. I decided to ignore my hunger and focus on the task at hand. I came to the first gallery, with the inane name Art People, whatever that meant. I peeked inside their large windows and saw huge canvases of faces painted in vibrant, unnatural colors. It didn't seem to be the kind of place Cecil, with his taste in abstract art ,would own. But, then again, as owner, he might have to be flexible, not his strong suit. I walked in.

A young, anorectic-looking woman with yellow hair sat at her desk eating a salad. She welcomed me and asked if she could be of any help. I said I was just browsing and pretended to admire the paintings as I made non-committal murmurs while I walked from painting to painting. She handed me a brochure and told me about the young artist they were featuring. She went on and on enthusiastically. I glanced at my watch; this was taking too much time and I had a long list of galleries to check out. I finally asked her point blank if she knew the gallery owner because I was new in town and was looking to reconnect with an old friend. Turned out it wasn't Cecil. I thanked her and walked out. I'd have to make this process quicker, I realized as I went in search of the next gallery on my list. Meanwhile, I rehearsed in my mind that if I should find his gallery, I'd pretend to have developed a sudden interest in art and that I was even thinking of taking watercolor classes. I was amazed at how easily these little fibs occurred to me even though I'd been raised not to lie.

I went through half a dozen galleries and came up empty. *Bubkes,*

Mr. S would say. It was an idiotic idea. Even if I *had* located Cecil's gallery, he probably wouldn't believe I'd just happened to walk by. I'd have to find another way to accidentally run into him. If I could only get the opportunity, I felt sure I could prove to him that I was a changed woman. That I had matured tremendously in the three years we'd been apart, and I was worthy of a second chance. This time around, I'd be more accommodating, too. I'd let him have his way in all things. I thought of one of Mom's saying: first get the horse, worry about the cart later. Message clear. Get your man first, worry about the rest later.

I turned and walked dejectedly back uptown on East Central Park. The park benches were taken by people eating their lunches, sandwiches or salads, from greasy bags brought from home or nearby delis. A man in a baseball cap looked up from his plastic container at me and smiled a crooked smile. The smile reminded me of Cecil, but, then, the sun was in my eye and I figured it only looked like him because I'd been thinking of him. I must have conjured him up. I looked again. He raised his hand and waved tentatively. It was him. I froze. Then my heart started pounding.

Instinctively, I wanted to duck behind a shrub to gather my wits. Despite praying for this moment, playing it out a million times in my mind's eye, now that I had him in my sight, I was paralyzed. But surely it was an omen of some sort that I'd actually found him, given the odds. Remember, "The world is your oyster," Mr. S had said. I wiped my sweaty hands on my pants and walked over.

He rose to his feet, and we stood awkwardly, facing each other. Thankfully, our sunglasses helped avoid eye contact. He hesitated, then held his arms out. I took an abrupt step forward and my head hit his chin as he bent down. It was a short, stiff hug. We chuckled as he rubbed his chin. I hoped he couldn't hear my heartbeat.

I rummaged in my brain for an appropriate movie line to throw at him, make him see how blasé I was about this chance encounter. "Of all the benches in all the parks, in all the cities, you had to sit on this old bench," I said, imitating Bogart.

He shifted his feet. A little frown appeared on his forehead before he grinned. "You can still come up with movie lines for every occasion." He shook his head in disbelief.

He remembered. He remembered how I used to quote or paraphrase lines from my favorite movies, seeing how far I could carry a conversation that way. My insides vibrated as a bolt of lightning spread a warm glow through my body. Until this moment, I hadn't actually believed in my Cecil Project. Now I was flushed with hope.

"What in heavens name brings you to this park bench?" I babbled on.

He sat again, and I sat next to him. "I work nearby. What are *you* doing here? Still work at that same old methadone clinic?"

"Yes. I've been promoted. I'm the clinical supervisor now. A lot more responsibility."

"Good for you. Although you know I always felt that you ought to stop working with those people." He dug his fork into his salad. "They don't get any better and the place is a dump."

Yes. I knew that. He'd been on my case to start a private practice, work with *worthy* people, the kind who actually wanted therapy and could pay handsomely for it. It had been a bone of contention. I didn't want to be reminded of it now.

"We're going to be renovating the clinic soon, spruce it up. Anyhoo, I've been taking walks at lunchtime and today was such a perfect day I wandered all the way here. So, what about you? Still at Sotheby's?"

He waved his hand dismissively. "I left them a few months ago. Been wanting to do it for a long time. I own my own art gallery now. Not too far from here, actually." His dainty little nose twitched the way it did when he was pleased with himself. Another little habit I'd forgotten about.

"So no more of those interminable three-martini lunches?" I joked. How he used to boast about those lunches at exorbitant restaurants, but in a disparaging way, as if he hated them.

He patted his flat stomach. "I'm much happier, eating healthier now." He shoved a large piece of lettuce into his mouth. A dab of Russian salad dressing landed on his lower lip and I was tempted to wipe it off, but he licked it off and the opportunity for the little intimate gesture was lost. "And you? Still dieting?"

"Who, me? No way. I was just thinking of getting a hot dog." I hated hot dogs and prayed he wouldn't point to the nearby vendor and offer to buy me one. Thank goodness generosity was not one of his traits.

His eyes widened as he looked me up and down. "Still look pretty skinny to me. As a matter of fact, I'd say you've lost weight."

*Of course I did*, I wanted to hurl at him. *You dumped me, and I went on the I'm-worthless-and-my-life-is-out-of-control diet.* But I knew he liked me thin, so I held my tongue. Besides, people who live in glass house. Cecil had been a chubby child and was always conscious of how he looked. He'd check his abs in front of the mirror while sucking his stomach in. And when I gained a few pounds one year, he was on me like a bulldog, making fun of my "little adorable tummy bulge." I dismissed those memories from my mind. I had to make the most of this opportunity.

"So, what else is new with you? How's it going with your new gallery?"

He wasn't wearing a ring on his left finger, which reaffirmed my previous conclusion.

He told me the name of his gallery and I swallowed a giggle that threatened to burble out of my mouth. "The Abstractionists," I repeated. "Sounds a bit like a band of artistic musicians." Of course, as soon as I said that, I regretted it. He never had appreciated my caustic humor. And really what did I know of art? Nothing.

His nose twitched. "There's more to art than Van Gogh, you know."

This was going all wrong. Not the way I envisioned it. "You're right, of course. I'd love to see your gallery, I truly would." For the second time, I was glad I had sunshades on as I felt tears well up. "How are you otherwise?" I went on, hoping to soothe his ego.

"Life's good," he said in a noncommittal way. "What about you? Are you seeing anyone?"

Why couldn't I be that direct? "I'm not lonely, if that's what you mean. I'm fine. More than fine. I'm loving my independence." Sweat trickled down my back.

"Great. See, breaking up was what we both needed. Figure out who we were. Gave us a chance to … to find ourselves."

Such a cliché. I didn't see why a person couldn't figure out who they were while they were in a relationship. Besides, I knew very well who I was. I was my mother's daughter. What I needed was security and marriage to forestall loneliness and bad things in general.

"Yes. I've also been thinking lately about what went wrong with us and realized that I … I was too insecure and probably insensitive to your needs," I said.

"Well, the past is past," he said. He got up and stretched to his lanky full six-foot height. He crumbled the napkin and tossed it into the trashcan with a little jump. "I really hope you'll find the man who'll make you happy."

The euphoric jolt that had entered my body earlier whooshed right out, leaving me deflated. Other than throwing myself at his mercy and begging him to give me another chance, I could think of nothing to say to keep him from leaving.

"I meant it, Cecil. I'd love to see your gallery," I said, biting my lower lip. I remembered all too clearly his words when he broke up with me. "I can't be your Prince Charming." He never had been, but he was the man who was going to be my husband and keep loneliness at bay.

"And here's looking at you, kid." He saluted as he turned to go. Then he swung around and waved. "I'll put you on our gallery's mailing list," he called before he walked away.

"Send it to my work address," I yelled after him, remembering he didn't know where I lived.

I sat on the bench for a few minutes longer, surrounded by a riot of

June flowers mocking me. My mind twisted and turned. I had let a momentous opportunity slip by. I was an idiot.

My stomach rumbled from lack of food, but the thought of eating made me sick. I walked back to work, feeling empty at first. But with each step, I felt lighter as hope returned. I went over every word he'd said and realized that there was nothing to be negative about. Today was just the *start* of my Project and somehow, something I did, caused me to run into him. I'd *made* it happen. The power suit worked. Now that I knew where he worked, I would find a way to get back into his life. The world *was* my oyster and today was nothing short of serendipitous.

# ~CHAPTER EIGHT~

When I returned to the clinic, I found that the staff had left. It was a little after two; I'd lingered longer at lunch than usual. The only one still there was Derrick. He was sitting in his office, his legs propped up on his desk, again, a thick volume of OASAS state regulations resting on his thighs. Worse yet, a lit cigarette was dangling from his ashtray. Such a filthy habit. I hoped that that was the only thing he had in common with Phoebe. But, as a doctor, he should have known better. On closer look, I saw his chest rising and falling rhythmically. His eyes were shut. I rapped on his door and his head jerked up. He put the heavy volume down on the desk, yawned, and stretched his arms up over his head, not even pretending he hadn't fallen asleep. He stabbed out his cigarette.

"State regulations are not exactly riveting reading," he said, scratching his head and tugging at his dreadlocks.

"Where is everyone?" I asked.

"Theresa locked up the meds, so I let her go home early," he said. "Same with Kumar and Dinesh. They said they had exams coming up. Don't envy them that, studying for the boards. Brrrr." He shook his whole body.

I bit the inside of my lip. I realized that as the medical director he was technically our boss, but still, this was his second week on the job, and it would have been nice if he had consulted with me. After all, he didn't know the ins and outs of our clinic yet. And I was still the clinical director, and as such I was the counselors' immediate supervisor. It had taken a long time for me to exert some authority over them and I wasn't going to roll over and let him take charge.

"They are woefully behind in their chart work," I said.

"Sorry," he smiled, showing his dimple. "I probably shouldn't have, but I felt sorry for them, and they asked me. And since you weren't here …." His shoulders went up.

"We're due for an inspection later this year and I'll end up doing much of their chartwork. I know they're trying to pass their exams, that they're just treading water here. They do try, but it's been an ongoing problem. First they had to pass part one; now part two; then there will be part three."

He looked at me intently with his cat eyes, appraising, and waited for me to go on. I just shook my head. What was the use?

"Sorry, I didn't mean to step on your toes," he finally said. "I didn't think it was a big deal, but you're right, I ought to have consulted with you."

My shoulders relaxed. Maybe he wasn't going to be exactly like Phoebe. He was smoother, but that was no reason to let my guard down. "Phoebe thinks I'm way too lax, that I need to get the staff to do their jobs. She knows their chartwork isn't up to par, but she hired them because they're working below wages. She's taking advantage of their situation and wants me to be the bad cop."

"Maybe you shouldn't worry so much about Phoebe. Relax."

I liked the way he drew out his vowels and said "relaaax" But I didn't like being *told* to relax. He was too laid back, with his battered jeans and dreadlocks. Who was he to tell *me* I needed to relax? He didn't know me.

"Earlier you suggested that I needed to be tougher with the patients, give them consequences, now you're telling me to relax?"

He seemed to be trying to decide something, tapping his full lips with a pen reflectively. "Hmm," he said. "I take your point. I've got a lot to learn about this clinic. As you know, I was mostly a researcher in my prior jobs."

I laughed. "You mean like working in a lab with little mice running around in cages?"

"Well, if you put it like that." The corners of his eyes crinkled. "Actually, we were testing the efficacy of various drugs, like Naltrexone, in reducing cravings for alcohol and drugs."

"With mice? So now what, use our clients as guinea pigs? Well, I better get back to my office and do *my* chartwork," I said. I turned on my heels, leaving him with his mouth slightly agape.

I wasn't sure what had gotten into me. I wasn't normally bitchy. It was just that I didn't know what to make of him. I didn't know what to do with someone from a Caribbean island where the sun always shone and the living was easy. Not like the darkness I'd grown up with. He wouldn't relate. Most people couldn't.

I went into my office to face all the charts from the morning's group, which felt like ages ago. Writing in charts takes a special kind of talent. Say as little as possible in so many words. Justify the patients' continued need for treatment and at the same time imply that some progress had been made. It *was* a fine line.

At the end of the day, I rushed to leave so that I wouldn't run into Derrick and be tortured with any small talk, but there he was, right outside my office, asking me if I was heading home. Luckily, I remembered that I was still in need of new make-up to go with my new look, so I told him I had an appointment. Thankfully he didn't ask about it, and I didn't have to come up with a little white lie.

I was deep in thought, still mulling over the events of the day, when I arrived home and walked up the stairs. I stopped by Mr. S's to give him the newspaper.

The door was open a crack, which was quite unusual. "Hey, Gramps, your crossword's here," I called, knocking on his door.

"Come in, come in," I heard his muffled voice. "I left it open for you."

I let myself in. "Where are you?"

"In here," came his muted voice.

I found him in the kitchen, by the sink, his head covered in a towel, bent over a pot spewing steam. He was still in his bathrobe. This was the first time I'd seen him not looking meticulous in his starched white shirt and tie. I'd often wondered why he bothered to take such trouble with his attire. His only known outings were to the corner to get his morning rag, *The Daily*, and a pastry, or to the supermarket. When I'd asked him about it once, he'd chuckled and said that just because he was old there was no need to relax his standards. "It's a slippery slope," he'd said.

"Are you all right, Gramps?" I asked feeling a bit alarmed.

He raised his head, his face red, sweat dripping. "I'm eighty-five years old, how all right can I be already? But not to worry, just a little congestion."

"Shouldn't you see a doctor?"

He waved his hand dismissively. "Doctor schmoctor! This is the best medicine, a good *shvits*. Sweat it out. Opens up all the things that should be open. See, I can breathe through my nose." He inhaled deeply before a phlegmy cough convulsed him.

"Gramps, you're not fine at all."

The spasm passed and he regained his breath and dried his face. He hacked again, spit into the sink and rinsed his face with water. "Good to get rid of the phlegm. With all the modern fancy medicine, they still don't have a cure for the cold. Now, how about a nice cup of tea?"

"If you're not better by tomorrow, promise to see a doctor. First thing," I scolded as I set the kettle on the stove.

"Now you're being, a nag, a *noodnik*, like my poor wife, may she rest in peace," he said. Dad had often called me *noodnik*, as a term of endearment, accompanied by a pinch to my cheek.

\*\*\*

That night I woke up with a start. I thought I heard Mr. S cough. But of course, I couldn't have, as he was one floor below me, and I tried to calm down. I put on my robe and tiptoed down the stairs. I stood outside his door and listened. All was quiet. Relieved, I went back to bed, but sleep eluded me as thoughts of Cecil invaded my head, crowding out my worries for Gramps.

I got up from the rumpled bed again and went to the kitchen. My stomach rumbled and I calculated how many calories I had consumed that day, including the dressing-free salad I'd had for dinner. I opened the fridge and scanned the empty shelves. Yesterday's steamed vegetables were limp and lifeless. I tossed them out and put some fat free popcorn into the microwave. While it was popping, I poured myself a thimbleful glass of wine. Something to take the edge off while I waited for the popcorn.

I know that Cecil hadn't been totally wrong. I'd needed to mature. My parents' demise at my relatively young age had traumatized me, and there were other wounds on my psyche. There were some scars that went back to even before their violent deaths. They were there even if I couldn't see them. But I hoped there were enough healthy parts left of my mind that were undamaged, parts that could find happiness. I clung to that hope.

# ~CHAPTER NINE~

I popped my head into Derrick's office shortly before our staff meeting on Friday.

"Can we hold off the meeting by twenty minutes or so? It's Kumar's birthday and I'm running out to get a cake," I said.

"Are you collecting money for it or is it a petty cash thing?" he asked, reaching for his wallet.

"Petty cash." I laughed. "D'ya think Phoebe would pry her fingers loose for something like this? She'd think it a waste of time and money to celebrate birthdays. Thanks, but I buy the cakes for all birthday celebrations. We never had them until I became the supervisor. I figure everyone deserves a birthday treat. Anyway, I wouldn't ask Kumar and Dinesh for money."

Derrick's eyes lit up, greener than green. "Nice of you. I'm more than willing to contribute." His fingers pulled out some bills.

I held up my hand. "Not necessary," I said and walked out, although I could have used the cash.

It was true that before my promotion we'd never celebrated anyone's birthday or any other staff achievement. I'd implemented little things like potluck lunches at holidays and cakes for birthdays. It was the little things that make the difference between a heartless workplace and a caring one. I was still working on making us more harmonious, but I felt like I was making headway, especially with Kumar, and, since it was his birthday, I'd make sure I'd buy him his favorite vanilla cake, even though I hated all things vanilla.

***

The following weekend, the last of June, I had to put the Cecil Project on hold. It was the weekend Daphne had invited me over for the arranged blind date. I wasn't thrilled about the distraction, especially since the past blind dates Daphne had fixed me up with, mostly lawyers from her firm, hadn't worked out so well. As a matter of fact, they'd been quite torturous. The young ambitious lawyers found me wanting; I didn't measure up to their expectations. They were Jewish men looking for gorgeous *shiksas*. I knew the type. I flat out didn't belong to that set and I couldn't figure out why. It wasn't for lack of cheekbones, but perhaps there was something about my attitude. I couldn't put my finger on it, whatever to was.

The train car was relatively empty, as I had purposefully decided to take a late train to Westchester to avoid the hordes of New Yorkers scrambling to get out of town for the summer weekend. I tossed my luggage on the seat next to me in the hope of dissuading anyone from sitting there, and plopped down. I started daydreaming about what I'd look like in the neon green dress I'd bought at Saks, the one with the Krystal Carrington shoulder pads. Perhaps it was a little trashy, barely covering my butt, but who was I, with no sense of fashion, to argue about it? This was a test run for when I'd wear it for Cecil.

Just before the train pulled away from the station, a few more stragglers entered the car and I closed my eyes, pretending to be asleep so as not to have to remove the suitcase from the seat next to me. Impulsive intimacies that occur between passengers on a journey were one of the things I shied away from.

Images from a trip I'd taken long ago with Mom flooded me. I must have been six or seven and we were going on a trip to New York City, just the two of us, to see the *Nutcracker* at a Sunday matinee. Not sure why Daphne and Dad didn't come too, but it was often Daph and Dad, the two D's, we called them, and me and Mom. A stranger joined us and began to talk to Mom. I put my head on her shoulder and nodded off, but through my haze, I heard the stranger tell Mom how pretty she was, and at some point, I thought I saw his hand hover on her knee. Mom woke me up and yanked my arm as she jumped up. We moved to another car. That taught me to keep to myself on trains. Yet, I loved train rides, or any sort of travel. That lovely combination of being suspended in time and the forward motion lubricated my mind, giving me the feeling of freedom from my daily angst.

The train jerked and I opened my eyes to discover a woman sitting in the seat facing me. A scrawny little girl, no more than six, sat next to the woman, her daughter I presumed. The child looked at me and quickly averted her eyes shyly. A homely girl, her freckled face was ringed by yellow curls. She reminded me of myself at that age. The mother bent down and whispered something to the little girl. She then put her arm around the child and laid the golden head on her lap.

I shifted in my seat. My eyes grew hot, in sharp contrast to the tightening cold weight I felt pushing against my chest. I couldn't breathe. I tried to look away, not wanting to intrude on the intimate scene, but my eyes kept darting back to the two. The mother bent down and kissed her daughter's cheek. I grabbed my bag and scampered from my seat, unintentionally hitting the woman in the knee. Mumbling an apology, I went to the next car and found another window seat. The sun dipped below the horizon as we pulled out of the tunnel and the train picked up speed. I leaned my head back and shut my eyes again. Memories flowed over me like cool fresh spring water.

***

I am five years old, sitting on Mom's lap, while she sings to me softly in her melodious voice. These are the moments that I feel so special, her stroking my hair, her sweet smell, her delicate hands warm on my face. She rains kisses on me. I giggle and squirm. I follow her fingers as they flow over a picture book as she teaches me to read. By the time I start first grade, I can read so well the teacher seems upset and says it's best if my mom stops teaching me. Not that it matters anyway, because by then Mom doesn't feel like getting out of bed on many days, let alone teaching me to read. I no longer sit on her lap very often. On these days, she moves from room to room as if looking for something she can never find, or she yells at us for every little infraction. My sister and I walk on tiptoes on such days, careful not to make any noise, not to upset Mom. We check with each other, every morning, to see what kind of day it will be.

Oh, my mother. I was sure she was much more complicated than I'd ever understood. I wondered if I ever really knew her at all. She was beautiful, she was melodramatic, she took all the oxygen out of the room, while Dad was dull and quiet and stayed in the background. He was serious, watchful, and worried about Mom.

I shoved down these intrusive images and focused on the passing scenery. I'm used to looking through my apartment windows in the city. People can be lonely anywhere, but there's a special aroma to city loneliness that comes from being surrounded by millions of people. I felt like one of the women in an Edward Hopper painting, looking out the window from a bare room, gazing outside at the people who threw dinner parties, whose homes were filled with laughter. People get a whiff of your loneliness and they stay away out of fear of catching it, like it was cancer. It radiates shame, so I hide it and pretend otherwise. I've made up little stories about my social life. I've even lied to Theresa about non-existent dates. Daphne's the only one who suspects the truth; she knows me too well.

The train slowed and then lurched to a stop. Across the platform at the Briarcliff Manor station, an old woman in sensible shoes was waiting to get on the train. I hoped she had a family waiting for her, wherever her destination. I picked up my suitcase and hopped off . Going back to the town I grew up in, and where Daphne still lived, made me queasy, so I didn't do it as often as I probably should. I make it a point not to go past the old house where we used to live, but I feel drawn to it, and on each visit, I walk to the corner of our old block, look down the street and up to the second story bathroom window, and then quickly scram out of there.

It happened to me each time I went by our old house: the flood of memories. I'm no more than eight years old and I've just woken up from a nightmare. Daphne, in the twin bed next to mine, is fast asleep. I'm tempted to wake her up but whenever I do, she gets mad at me. So I tiptoe out of the room and down the hallway to get a glass of water. I notice the light is on in my parents' bathroom. Must be Mom. She's always complaining of not sleeping much. I walk over and knock softly on the door, but there's no answer. I knock again, still nothing. Someone must have left the light on, though we've been taught to always turn off the lights when we leave a room. Electricity is expensive. I try the doorknob and the door opens. Mom is lying in her nightgown in the half-filled bathtub. Something's not right. Her head is slumped on her chest, as if she's sleeping.

"Mom," I whisper. She doesn't hear me. I get closer. I could touch her, but I don't. "Mom," I call louder. She doesn't move. "Mom," I screech. She still doesn't move. Luckily, Dad hears my scream and comes running.

He shoves me out of the room and yells for Daphne to get up. "Call an ambulance. 911."

After the ambulance came and took Mom to the hospital, Dad told us that Mommy got sick and she'd have to stay in a special hospital for a while. When she finally came back home after a few weeks, she looked the same, yet she was different. Not the same mom who'd played with me and taught me to read. This mom had a vague, distant look in her eyes, as if she was somewhere else even when she was there with us. As if she didn't really see me. And that's when I became her shadow, following her around. I worried if I let her out of my sight, she might get sick again.

I'd thought that love meant everything, and that nothing was stronger than the love of a mother for her child. Until that day when I found Mom unconscious in the bathtub. It was then that I realized, even at that young age, that love could cause pain rather than make you better. And that, in any case, love didn't last.

I shook my head and dismissed the old memory, banished it from my mind. I was on the verge of reinventing myself. No more depressive Marika, the one Cecil didn't want. The new me was leaving all that sadness behind.

I went in search of Daphne.

I found her standing next to her Volvo station wagon, waving and jumping up and down. Looking at us, no one would have guessed we were sisters. She with her large dark eyes and big frame, and I fair and petite. I ran over and we hugged a little stiffly, as if we were distant acquaintances. Even though we loved each other deeply, we'd never been a family of huggers, nor were we effusive with our emotions. Except for Mom, whose moods had changed with little warning. She loved us with abandon, until she'd get angry and yell at us with the same lack of restraint.

"Let's get you home so you can visit with the kids. They're so excited about seeing Aunty Rika. I'll try to get them to bed early, but Gerald's been feeding them Skittles and God knows what else, so we'll see how that goes," she said in her no-nonsense manner.

"I'm sorry I don't get to see them more often. They're growing so fast. I can't believe Davey's eight and Nina's turning five in December. Can never forget her birthday since we share one, haha," I said. The thought of our upcoming same-day birthday sent a shiver up my spine, what with my goal not yet within reach. And what would happen if I didn't reach it.

Daphne waved her hand dismissively as she revved up the car engine. "Can't wait for you to meet Nathan tomorrow. He's so nice, not like the shmucky lawyers we've introduced you to."

I smiled weakly. Daphne was such a romantic. It was astonishing that we came from the same home. She believed in the power of love to heal all wounds, that love could surmount all obstacles. She'd been quite happy when Cecil and I broke up because I had mistakenly confided in her that he wasn't the love of my life, like Gerald was hers. She thought I'd been spared a life of misery.

"So, what makes this Nathan guy different from all the others?" I asked.

"He's sweet. A real *mensch*."

I sighed. "Nice, hmm. Must mean he's not exactly a heartthrob, not that I'm opposed to nice guys."

"Yes, I know, you're the cold-hearted Marika who doesn't need love. Determined to find your happiness by marrying into wealth. How's it working so far?"

I chafed at being so described. "To each his own," I said. "Anyway, the whole dating thing is getting old. Tedious. I'm sick of it and all the rejections. So, no, I can't get excited about meeting Nathan, nice though he may be."

"Come on," Daphne said. "No negativity. You're beginning to sound more like Mom every day." She gave a mirthless chuckle.

"What's wrong with that?" I barked.

"If you have to ask ...." She paused, then sighed. "You can't bring Mom back by being like her, you know that, don't you? Besides, Mom wasn't the saint you make her out to be."

"I know that." I shrugged and looked straight ahead. Daphne gets these strange ideas about me idolizing Mom. Of course, Daphne worshipped Dad and would bite my head off if I ever said anything remotely critical of the way he was. I bit my lower lip, a habit that intensified whenever I was with Daphne.

"Seriously, Rika, stop being so negative. You'll meet the right man. I know you will. Every pot has a lid."

I hated that cliché. "Of course. And everybody lives happily ever after." I rolled my eyes. Would she now break into song, "Tomorrow" from *Annie* perhaps? "Are you sure one of us wasn't adopted?"

She looked at me wearily. Ever since our parents died, Daphne'd done her best to step in and take care of me, despite having a family of her own. It couldn't have been easy for her. After all, she lost as much as I did, and on top of that she lost her first baby, but at least she had Gerald and a family now.

*** 

After dinner, Gerald went off to his man cave to watch a testosterone-laden movie, while Daphne dispatched the kids to bed early with promises of treats the next day. Luckily, the G.I. Joe and Cabbage Patch doll I'd brought were big hits, though I'd noticed Daphne's mouth twitch sideways when I took out the military toy.

The two of us settled in the family room, which was decorated with homespun rugs and antique furniture. Mom scoffed at antiques and called them *alte sachen*, old stuff. I also preferred modern design, but one of Daphne's and my favorite activities was rummaging through estate or garage sales. We'd get competitive, daring each other to find the best bargain ever. One of our finds, a vintage walnut sideboard, was prominently displayed in the dining room. I'd seen it first, but now it was hers. Not that I could have afforded it in any case, so I was glad she had it. Daphne sipped her hot chocolate, and I stuck to my Diet Coke.

"Why didn't you get a manicure?" Daphne asked, eyeing my chipped and bitten-to-the-quick nails.

I had meant to do so as part of my makeover project but changed my mind. "What for? It's a waste of money on me." I tucked my hands under my thighs to hide the horrible condition of my nails.

"It would help you stop biting your nails."

"I'll just pick at the polish. Not worth the expense." I was still smarting from all the money I'd spent on my Cecil Project makeover.

Daphne wiggled her heavy dark brows. "Tomorrow I'm treating you to a mani-pedi."

"You really think that my having pretty nails is going to make a lick of difference with this Nathan?"

"Of course not, silly. Don't think of it like that. You should do these things to please yourself."

I thought of the painful leg and crotch waxing I'd recently endured, the latest in my preparations to rekindle Cecil's interest. "Spare me the homilies about how we should dress for ourselves, 'cause it ain't so. We jump through hoops to impress a man, and only after we've got that ring do we exhale and maybe let ourselves go a little."

Daphne raised her hands in surrender and gave a tight little laugh. "Are you implying that I've let myself go?"

"Never. You're as put together as ever," I lied. Daphne's clothes were cheap and utilitarian rather than fashionable. It was time to change the subject. "Tell me about this Nathan. A nurse? Seriously? What, they've run out of doctors at the hospital?" A doctor might have been worth giving up my Project.

"Gerald says Nathan's the shy sort, but that he's really super sweet," she repeated what she'd told me earlier.

"Two shy people making stilted conversation. That ought to be fun," I said. I was ready to get this unpleasant date over with and get back to my Project. "I wonder if we should eat outside tomorrow. It's awfully humid and may even rain." Humidity, a curse for my hair.

Daphne got up and stretched. "I'm off to bed. And you, stop being such an Eeyore."

"Hey, what's wrong with Eeyore? He's a realist," I said. I don't like anyone picking on one of my favorite fictional characters from childhood. "And don't blame me if it rains tomorrow," I called after her.

True, I wasn't a ray of sunshine, but that was what life had taught me. Expect rain and you'll never be disappointed when it pours.

# ~CHAPTER TEN~

The following morning, after breakfast with the two little rambunctious urchins, Nina and Davey, Daphne and I went to get our mani-pedis. This despite grumbling from Gerald about having to babysit for the entire morning, as if the cherubs were not his progeny. Daphne pursed her lips in annoyance but said nothing and off we went.

When we got back with my shiny Cruella de Ville red nails, I took over babysitting duties. I find babies cute; however, there's only so much cooing and babbling I can tolerate. Now that my niece and nephew were older, they were much more fun. They were exuberant, hilarious, and delightful, until they inevitably took a turn and suddenly became cranky and boisterous. Daphne was busy cooking and baking, and I had to manage as best I could. Of course, if they were my kids, I'd be less self-conscious about disciplining them. But my sister believed in reasoning with them. Not sure why, because Mom had been the queen of yelling, and it seemed to work with us. We were always well behaved.

In the afternoon, Gerald set off to buy steaks. "I promised Nathan a good steak and he shall have it. That way, if it doesn't work out with Marika, he'll at least have had a good meal, ha-ha," he said.

Although Gerald and I weren't really as close as I'd hoped we would be, he was my brother-in-law and had gone to the trouble of setting up this date. And we had an established relationship. He'd throw his little jabs, Daphne'd jump to my defense, and although I sometimes stung back, I mostly bit my lips and kept my mouth shut for Daphne's sake.

By six o'clock, I could procrastinate no longer. Daphne and the kids were all dressed, and I slogged upstairs to get ready. I inspected my dress. What had looked trendy in the store now seemed garish and downright campy. The exaggerated shoulders, the neon green, the ultra-short hemline, none of it signaled stylish. But it was too late to do anything but put the bright concoction on. What I saw in the mirror was a walking neon sign. I tugged the dress downward in a futile attempt to lengthen it. Daphne came into the room, took one look at me, and stopped in her tracks. Her eyes popped wide open and the edges of her lips twitched upward.

"What? I look ridiculous, I know," I groaned.

"Eh, no. You're very hip," she said, inspecting me critically. She cleared her throat before going on. "I … wonder if you could take some of the shoulder padding out."

"No, they're sewn in, not taped," I said. "They're supposedly the height of fashion." I flopped down on the bed. "Oh, what's the use, go ahead and say it, I look ludicrous, and I can barely breathe, it's so tight."

"Don't be silly, you look very chic. Like what's her name, Krystle from Dynasty." This was the second time I'd been compared to the actress, so maybe there was something to this dress. Daphne patted my big shoulders. "It sets off your beeootiful eyes." The doorbell chimed. "It's probably Nathan. Want to get it?"

"God, no! You go. I'm not ready. Mascara, blush, and hair," I said, my hands fluttering over my hair.

"You're so cute, you don't even need makeup, but maybe you can dampen your hair down a bit? It's kind of big," she said. Seeing my face, she quickly added, "Never mind, it looks perfect. Anyway, don't take too long. It's not nice to keep a man waiting."

I shook my head. "Don't worry," I reassured her as much as myself. "I'm gonna make a grand entrance."

She ran downstairs and I slathered on my new make-up, mascara, eye liner, and lipstick, before inspecting myself in the mirror one last time. Maybe I did go overboard with the purplish eye shadow and black eyeliner. But my eyes certainly popped. Overall, the effect was more Cyndi Lauper than Krystal Carrington. Unfortunately.

I inhaled one deep breath, let it out slowly, and meandered down the stairs, reminding myself that I had my Project and an escape plan. It was almost a comforting thought to cling to, and there was no need sweat about Nathan or anything else. This was a test run for my new, self-assured persona. I was aiming for a woman with that certain *je ne sais quoi*. Self-assured and charming.

Gerald greeted me at the bottom of the stairs with a hearty smile. "Hey, Marika, meet my buddy, Nathan. Great guy." He clapped Nathan on the back vigorously.

A short, slightly overweight, balding man, with a proboscis the likes of which I have never encountered, greeted me with a wide grin. I tried, but it was impossible not to stare at his appendage. Fascinated, I found myself wondering how he ever managed to get through a common cold, or, worse, plant a kiss.

"Marika," Nathan said, "that's an unusual name. I actually looked it up. It means bitter. But I'm sure you're not." He laughed at his little joke.

A non sequitur. My parents had told me my name meant grace in Hungarian, and that I was named after my grandmother, but I decided not to disabuse him of his notion. I smiled enigmatically. "My parents were unusual people. Maybe I was born with a grimace, so they named me accordingly," I added with a shrug. The cool new me.

"Oh, sorry to hear that," he said solemnly.

*God, some people have no sense of humor.* "It was a joke. They were normal parents, as normal as can be." I wanted to ask him how he managed to get through life without humor, especially given how homely he was. He seemed like one of those nice fellas who was probably the easy butt of jokes.

An awkward silence descended and I was thankful for the distraction the kids provided before Daphne scurried them off with a Winnie the Pooh movie and promises of more Hershey's Kisses. I wished I could run off with the kids. How sweet it would be to take off the tight dress, watch Eeyore and Pooh, and relax. This finding a husband business was getting on my nerves. What if I gave it up altogether and accepted the cozy company of women? Would that be so bad? Problem was the only women I knew who were single were unhappy rather than cozy. We were all lonely.

Gerald went to get the wine. He came back and struggled with the corkscrew. "Hey, I think you two have a lot in common. You're both in the helping profession. As am I, of course. My wife *thinks* she helps, but, then, we know the world has too many lawyers, ha-ha."

I felt my cheeks burn for my sister. Until today I hadn't noticed Gerald's lack of tact and wondered if Daphne had settled when she fell in love as a freshman in college. I snatched the offered glass and chugged it as if it was water.

"So, I hear you're saving the world from drug addicts. Or is it they who need to be saved," Nathan said.

I didn't think he meant it in any disparaging way, but I disliked people's often glib comments about addicts or my profession. "I'm a therapist. A social worker therapist," I clarified, so he wouldn't think I was a psychologist. "And I don't think I'm saving anybody."

"She works with heroin addicts. Street people. It's a thankless job," Gerald interjected.

"I often see drug addicts when they land in the E.R.," Nathan said. "Really sad. But we do what we can."

"Yes, but I'm really not a do-gooder." I didn't want him to mistake me, as people often confused social workers with either humanitarians or evil people who snatched kids away from their parents and put them in foster care. I was neither and didn't pretend to have attributes I didn't possess.

I refilled my glass and went on to describe my job in the most uncharitable way I could think of, including the details of breaking up the lovers' quarrel in the clinic. "All in a day's work," I added with a shrug, as if it really was.

Nathan looked gobsmacked. "Sounds unpleasant. We often have to stop fights when addicts arrive at the hospital high or are coming down. The least pleasant part of my job as a nurse. They're often brought in by the police, already in handcuffs."

"Yeah, I'm sure," I said.

He didn't look the type who could hold his end in a fight. He was probably one of those super nice people who overcompensated because of their homeliness. For a moment I could even envision falling in love with him, in spite of his appearance, just out of pity. Thank goodness I wasn't the type who fell in love.

Gerald went outside to start the grill, carrying a tray with steaks, and, thankfully, Daphne came in. She was a much better conversationalist than I was. Being a lawyer, she was used to plying people with questions. I left her to chat with Nathan, who was busy describing his nursing job, which apparently, he loved, while I went to get more wine.

By the time Gerald had finished grilling and Daphne had summoned the kids to the table, I was a little unsteady on my feet. But I was not so drunk as not to detect the tight smile on Daphne's mouth. She kept flashing me looks, raising her eyebrows meaningfully at me. At one point, she hissed at me to stop drinking. I blithely ignored her.

Conversation at dinner was less than brilliant with Nathan looking longingly at me. Perhaps he was dazzled by my neon green dress, or my purple lidded eyes, but I stiffened my resolve not to care. I had my potentially lucrative Cecil Project, and I wasn't going to be sidetracked by falling in love with a nurse, sweet as he was, and be alone at night while he worked his shift. I began to feel slightly sorry for Nathan, but the world was my oyster; I repeated my new mantra. I picked at the unappetizing bloody piece of meat on my plate, while Nathan masticated his with gusto. At last dessert was served and I gleefully ignored the caloric count of the wine and chocolate cake as I licked my fork. It had been ages since I'd permitted myself anything more than a whiff of cake. And never more than one glass of wine.

"Nathan, I was just wondering," I said, making sure to enunciate my words carefully, for I *had* consumed just a teeny bit too much wine and didn't want to appear inebriated. "Has anyone ever said anything to you about … that you should do something about … fix your … well, you know. This." I waved my hand in the direction of his face. "You'd be quite handsome. You've a very kind face." I meant to do good, to help him see that perhaps his nose was problematic, keeping him from finding his true love. If his mother had been anything like mine, she would have made sure that he fixed that problem. I only wanted to help.

"Mommy, is Auntie Rika drunk?" asked my angelic Davey, his eyes wide with wonder. Tiny Nina giggled and covered her mouth.

"Okay, kids, let's see who can get upstairs first for another treat," Daphne said, yanking her two cherubs by their hands.

"Marika, how … how rude. Are you drunk?" Gerald sputtered.

"Please, don't," Nathan cut him off, his lips turned downward. He looked at his plate, his eyes averted from mine. "I appreciate your honesty, Marika. You must be a good social worker," he said without a trace of sarcasm in his voice. He got up from the table. A little bead of perspiration appeared above his upper lip.

I felt hot, and a strange thrumming of pulsating blood whooshing in my ears. "I'm … I'm so sorry," I stuttered. "I was just …." But what was I? Tears pricked my eyes. I blinked them back. I wanted to help him. I didn't want him to be lonely, like me.

"Thanks for inviting me, Gerald, but I think I better go now. You've got a lovely wife," Nathan said. He nodded towards Daphne, who'd returned to the room, and left, giving me a tiny nod.

The three of us were stunned into a momentary silence.

Gerald was first to find his voice. "How could you embarrass us like that, Marika? This is the last time we'll try to fix you up with anyone. You're … you're no better than your patients," he bellowed.

"I … I don't know what got into me, honestly. But, really, I was trying to be helpful, point out something that was standing in his way of finding happiness. I've never in my life seen such a snout." I burst out in giggles, which quickly deteriorated into some sort of hysteria.

"Look at you." Gerald waved his hand up and down, pointing at my body. An ugly sneer crossed his face. "What makes you think you're such a great catch? Perhaps you should consider lowering your standards. Yes, you're cute, but cute women are a dime a dozen in New York."

I looked at Daphne; her face was impenetrable. "Stop it Gerald. There's no need for that. But you made me ashamed of you tonight, Marika," she said. Her words landed like a bucket of ice on my face. "I think it best you drink some coffee. Go have a lie down. Gerald and I will clean up."

I stumbled up the stairs, holding on to the banister, all my giddiness gone. I don't like people being angry with me, especially Daphne. It reminds me of Mom lashing out in her fury. In my room I ripped off my foolish dress. A dress like that would make anyone act stupid. I went to the bathroom and splashed cold water on my face, letting my mascara and purple shadow smear on my cheeks. I didn't care. I plopped on the bed and buried my smudged cheeks into the pillow. It was in this position, in my underwear, that Daphne found me some time later. I sat up and sniffled. She glanced at the make-up stained pillowcase but said nothing. I flipped the pillow over, as if by hiding the dirt it wouldn't be there. She shook her head from side to side and handed me a mug of coffee.

"Not sure I need it anymore," I said sheepishly. I'd sobered up pretty quickly.

"Drink it anyway." She waited for me to take a sip. "I don't know what's gotten into you. This is *not* how we were raised. You were so rude, and really shallow, going on about his nose. And what's with the drinking?"

"I didn't mean it like that. I wanted to help him. And I hardly ever drink, which is why I can't hold my liquor," I said.

"Well, you had a lot tonight. Not that getting drunk excuses your behavior. Wanting to help indeed!" Daphne sounded like the lawyer she was. "Something else is going on with you."

"What do you mean?"

"I bet this has something to do with Cecil, doesn't it? Ever since you mentioned that you ran into him, I've had this gnawing feeling about it."

She certainly had a sixth sense, because I'd never actually mentioned my Project to her. "He's got nothing to do with it," I mumbled.

"I hope you're not fantasizing about getting back together." Daphne paused and when I didn't answer she went on. "I think you've truly lost your mind if that's what you're thinking of doing. Did you forget how he treated you?"

"He wasn't *all* bad. As a matter of fact, we were good together, most of the time. We loved each other, in our way. I'm the one to blame for the breakup. I was too clingy. Needy and immature."

"Just listen to yourself." Daphne looked apoplectic.

I fixed my gaze on my manicured fingernails, temped to bite them. One of the nails had already chipped. "I don't know why you set me up with Nathan. You know I'd like someone who … who has better financial prospects than I do. A nurse is almost as bad as a social worker."

"How about instead of trying to marry for money or get back with Cecil, you start thinking seriously about what matters in a relationship? How about you marry like most people, because they simply fall in love?"

"Spare me. The power of love to cure all, right." I made a face. "Besides, what's the point? Half of those who marry for love end up divorced."

I wasn't going to get into it with Daphne, who had her notions about love. I wasn't going to tell her that the more you loved the more you risked the pain of loss, and it wasn't worth it. I didn't want to disabuse her of her ideas, but they simply weren't mine.

Then there was Mom. There was always Mom. "Love didn't stop Mom from doing what she did. Didn't stop her from trying to kill herself once and then finally succeeding," I said. It wasn't until after our parents died that Daphne told me the truth about Mom's first suicide attempt, which wasn't an accident as I was led to believe, and it had taken me years before I could bring myself to say the word suicide out loud.

"Leave Mom out of this. She's way too much in your head anyway. Time you start thinking for yourself. And, yes, marry for love."

"Aha, I get it. Like the way Gerald loved you yet it didn't stop him from cheating on you. And not like you'd been married long enough for him to get that seven-year itch." I regretted those words as soon as they escaped my mouth. When Daphne was pregnant with Nina, Gerald was unfaithful. I'd been having my own issues with Cecil at the time and probably wasn't there enough for her. It was an episode in her life we never talked about. In any case, Daphne wasn't one to pour her heart out to me; I'm the fragile one. We played our roles: she the wise, mature sister, I the needy one. I supposed it made her feel superior to me.

Daphne gasped. Her tone turned chilly. "I can't believe you said that. You know nothing about my married life or about love. I had three-year old Davey at the time and just gotten pregnant with Nina. What was I to do? Leave? Besides, Gerald was very remorseful. And, yes, being in love means being able to forgive. The sooner you learn that, the sooner you'll find happiness."

Her self-righteous, holier-than-thou attitude, made me sick. "Oh, sure, staying with a man who cheats on you is okay, and *I'm* the screwed up one. You're my perfect sister with your law degree who latched onto your first boyfriend ever and wouldn't let him go. You think *I'm* looking for a savior?" My voice got louder. "And what are you? Like Dad clinging to Mom?"

Splotches of red spread on Daphne's face. She sprung up from the bed. "Really! Really," she sputtered. "Do as you please. It's your life. Just don't come crying to me when it all explodes in your face. Again."

"Don't worry, you're the last person on earth I'll come to." I started hyperventilating as I watched her walk out the room—and probably out of my life. We hadn't fought since our parents died. What would I do without her?

A whimper escaped my lips, and I folded my body over, making myself small. My hands shook, my blood pounded in my ears. After a while, I lost sense of time. I sprung up from bed and started pacing the room, wrapping my hands tight around my shoulders in an attempt to still my shaking body. Gerald's right, I'm no great catch and the idea that the world was my oyster was laughable. I should grab the first guy who bestowed attention on me and marry him. But I couldn't stay here and face Gerald or Daphne in the morning. I snatched my weekender and stuffed the clownish dress inside, then dumped in the rest of my clothes. Not even folding. I needed to make a quick getaway, escape back to my own little hole. I called a taxi and tiptoed out of the house without waking the sleeping innocents. Why disturb them? They were sick of me and would no doubt breathe a sigh of relief not to have to deal with me in the morning.

I didn't check the train schedule and had a long wait at the nearly empty train station at that hour of the very early morning. It gave me plenty of time to think about my life. A young couple, lovers, were standing in a corner, kissing hungrily. I quickly averted my eyes from the intimate scene. A man, a vagabond by the look of his clothes, was fighting to stand up straight. His knees buckled under him but, just when he was on the verge of falling, he straightened up. I recognized that heroin shuffle so familiar in our patients. If I'd been a do-gooder I'd have gone over and offered him advice about getting on a methadone program, but I didn't. I moved further down the platform.

I recognized that I wasn't a very nice person or I wouldn't have acted like I had. Not with Nathan and certainly not with Daphne. But I wasn't cold or heartless as Daphne seemed to think. I had every intention of being a good wife to Cecil if he'd ever give me the chance. I'd even agree to have a child if he wanted me to, although I was ambivalent about having kids. Parental love was the most unfathomable of human emotions to me. You had to love somebody relentlessly and utterly, regardless the circumstances. It was the most reckless, dangerous love of all, and bound to hurt accordingly.

I carried scars that Daphne was familiar with, as hers were probably not so dissimilar to mine. And since my mom's death, I'd often felt as if I was barely connected to anything or anyone. If not for Daphne, I might have been blown away, like a weightless feather, drifting aimless. And yet, even Daphne didn't know how alone I felt. That was why my only way out was redoubling my efforts on the Cecil Project.

# ~CHAPTER ELEVEN~

I emerged from the train station in the still-early hours of Sunday morning, bleary eyed and disheveled, my mouth tasting like yesterday's coffee, sour. The city was still, hibernating, in deep slumber. Nothing is more eerie than New York City on a Sunday morning, the streets deserted while everyone's sleeping off Saturday night's bacchanal. I was going to treat myself to a taxi home. It had started to rain, a light drizzle, all the more reason to get door to door service. But at that hour, finding a cab in the rain was like wining the lotto: unlikely. And after standing at the curb for a few minutes, my T-shirt getting wet, I lugged my suitcase back downstairs to await the train. It was a long wait, but at least I wasn't rained on.

I didn't like Sundays. They stretched on endlessly and at their tail end comes that gnawing anxiety about the looming workweek. The patients with their endless demands and needs. I found their wants at times so great, and we offered so little. And a rainy, humid summer Sunday was the worst. Thankfully, it had stopped raining when I got out of the subway. As I hauled my suitcase down my street, I started thinking of the long dreary day ahead of me. I had little to look forward to. Even my Cecil Project held little hope this morning. There was a heavy lump at the pit of my stomach. I was fresh out of ideas on how to proceed with Cecil.

In the distance, down the block, I noticed a man walking his dog and figured it had to be Derrick, his dreadlocks giving him away. I skootched into my building hoping to avoid him as I suddenly remembered my appearance. I hadn't even washed my face from the night before and still had mascara smudged down my cheeks. Mom would have been horrified at the idea of meeting a man looking like I did. One should always look presentable, or even alluring, at the ready, she had counseled. Somebody— by which she meant a man— might one day show up at your doorstep and that would be a lost opportunity. However, such an emergency had yet to arise in my experience.

I was dying to brush my teeth and get into a nice soothing bath, followed hopefully by a long nap. I even thought of treating myself to chocolate, a little succor after my ordeal. When I passed Mr. S's apartment, a twinge of guilt surged through me at having abandoned him to his cold. He'd had a hacking cough for the past week, but he was too stubborn to see a doctor. It worried me, but each day when I stopped by, he waved off my concerns. In the movies, if someone gets a cough, you know they're going to die, and probably within the next couple of scenes.

I ran upstairs, dumped my bag without unpacking, quickly splashed water on the dried, caked-on makeup to get it off my face, and went down to the corner bodega to get coffee and churros. A treat for both of us. Mr. S had such a sweet tooth. Balancing everything in one hand, I knocked on his door. There was no answer. Odd, because he was an early riser. I knocked harder. Still no answer.

I began to feel uneasy. I raced upstairs and retrieved the key he'd given me a while back, just in case he ever fell and couldn't get up, like on that television commercial. We'd laughed at the time. I left the breakfast goodies on my kitchen table and scrambled back down the stairs. I fiddled with the lock with shaking fingers, hoping he hadn't latched the chain from the inside as he sometimes did, thus defeating the point of giving me a key. Luckily the door opened. I walked in and called him. Nothing.

I tiptoed to his bedroom and found him lying in his bed, his face white, his chin sprouting stubbles. His mouth was agape, emitting barely audible little croaks, gasping for air. His skin was so translucent I could see the veins in his gnarled hands, lying lifeless by his side. I took his hand in mine. It was dry, papery thin, and cool. Fear gripped me and goosebumps covered my arms. He used to tell me that no way would he ever want to die in a hospital; that he'd lived and suffered enough and earned the right to die at home, in his bed. The one he had shared with his beloved Esther. What was I supposed to do? If I called an ambulance, he'd end up in the hospital for who knew how long, and he'd be so disappointed in me.

Mr. S was my savior when I felt overwhelmed or incompetent, which was all too often. Like the time I locked myself out of my apartment and he jimmied the door open, saving me the cost of a locksmith.

Then the sight of Derrick calmly walking his dog popped into my head. He was a doctor, albeit the wrong kind; still, there was an M.D. after his name. And he did tell me I could come to him if I ever needed — well, yeah, he'd said a toilet plunger, but I assumed his offer wasn't confined to that. Besides, he was the only doctor I knew within walking distance. I'd make a run for him rather than phone, because he'd be less likely to turn me down in person. People were much kinder in person; phones made it easier to be rude.

"I'll be right back, Mr. S," I shouted.

He murmured something or other, which I took to mean he understood me. I tucked his hand inside the sheet to keep it warm and scrambled down the stairs. My head was pounding so hard I thought it might explode.

Once outside Derrick's building, I realized I didn't know which apartment he lived in. I paced on the stoop. Luckily, a young woman came out and I slunk through the opened door. Now all I had to do was read the names on the mailboxes. He was on the third floor. Great. I leaped up the stairs, two at a time, and buzzed his door. I heard the dog barking and its paws scratching on the floor before the door opened.

Derrick stood there, eyes wide, eyebrows raised. The dog watched him, then me, ears up, head slightly cocked. "What's up?" he asked.

"Thank God you're home," I gushed. "I need a doctor. It's Gramps, he's old and he's sick. Could you come and have a look at him? It won't take long. He's in a bad way."

"Shouldn't you call an ambulance? I'm a psychiatrist—"

"You're a doctor, aren't you? And he's old, he doesn't want to go to a hospital."

"It's really not in my scope. Take him to the hospital."

"I can't. You don't understand. I can't. Please, it won't take you a moment, just look him over," I pleaded. "You know they keep you for hours the E.R. before they do anything."

"But—" He stopped and shook his head. I felt tears prick and swallowed hard. "All right, let's go. Be right back, Brucie." He fondled his dog briefly before locking his door and followed me.

We jogged across the empty street. It was still uncannily quiet and Kris Kristofferson's haunting "Sunday Morning Coming Down" reached my ears from somewhere. We got to the apartment and crept quietly into Mr. S's bedroom.

Mr. S's eyes were closed, but his breathing seemed less labored. He was lying on his side, all scrunched up like a baby. He looked so small.

"Is he your grandfather?" Derrick asked.

"No, but ... sort of, the grandpa I never had." I edged cautiously closer to his bed.

Suddenly Mr. S's eyes shot wide open. "Esther? Esther, I've been waiting for you," he whispered.

"It's me, Marika," I said, and gently put my hand on his shoulder, afraid I'd startle him.

"Eh? I thought for a moment that you were—" He stopped, overcome by a phlegmy cough. "Who's this? You found your new fiancé?"

I turned to Derrick, embarrassed. "He's confused," I said. I made the quick introductions. "Derrick's the new doctor at my office."

Derrick came forward. "Actually, I'm a psychiatrist."

Mr. S looked at us with his rheumy eyes. "A psychiatrist? Where does it say an old man isn't allowed to think or even hallucinate about his late wife? That don't make me crazy." He wheezed.

"Gramps, you're sick. You need a doctor. I came in earlier and you weren't very responsive. You gave me such a fright. I got Derrick here to check you over," I said.

"I heard you, I heard you. I just didn't feel like talking. And this guy said he's a psychiatrist. What's he going to do, analyze me?"

I turned to Derrick and raised my palms up. "Say something," I said *sotto voce*.

"Mr. Saperstein, let me at least give you a quick look over. Otherwise I'll conclude that perhaps you do need a psychiatrist," he said with a crooked grin.

"Huh, you got a funny one here." Mr. S began, but quickly devolved into another fit of hacking.

"Got a thermometer around?" Derrick asked.

"I'm not primitive, of course I have a thermometer," Mr. S said.

I went to the bathroom in search of it. When I returned, Mr. S's pajama top was rolled up and Derrick was bent over him, ear to his chest. It was a sad little chest, caved in, with a few tufts of white hair bearing the last hint of what once had probably been manly. He then did the same thing to his back. Derrick straightened up and took his pulse.

He turned to me. "We need to get a move on. He should be in hospital."

"No hospital," Mr. S wheezed. "No hospital."

"I think you may have pneumonia and need antibiotics, intravenously, asap," Derrick said. "If you don't go, it may not end well."

"At my age, it never ends well. I don't mind dying. We've all got to go sometimes. I've lived long enough. Too long." He dropped his head back on his pillow.

My knees shook. Didn't he care about leaving me? I crossed my arms and starred at him. "Fine, don't go. But don't expect me to bring you any crosswords, or churros, or, or ...." I couldn't finish my sentence. I took a deep breath. "So, you want to leave me, too?"

"Okay, okay, you sound like my Esther, bossy. I'll go. But don't let them prod and stick me with needles. They like to take your blood all the time and I don't got too much left."

I looked at Derrick helplessly. He already had the receiver in his hand. "I'm getting an ambulance. Not to worry, we'll stay with you. I'll say we're family."

The old man's face broke into his Yoda grin. "Sure, one look at us and they'll see the family resemblance."

"Ha-ha," I said, but my stomach clenched.

Within minutes, we heard the ambulance's wail. Sunday morning must be a dead time for emergencies. I looked out the window and saw it had pulled up alongside the building and two men were getting out. They looked barely old enough to be out of school.

"Apartment 3-G," I called out the window. Derrick went to buzz them in.

Once the medics had set down their gear, the younger of the two asked, "Okay, what have we here? How are we feeling, sir?" He raised his voice at Mr. S, as if he were hard of hearing.

Derrick filled them in, and I watched closely as they started working around the old man, moving quickly. One bent over Mr. S, taking his pulse, while the other put a stethoscope to his chest and asked him to cough.

"We'd best take you to the hospital," the younger one said. "Looks like we got ourselves pneumonia, but we'll take good care of you."

"Can't you give me a shot or something? I'm an old man and hospitals are full of germs," Mr. S said.

"Don't worry, we'll be with you," Derrick said. I should have been the one to reassure; after all, Mr. S was my adoptive Gramps, but I hated hospitals even more than he did. They were full of people all sick or, worse, dying, leaving loved ones behind.

"You coming with him?" one of the paramedics asked me. "We can only take one of you in the back."

Derrick looked at me. I wondered if he could see the rising panic in my eyes. He reassured me that he'd walk on over to the hospital and meet me there. He put his hand on my shoulder, ever so briefly, and looked at me as if he saw me in a new light.

I climbed into the back of the ambulance behind one of the paramedics. He put an oxygen mask on Mr. S, and I took his hand. "There, there, *meydele*," he said removing his mask for a moment. "It will be all right. I don't think God is ready for me. Not yet."

I looked the other way so he wouldn't see my eyes welling up, my lips quivering. I was supposed to reassure *him*, not the other way around.

I'd had very little experience with sickness. In our little family, no one ever got sick. All the feeble or sick people, the would-be aunts, uncles, and grandparents, had been disposed of by the Nazis. My parents were strong and healthy until cancer snuffed out my dad.

Dad was right. Life was fragile and fleeting. I knew all that. Still, I wasn't prepared for another loss. It was my bad for allowing myself to get close to Mr. S. That's what happens to people I'm close to. They die.

# ~CHAPTER TWELVE~

I was feeling groggy as I walked into the clinic the next morning after a fitful sleepless night worrying about Gramps. I had little energy to try and figure out my next move in the stalled Cecil Project. Also keeping me up was a heavy gnawing feeling that I'd have to make up with Daphne. I owed her an apology. I intended on doing that soon, because if there was one lesson Dad had taught me it was that the best way to get rid of an unpleasant task was to do it quickly. He was forever apologizing to Mom, even if he'd done nothing to warrant an apology. Perhaps that was why Daphne and I never fought. We simply avoided difficult subjects. And although I knew I owed her an apology, it stuck in my craw, for whenever we did have a little disagreement, inevitably I had to be the one to take the first step.

"Brace yourself," Theresa said as I passed her office. "Phoebe called down and wasn't thrilled you weren't in yet."

I looked up at the clock. It had just turned nine, so I wasn't late. "What now?" I grimaced. My head was threatening to split open.

Theresa shrugged. "Don't know. But she wants you and Derrick in her office, like now."

"Good. At least whatever I've done, I'm not the only culprit."

I dropped my things off in my office, tossed my half-eaten apple in the garbage, and took the final swig of my coffee. I also popped a Tums in my mouth as a preventative and marched to Derrick's office.

I poked my head through his door. "Ready to see the old battleax?"

He chuckled. "How's the old man," he asked. I raised my shoulders. I had nothing new to report, the nurse at the hospital had only given me a cryptic report. Derrick acknowledged that hospitals' communications were unsatisfactory.

He followed me out the door. "Not sure why you dread Phoebe so much, she's not that bad," he said. But I noticed that he had his dreadlocks tied into a neat ponytail so that he looked less like a reggae star, more professional. His jeans and scruffy sneakers, however, were as shabby as ever. I was glad I was wearing my power suit with its humongous shoulders.

"Do you have any clue what she wants?" I asked when we climbed the stairs.

"Nope. But we'll find out soon enough." He didn't seem concerned in the least bit. I wished some of his serene unflappable manner would rub off on me.

"Come in, come in," Phoebe called when we presented ourselves at her office door. "How are you settling in? I hope everything's to your liking?" She smiled brightly at Derrick. "I've been meaning to check in with you but have been inundated, as you can see." She pointed at her messy desk, as if an untidy desk was an indication of the significance or urgency of her work.

"I've been well looked after by Marika and Theresa, so I'm good," he said, smiling.

"Well." Her eyes narrowed as she looked at me as if she couldn't believe I had been very useful. "Anyway, do sit down."

The two chairs across her desk were cleared of all files. Also, her ashtray had been recently emptied. Even her hedgehog hair seemed softer, as if she'd actually used a hair dryer on it.

"You're probably wondering why I called you both up here. It's come to my attention," she began with her usual line, "that a few of our patients have tested positive for AIDS." She reached for a cigarette and offered one to Derrick, who declined.

"Doctor Bird mentioned that we've had a few patients who are HIV positive, though probably not yet full-blown AIDS," Derrick corrected her.

"Six of one." Phoebe let the thought trail. "In any case, some of our board members, who are doctors, are pretty adamant that we should test our entire population as soon as possible."

"As you know, we can and do offer the test whenever they have a physical due, or simply ask for it. We highly recommend and encourage them to get tested," I chimed in, annoyed that she hadn't given me credit for implementing the policy already.

"We're in the midst of what may turn out to be a crisis, so we need to get ahead of the curve and test *everyone*, physicals or no physicals. Not just *encourage* it." She shot me a scathing look.

"However, we can't force anyone to be tested if they don't want to. They have the freedom to choose," Derrick said. There was no edge to his voice; it was as calm as if he was discussing the weather.

"Of course, I didn't imply that you'd force anyone. Certainly not. I'm merely suggesting that we do what we can to make them get tested. It should be matter of policy," she said, a tight smile on her thin red lips. "Our doctor comes only once a month to do physicals, so we'll have to ramp up the blood tests without his presence. I thought you and Theresa could do that and send them to the lab."

This courteous, agreeable Phoebe was new to me. "Perhaps we can increase counseling them about the benefits of testing," I ventured.

"That's precisely why I wanted you in this meeting." She turned to me. "It's *your* job to do what's necessary to bring the patients around. *You're* the therapist and have to be the persuasive one. As the clinical director, you have much more day-to-day contact with them than Derrick."

I felt my ears burn as I sat there chewing the inside of my cheek thinking of her reprimand.

Derrick leaned back in his chair and sighed. "This will require teamwork, Phoebe. But no worries, we've got it. Marika and I, we'll tag team it." He gave me a tiny wink and sat upright. "Anything else we can do for you?" I almost expected him to call her Pheebs.

Phoebe's mouth clammed shut and her lips disappeared. She cleared her throat and stabbed the cigarette in the ashtray. "Good. Very good. I knew I could count on you, Derrick, to come through." The muscles in Derrick's jaws tightened, but if he was angry, he didn't let on.

Back in his office, I tossed my hair and laughed with a certain insouciance. "You're right, Phoebe's not so bad. She's really a pussycat." I bit my lower lip, glad he couldn't see the thumping of my veins. "Thank you, Derrick, I knew I could count on you, Derrick," I mimicked her. "What am I, chopped liver?"

His eyebrows drew together and he scratched his head before opening his mouth to speak, but then didn't. When he finally spoke, surprisingly, he ignored my comment altogether.

"Why don't I come as a guest speaker to your group one day, after you've talked to them about the HIV test? Then they can ask me medical questions about it," he said.

I was grateful for his offer, for although Derrick was not our medical doctor, he was still a doctor, and knew our patients much more intimately than our once-a-month physician who provided quick, bare minimum physicals and didn't have much of a rapport with them. Perhaps other methadone clinics were better equipped to deal with this new plague, and any other medical issues, but not us. Our patients ended up in the E.R. all too often when they needed medical care.

"Sure, sure. Let's tag team it. I've got group in a few minutes, so I better get prepared to broach the subject with them today." I didn't really see the point of the whole exercise. If I was in their shoes, I wouldn't jump to take a test to find out I had a disease that had no cure.

"Do you want me to come to your group today, in case they want to ask medical questions?"

"That won't be necessary," I said. I wasn't prepared for him to see how fractured my group was, nor did I want to spring anything on my women. "I'll talk to them about it, and you'll be the guest speaker next week."

"Next week it is." He coughed a tiny cough.

"And maybe you should give up smoking or soon you'll compete with Phoebe's hack."

He looked offended. "Didn't you see me turn down her offered cigarette?"

I shrugged. "Early days." I'd seen too many people battle giving up smoking and lose. I turned to go.

"Hey," he called. "If you're going to visit your Mr. Saperstein this evening, I'd like to come with you. I like the old codger."

His offer surprised me, but I gladly accepted it. He'd turned out to be not a bad sort, after all. Perhaps I'd been too quick to judge. We settled on the time after work, and I marched on to do battle with my group.

It was the usual group meeting, full of little squabbles interspersed with heartening, meaningful moments. I told them about our new program offering HIV testing for all, with the familiar drivel about the importance of using precautions and not sharing needles. And they responded with their customary cynicism and distrust. My comment about the total confidentiality of the tests was met with snickering and scorn, especially from Rosie. She'd been looking much better in the past few weeks. I noticed that she had on clean clothes, and her eyes were alert and bright. She laughed lustily and often.

"If you don't know by now that nothing that goes on in this place stays confidential for more than a minute, then you ain't learned a thing I been trying to teach you." She laughed her raucous laugh. When Rosie laughed, you couldn't help but join in.

"I know, I know," I conceded the obvious. "But you can't make important decisions about your life and health based on such worries." And yet, even as I said that I wondered what I'd do in their shoes. If I tested positive, I wouldn't want anyone to know. There was so much stigma and shame attached to that disease.

"As soon as somebody loses some weight around here, the rumors start flying that they have AIDS," Carmen said. "I ain't interested in no test. If I got it, I got it."

"Hmm. Most likely cause of weight loss around here is cocaine use," I said.

The mood didn't improve after my last comment. We ended soon thereafter. Rosie followed me as I walked to my office.

"Do you have a sec?" she asked.

I opened my office door and we walked in. I was glad to see her happy. "Sit down," I said.

"No, this won't take a min. Besides, Carmen's waiting for me. I just wanted to tell you that I been sending around my resume and I have an interview next week for sub teaching for summer school up in the Bronx. Gonna have to wear long sleeves no matter how hot it gets, though," she said, holding up her arms with their track marks running their full length.

I felt my heart expand. I wanted to envelope her in a hug but remembered my boundaries. "That is terrific news."

"Let's not celebrate. I ain't got the job yet. It's gonna be hard if they ask for any recent references. But I got some good old ones and I hear they're pretty relaxed with subs anyway. They just lookin' for a body to babysit."

"Don't sell yourself short. You were a good teacher. Just remember not to lapse into your street jive."

"Why you always worry 'bout that? I can talk like a college grad when I need to, Ma-Rika." She was the only patient who had a nickname for me, and only used it when she was in an exceptionally good mood. "Thanks for never stopping believing in me."

"I won't take the credit for your successes." Although, in truth, I probably did, a little.

"Let me know how it goes, but I'm sure you'll nail it," I called after her as she left. Honestly, I had my doubts, although Rosie, before her downfall, had been a successful math teacher, but that was a good number of years ago, and it had been only a few weeks since she was still using cocaine.

After Rosie's good news, it was time to focus on my own messed up life. I grabbed the phone and dialed Daphne. My heart raced when she answered.

"Hi," I said and waited. It was quiet on the other side of the line. As I figured, Daphne hadn't forgiven me my unforgivable behavior. "Look, Daph, I'm sorry. I really am. I don't know what got into me. I … I wish I could take it all back, but I can't."

"Yes, what's said cannot be unsaid." She sounded as cold as Mom used to whenever one of us asked for forgiveness before she was ready to bestow her pardon. "And on top of that, you didn't bother to let us know you were leaving. Didn't you think we'd be worried about you?" Her voice rose. "You didn't even say 'bye to the kids."

I swallowed hard. Crying would be too pathetic, a low and underhanded way to get sympathy. "I wasn't thinking clearly. I was so embarrassed."

"Whatever."

"I was going to ask you for Nathan's phone number. I want to apologize to him."

"I'll ask Gerald for it. But, honestly, I don't think an apology will do much, do you?"

I'd never known Daphne to be that angry with me, although I've given her plenty of cause in the past. "What do you think I should do?" I asked.

"Truth is I don't know. And right now, I don't really care. I need a break. I'm going to focus on me and my family. So, if you don't mind, let's keep some distance for a while." Her voice broke ever so slightly, but then she went on. "I'll call you when I'm ready to talk."

I was stunned into a momentary silence. "You ... you don't mean that, Daph. I'm really—"

"Don't Marika. Ever since Mom and Dad died, I've been taking care of *your* needs, *your* pain, *your* everything. I can't anymore. I need a break. I'll call you." Softening her tone a little, she added, "Give me some time." Then she hung up.

I clutched myself in an attempt to stop the shivers that rocked my body. I was suddenly overcome by fatigue and would have climbed on top of my desk and curled up in a fetal position, had someone not knocked on my door at that moment.

"Been thinking about what you said in group," Carmen said without preamble. "And I'm worried about Rosie. She ain't been right. I want her to get tested."

"Did you talk to *her* about it?" I asked, astounded. "In group, you were so against testing." I wondered if she was trying to sabotage Rosie's attempt to get a job. Afraid she's straighten her life out and leave Carmen behind.

"Fock. What I say in group is in group. Anyway, I can't talk to her, she don't listen to me. She only listen to you. I want you should talk to her." Carmen always had an edge when she spoke to me. We'd never gotten along, and I blamed myself because I was the therapist and it was up to me to make the relationship a therapeutic one.

"I'll be happy to talk to her. Better yet, how about the both of you talk to Doctor Scott? He'll explain the whole testing process much better than I can. Maybe if you agree to test, too, Rosie'll be more open to it. After all, you two have shared needles and ... other things," I said.

"I ain't the one losing weight, I tell you. Anyway, talk to Rosie," she said with finality and left.

Daphne, Rosie, Mr. S, Cecil, nothing was right. I wanted to go home and crawl under the covers. Even the thought of my Cecil Project didn't excite me. But I had to go to the hospital to visit Mr. S. I hoped seeing him improving would change the trajectory of this unpleasant day.

# ~CHAPTER THIRTEEN~

The subway stopped a block from the hospital and as we climbed up the stairs, Derrick suggested that we get Mr. S a little present. I was ashamed the idea hadn't occurred to me, for it should have. I hadn't even brought any crosswords for him. We agreed that Mr. S wasn't the flowers kind of guy, being much too practical and unsentimental.

"How about some toiletries," Derrick suggested.

"I should have gotten them from his apartment," I said. "He wouldn't want me to waste money needlessly." Derrick looked at me as if I was from some strange planet. Obviously, he hadn't a clue about my parents' nor Mr. S's one-bag-for-three-cups-of-tea ways.

"Seriously? A tube of toothpaste and a razor? How much could it cost?"

"Waste not." I let the cliché trail off. "Anyway, he's probably not up to shaving yet. Why don't we get him a little treat? Chocolates or something. He's got an awful sweet tooth." I remembered when I was sick as a child, which was quite often, Mom always brought me chocolates.

"Fine, if you think he'd be up to eating."

"Oh, it's the thought that counts, the gesture. Besides, chocolates last," I said, beginning to feel unaccountably irritated.

We wandered into the little shop across the street from the hospital. The shop carried a small range of cheap chocolates.

"They're all made in the U.S." I scrunched my face.

"And?"

"Mr. S is Viennese," I remarked, as if that should explain everything. He and I shared a love for finer chocolates, although for some unknown reason he loved Ding Dongs. I got a couple of Hershey bars with almonds and a couple of Hostess Cupcakes. Derrick picked up a newspaper and a *People* magazine, which I thought was ludicrous, but resisted the temptation of saying so. We paid and walked out with our meager gifts.

As soon as we walked into the hospital, I wanted to turn and run. All the hairless, toothless old people in the hallway and rooms, either dozing or starring at the television sets overhead were ghostly reminders of our mortality. We found Mr. S's room, which he shared with another man. He was lying in bed, his eyes shut, with an oxygen mask over his face. Two intravenous drips were hanging from a pole; their fluid seeped through the feeding tubes into his veins while a heart monitor beeped in the background. He looked frail and small, childlike. I struggled to squelch the fear in my heart and went to pull the dividing curtain for some privacy. The man in the next bed starred vacantly at the ceiling. I reached out to pat Mr. S's hand in a pathetic attempt at reassuring him all would be fine.

Derrick picked up the chart dangling from the foot of the bed.

"I don't think you should read it," I whispered.

"He can read it. It's not a state secret. That's why it's out in the open for everyone to see."

I jumped at Mr. S's muffled voice. "How are you feeling, Gramps?" I said with the same fake cheeriness I'd hated hearing other people use when talking to the sick. "I thought you were asleep. Hope we didn't wake you."

He removed his mask with his wrinkled, spindly hand. "You can't sleep in hospitals. They poke at you all night long with their needles. Every five minutes someone else comes to take your blood. I probably have little left and will soon need a transfusion."

Derrick laughed. "I see you still have your sense of humor. How *are* you feeling?"

"You brought the shrink with you, good. Maybe you can tell me what it says in the chart. The doctors don't tell you anything around here."

"Doesn't say much, just that you have pneumonia. Double pneumonia."

"Does it say when they expect me to die?" He wheezed; perhaps it was an attempt to laugh.

"Stop it, Gramps. None of that kind of talk," I said.

"All I'm saying is don't buy me green bananas." He let out another wheezy laugh.

I changed the subject. "No bananas at all, but we did get you a few sweets." I put the bag on his tiny bedside table. "Did the doctors say anything about when you'll be leaving?"

"I'm not sure the kid who came to see me was even a doctor. Looked like he hadn't started to shave yet. He poked, prodded and left."

"They're waiting for the antibiotics to kick in. You'll probably be here quite a few days, count on at least a week, maybe two," Derrick said in his calm, sing-song accent. "I think you should put the mask back on, so you don't tire yourself."

"But you're my guests. I have to be a good host." He held out his bony hand to me. It felt so cool in mine. I choked back the tears threatening to well up.

"We got you some magazines and chocolates. Cupcakes. Couldn't find Ding-Dongs," I said.

He peeked into the bag. "I love Hershey's imitation chocolate. Sweet." I didn't know if he meant me or the chocolate, but I thought I saw his eyes water. Derrick's eyes lit up, too.

"I think Derrick's right. You should put the mask back on, and we should let you rest," I said. "I'll be back tomorrow."

Mr. S let his head drop back on his pillow and shut his eyes again. His breathing was shallow, his face flushed. "You're busy, no need to come every day to see a boring old man."

Derrick motioned to me and we started toward the door. Mr. S rasped, "Hey, this new boyfriend, you could do worse."

I waved my hand dismissively to hide my embarrassment and hoped Derrick hadn't heard him as I dashed out, after promising to come the next day.

We rode the elevator down in silence. My hands were sweaty, and I felt hot. I was glad to be out of there. We stepped out into humid damp evening air and I inhaled deeply, finally feeling the tightness in my chest loosen. There was still some soft light. I wished for a little rain to clear the air.

Derrick hoisted his battered backpack on his shoulder and looked up at the sky. "There's a nice little burger joint nearby, want a quick bite?" he asked.

I hesitated. I wasn't prepared for this, whatever *this* was.

"Unless, of course, you have other plans," he quickly added.

I didn't relish the idea of having to make conversation with him for an entire meal. It had been an upsetting day and even in the best of times I'm not much of a conversationalist. On the other hand, I thought it would be rude to turn him down after he'd been so helpful with Mr. S. Besides, I might need his help again. And there was nothing waiting for me at home. All told, I quickly realized that it would be sensible to accept his offer.

"Sure," I said. "But I don't eat burgers."

"You're not a vegetarian, are you?"

"No. Just a fussy eater. Used to drive my mom crazy."

We ended up at a little bistro in the West Village. It had been one of Cecil's and my favorite little haunts, but that was no reason not to go in. I was familiar with their menu and knew they had low-calorie soups and salads.

We took our seats at a tiny table by the window and sat in not quite companionable silence, fiddling with the menus. I looked around, as if I expected to see Cecil, but of course he had probably stopped coming here. The waitress came over to take our drink orders. Derrick got a beer and I stuck to water. I didn't expect him to pay for my meal; that would have made this a real date, and Phoebe had a no dating policy at the clinic.

The drinks arrived and I ordered my carrot soup. He got one of those grotesque half-pounder burgers, fries, onion rings, the works. I watched him take a swig of his beer and wondered how he maintained his slim physique. The light from the window behind him cast his profile into view: his powerful nose, full lips, and chiseled chin.

"Ahem." He cleared his throat and gazed intently into my face. "Not sure how to break this to you, but your neighbor, Mr. S, may not survive. He's got double pneumonia and at his age ...." He surveyed his hands, as if he found them fascinating. His fingers were long and sinewy.

"But ... but he looked much better today. He even joked a little."

"It always gets better before the end, they say."

"That's ridiculous. I've never heard that. And who's the 'they' anyway," I scoffed.

"Sorry. You're right. Just an old wives' tale. My mom's full of them." He smiled, and his dimple appeared. "He means a lot to you, doesn't he?"

"He's my neighbor," I said keeping my voice casual. "We look out for each other. Besides, he doesn't have any relatives nearby. He had a large family before the war. They all died."

"That's so sad. Good that he has you."

I thought he was about to pat my hand, but our food arrived and we busied ourselves for a few moments. Derrick poured a huge dollop of ketchup, followed by another dollop of mustard and some hot sauce on his burger.

"So you like a little burger with your ketchup." I chuckled.

"American food is too bland. I like mine spicy." He piled fried onions on top of his burger and popped the bun on top. "Watch out. Fair warning, this ain't gonna be pretty." He grinned.

I looked away as he opened his mouth wide and took a colossal bite. Mustard and ketchup squirted out onto his plate and fingers. "Mmm." He licked the mess from his fingers. "You don't know what you're missing."

I sipped my soup slowly and daintily and toyed with the idea of taking a slice of bread, but carbs fatten my thighs instantaneously.

"So, your mom was full of good old wives' tales, huh?" I asked.

"Oh, yeah. There isn't a problem or issue that she doesn't have a wise old saying for. And she clings to them; there's no reasoning with her. She's a tough cookie, though."

My ears perked up. This was the first I'd heard him say anything remotely personal. "And your father?" I asked.

"My father?" His eyes narrowed. He chewed slowly and swallowed. "He's … I have very little to do with him. He wasn't around when I was growing up. What about your parents?"

This was rather titillating, and I would have liked to ask him more, but he'd cut off talking about his father deliberately. "My parents are dead," I said, keeping my voice indifferent to forestall sympathy. "Dad died of cancer in my senior year of high school, and Mom followed a year later."

He studied me closely as if he now noticed something he hadn't seen before, but thankfully he didn't offer the usual platitudes. "Sorry about that. I'm glad you have Mr. Saperstein."

I shrugged. "Don't make too much of it. I've only known him for three years. He's a jokester, and I like the old man, the gramps I never had. Do you have a grandfather?" I attempted to get back to him.

"I grew up in a household of women. My *white* father had his *white* family, and my mom was just someone he fucked. Very cliché. So it's been me, my mom, and grandma and an assortment of aunts and cousins. You can't always get what you want, as the wise Jagger put it." He inclined his head, looking puzzled, then tucked one of his dreadlocks behind his ear. "What happened to you and your fiancé?"

"Me and my what?" I was thinking about what he'd just revealed. How sad it was.

"Mr. Saperstein asked if I was your new fiancé, so I figured there was an old one."

"Oh, you know. We broke up." I waved my hand in attempt to show it was no big deal. "We moved on." I slurped the last of my soup and pushed the plate away.

"I get it." A small grin played on his generous mouth. "Engagements break up, marriages break up, which is why I don't see the point of getting married in the first place."

"That's a little dismissive of an old institution that most people still want," I said, a bit aghast, since marriage was, to me, the ultimate goal.

"How long were you two together?"

"About three years." It was two years and eight months, but I had a right to round it off to the nearest number.

"Three years," he said. "I don't think I've been with one woman three months." Seeing my face, he went on, "I think women more than men insist on monogamy and we're probably not built for that. Maybe I got that attitude from my father. Best to be together with someone for as long as it works, and then when it's over, make a clean break."

"That sounds so callous."

"Maybe, but I think most people secretly believe it, they just won't admit it to themselves. But here's the thing, we'd be much healthier if we did. If we allowed each other to do exactly what we wanted and with whom we wanted. We could still live with the one we loved for companionship, but we could have sex with others. We could even talk about it openly. Wouldn't that be more honest? Eliminate all the cheating and sneaking around."

"I don't know about that. Easy thing to say, but most people get awfully hurt when their spouses cheat," I said. "I bet you wouldn't like it if your girlfriend cheated on you."

"Honestly. I'm not so sure. I haven't a jealous bone in my body. Jealousy is an utterly pointless emotion."

"Emotions may be pointless, but they're still there." I was astonished at his attitude. Surely a shrink ought to have a more nuanced perspective on relationships. "Is everybody so laid back about marriages in Jamaica?"

"Not really. People get married all the time. Most Jamaican *men* probably believe like I do, that it's unnatural for men to be monogamous. As for women, well, it's true, men want and even expect their women to be faithful." He chuckled.

I didn't know if I should take him seriously. It was hard to tell. What was certain was that he and I were different animals. Or different planets. His relaxed attitude about everything, especially infidelity was hard for me to accept. I was therefore surprised when he insisted on paying for my dinner, and I let him, because even though I didn't expect him— or any man—to pay for my meals, it was a welcome gesture.

We got up to leave when I heard my name. It was unmistakable. Cecil had a unique way of pronouncing it, with the emphasis on the R, MaRika. I turned and, sure enough, there he was. In the company of another man, an artistic type, with earrings: one in his ear and one in his eyebrow.

"Haven't seen you in years and now we run into each other twice in a month," he said. "How unlikely is that?"

"Yeah, of all the gin joints." I laughed. He walked over, bent down, and pecked my cheek. "Who's your friend?" His eyebrows arched upward.

I introduced Derrick as a colleague, and they shook hands. "We also happen to be neighbors. This city is really a bunch of tiny villages strung together," I said.

Cecil introduced the man he was with as an amazingly talented new artist and added that his gallery would be having a one-man show of his work in a few weeks. "I hope you'll come to the opening, Marika," he said. Then he added as an afterthought, "As a matter of fact, you, too, Derrick. You're an art lover, I hope."

"How exciting. I'd love to come," I gushed. "Don't forget to send me the invitation. You can send it to my office address," I reminded him as Derrick and I turned to go. Cecil had promised before to send me invites to gallery openings, but so far, nothing.

I practically skipped on the way home as I chatted aimlessly about Cecil and his love for art. We got to our street and Derrick said he had to hustle. Poor Bruce was waiting for his walk. I thanked him for coming with me to see Mr. S.

"Like I told you, I like the man. He's good people." He turned to walk up his stoop, then stopped and turned around. "By the way, this Cecil, was he your former fiancé?"

"Yeah. Now that enough time passed, we can be friends again. We're being civilized."

"True."

"Would you like to come with me to the opening?"

"Why not? I like art as much as anyone." He waved and skipped up the stairs, taking two at a time.

I went home elated. Not only did old Gramps seem to be hanging in there just fine, despite what Derrick said, but the next phase in the Cecil Project had presented itself with no effort on my part. Like a gift, meant to be. It was better than anything I could have concocted. Now I'd not only go to the exhibit, but I'd have a pseudo date with Derrick. Perhaps that would make Cecil jealous.

# ~CHAPTER FOURTEEN~

"Gramps, what do you think of my hair?" I asked.

It was a muggy midsummer day and all my efforts at blow drying my hair that morning were for naught. I could feel it frizzing on my way to the hospital, actually feel it as if it was part of my skin. I gathered my mop into a scrunchy and pulled it on top of my head before I entered his room on Friday afternoon after work.

Poor Gramps had been in the hospital for three weeks, fighting for his life it seemed, so I was thrilled to see him sitting up in bed without the oxygen mask. I'd brought him a crossword puzzle as well as a churro, which he was scarfing down, licking his fingers. It was good to see his sweet tooth returning to him.

"Your hair? What's wrong with your hair? You've got beautiful curls." He smacked his lips and smiled. "Just like my little Rochel had."

I wasn't sure I wanted to remind him of his long dead daughter. "I hate my hair. It gets so frizzy in summer. Men hate frizzy hair," I said. Cecil had often tried to get me to straighten it.

"You've got ethnic hair and you want *shiksa* hair, right?" He looked at me knowingly. "If anyone doesn't like your hair, he's an idiot. Why don't you do it up in little braids, like that shrink of yours? And why didn't you bring him along?"

My laugh came out in little snorts. "You want me in dreadlocks? I'll look silly. Anyway, I don't know where Derrick is. You'll have to make do with me," I said. "He probably rushed home to walk his Brucie. He *loves* his dog."

"Hmm. A dog person. That's a good sign," he said. "It means he's got an open heart."

"Nonsense. So I'm not exactly a dog person, what does that make me a closed hearted person? No one in my family liked dogs, but they were all good people."

"I didn't say anything about people who don't like dogs; only about those who *do*," he said. "Now, let's talk about when I can get out of here. I asked the doctor today and he hemmed and hawed and wouldn't give me a straight answer, just something about still being under observation. But for God's sake, I've been here months."

"Don't exaggerate, but, yes, it's been a few weeks, longer than we anticipated, and I know it's been hard. But I'm sure they'll let you go as soon as they think you're healthy enough. Besides, you're being well looked after, so what's wrong with staying a few more days?" I shuddered at the thought of him leaving the hospital too soon and relapsing.

"Pshaw. I've been here months," he insisted, "and I'm ready to get sprung from the joint. I'm feeling good enough to go home. If I don't get out soon, I'll die here. I can feel it in my bones. Can you come and get me tomorrow?"

"You should do what the doctors say. What's this getting sprung talk? For goodness sake, you're not in prison. Anyway, tomorrow's Saturday, so they probably won't release you over the weekend."

"I'm telling you I'm not staying here another day. If you don't come, I'll just walk out tomorrow wearing these pajamas." It's the first time I'd heard him petulant, almost childlike.

I pretended to focus on the crossword, stalling for time. The sun was still high in the sky. It was promising to be another hot night and I'd have to crank the air conditioner on. "You can't leave against medical advice," I finally said.

"What are they going to do, arrest me? When you're my age, you've earned the right to do what you want." His looked at me, his eyes ablaze. I hoped it wasn't fever.

"Tell you what. Give me the weekend to organize your apartment, buy some food, and if by Monday they don't discharge you, I'll come and spring you, as you so delightfully put it."

"Good, like Bonnie and Clyde, we'll be fugitives from the hospital." His Yoda smile lit up both the dingy hospital room and my heart. Against my better judgment, I had gotten too attached to this old man. I reminded myself that I ought to harden, that he was *not* family. Speaking of which, my only family member, Daphne was still not talking to me, so, for the moment, Gramps was it.

On my way home from the hospital, I stopped by the local Duane Reade to get new hair products for myself as well as more toiletries for Mr. S, just in case he was released on Monday. I hoped he'd stay a few more days. While browsing amongst the shampoos and conditioners, each offering promises of gorgeous hair like the models pictured—and which I was a sucker for—I came upon the section Black people hair products. Why hadn't I thought of that before? If it can straighten really kinky hair, it could surely do the same for my curls. Cecil's gallery exhibit was on Saturday and I had no time to waste; my makeover project had to be revved up. I chose the straightener that showed a woman with dark, soft, flowing hair. That's exactly how I wanted mine to be: lush, shiny, and luxuriously bouncy. I couldn't wait to get home and put it on.

For once, I didn't mind being home alone on a Friday night. I had something to look forward to: the Cecil Project was going into high gear tomorrow. I pictured walking through the gallery, my hair swinging softly behind my back as Cecil's eyes followed me in admiration. I started fixing my dinner, chopping away at cucumbers, tomatoes, peppers, carrots. Chop, chop, chop to the beat of Tina Turner singing *What's Love Got to Do With It* wafting from my stereo.

"What's love but a second-hand emotion," I trilled as I filled the bowl with chopped veggies. I dumped a small chunk of goat cheese in, as well as a couple of hard-boiled eggs. I even toasted a thin slice of rye bread. A veritable feast, but I didn't care. I toyed with the idea of a glass of wine, but I couldn't find any. I was tempted to call Daphne again, just to hear her voice as well as consult with her about using the hair straightener, but decided not to. She'd made it clear that she needed a break from me and my problems when she gave me that don't call me, I'll call you admonition, and I had to honor her request. It had been almost a month.

I ate my meal, savoring every morsel, while watching a rerun of the *Mary Tyler Moore Show*. She was a single woman who, unlike me, was looking for love rather than making marriage the driving focus. I felt Mary was clueless for letting some pretty good prospects go all because she wasn't in love with them. She was a perfect example of women who fell into the trap of thinking love would make them happy, that it would even last. Mary should have married her overweight balding boss; he was a stable and good provider.

After I ate, I wasted no time in jumping into the shower with my miracle hair straightener, promising me mega sleek, silky hair. It was a messy process, requiring me to smear the thick, gooey concoction on my hair, combing it through, and then leaving it on for twenty to twenty-five minutes. I stayed in the bathroom so as not to drip goo all over the floor and waited for it to take. For good measure I waited an extra ten minutes before shampooing it out.

My hair felt a little stiff when I got out of the shower and towel dried it. But I calmed down by telling myself that once I'd blown it dry, it would look as soft and shiny and as full of life as the woman's in the photo. I took my time and blew it dry carefully, wrapping my hair section by small section around the brush. But when I was finished it still lay flat and stiff, like a wet helmet plastered on my head. The long strands hung rigid on my shoulders, as if my hair had ossified. A petrified forest of hair.

I stared at the sight in the mirror. I tugged at my stiff strands as if I could wake them into life, while I paced around my tiny bathroom frantically looking for products that could lend some shine and softness to my locks. I jumped back into the shower and savagely scrubbed my hair and rinsed it twice. I then applied half a bottle of softening conditioner. But halfway through my second blow dry, I realized it was useless. I wet my hair once again and let it dry naturally in hope that my curls would come back to life. Alas, true to its promise, the straightener had uncompromisingly straightened my hair.

There was nothing to do but hope against hope that after a night's sleep I'd wake up in the morning to find my hair had relaxed. Maybe that's what it needed, a good night's sleep. I certainly did.

However, once in bed, sleep refused to come. My mind was awhirl. What would I do if Mr. S insisted on leaving the hospital on Monday against medical advice? I'd be on the hook to take care of him. That's what I got for allowing myself to get too attached to the old man: a lot of pain and trouble. Just as I was going over the list of things I'd need to organize in his apartment before his return, a new thought crowded the old one out of my head. How would I face everyone at work on Monday with my hair plastered to my head, looking like it was painted on? I'd be the laughing stock amongst staff and clients alike. Worse still, how could I possibly show up at the art exhibit tomorrow?

That last thought kept me up the rest of the night. Yet, when the sun's rays finally shimmered through my bedroom window, I didn't want to get out of bed and face the inevitable mirror. Finally, when I could no longer avoid the unavoidable, I crawled out and shuffled to the bathroom, fluffing my hair maniacally with my hands. It was an exercise in futility. The strands were as stiff as they'd been the previous night, pasted onto my sculp. No amount of shampooing would bring the lifeless stringy mess back to life. I had to chop it off. All of it, without mercy. Perhaps I could pull off the Mia Farrow in *Rosemary's Baby* look.

I grabbed the phone book and called my hairdresser, the sweetest young man, right around the corner from my house. Unfortunately, he was on vacation and no one else could fit me in at such a short notice. This was a Saturday in New York City, what did I expect? I started cold calling a few other salons in the neighborhood to no avail, my hands shaking more with each call. Then I remembered my client Pam, the newly graduated hairdresser, the one Phoebe raked me over the coals for letting her style my hair. Normally, I wouldn't dream of disobeying Phoebe, but I couldn't let that stand in my way now. Pam worked in a ramshackle salon in the upper west side, way up. I decided to take my chances and just show up, partly because I couldn't remember the name of the salon, only the location, but also I thought maybe Pam would feel obligated to take me even if she had other clients waiting. That in itself would have normally deterred me, but, again, this was not normal times. I either had to do something about my hair or stand the risk of failing with my Project. And defeat was not an option.

Without losing any time on unwanted self-reflection or other worthless thoughts, I pulled on my shorts and T-shirt, grabbed my purse and a hat, and ran out. Perhaps I should have stopped to reconsider my actions, but, if anything, I faulted myself for having been the cautious type for too long. And what had that caution gotten me? Here I was, single, almost thirty, with a small job, in a small apartment, with a very small social life, and no obvious way out of my small existence. The clock was ticking. It was time to throw caution to the wind.

# ~CHAPTER FIFTEEN~

$P$am was a success story, if such could be claimed before one's life was fully over. I was well aware that someone with her background could backslide at any moment. Relapses were a common occurrence, so we couldn't become complacent. But when she'd first come to our clinic, Pam had been living on the streets for two years after being tossed out of her parents' home. It took a couple of years more before she stopped messing with drugs completely, and then another two before she enrolled in hairdressing school, after much cajoling by me. Finally, having graduated, she'd landed a job. I didn't regret having let her blow dry my hair that time.

Now Pam was ecstatic about her life, her professional achievement, and having a tiny apartment in the Bronx to call her own. It wasn't much but, as she constantly told me, it beat living on the streets. And if she wanted a steak, she could buy it rather than having to 'boost' it. We could now laugh at her story that she was once arrested for transporting stolen steaks across a state border. When she wasn't transporting stolen meat, she'd sold her body. She was still plagued by nightmares of getting high or living on the street and often after such nightmares would cry in my office. It was gratifying for me to hear the way she gave me credit for her achievements. Wrong, but nonetheless gratifying. I was relieved to see her short fiery spiked red hair as soon as I walked into the salon. It was kind of a dump, but I was in no position to be choosy.

"Marika." Pam clapped her hands upon seeing me. She ran over and gave me an effusive hug. I stiffened a little, for I'm not in the habit of hugging my clients. She bounced around me as if I was some sort of celebrity entering this less than exclusive establishment. "What are *you* doing here?"

Luckily, the salon was empty except for two Hispanic women sitting and chatting, their hair in tin foils sticking out at all angles, making them look like beings from another planet.

In answer to Pam, I took off my hat. "Oh, my God, what'd ya do to your hair?" Pam squealed, her blue eyes like round saucers.

"I straightened it with some awful product. But never mind. Do you think you can fix it?" I asked. I tried to hide my distress. "Sorry, normally I wouldn't do this, 'cause, as I've told you, I can't let you cut my hair, but I've got a function tonight and I can't go like this and my hairdresser is on vacation and I couldn't find another appointment right away." I said all this in one quick whoosh, for fear that if I'd slow down, I'd realize my folly and run out of there.

"Don't worry, Marika, I won't tell a soul. Your secret is safe. I'm so glad that you trust me to fix this. Let's see what we can do." She sounded calm, reassuring almost. A role reversal indeed.

I sat down at the chair while Pam went to get a towel and cape to put on me. My heart was thumping in my chest, and I tried to calm down. After all, there was nothing to be nervous about. It was just my hair. Once when I was in first grade I'd been in tears because the school nurse had sent me home because I had lice and my mom had to shave my head. I'd cried inconsolably, despite Mom's reassurance that my hair would grow back. A year from now, I decided, when I'm married to Cecil, I'll tell him the story and we'd have a good laugh. I might even tell it to our children, if we'll have them.

Pam came back and wrapped the towel and raggedy cape around my shoulders. "Have you thought about getting a wig?" she asked as she fingered my hair. "I mean, we can fix this for sure, but just in case."

"A wig?" I associated wigs with orthodox Jewish women. "No, I haven't. Wigs look so fake, unless they're real hair and that'd be too expensive."

"Of course, you're right. And don't worry, you won't need one. Let's see. I think I can cut it into short layers, lots and lots of layers. That should restore some of the bounce and volume. And I'll cut it dry, so we'll see exactly how much we'll have to chop off. I love the dry cut technique. It's a bit more difficult, but I've done it a few times in school," she said. Despite the situation, I felt something stir in me: pride at how far Pam had come in the years I'd known her.

She took her shears and cut a strand. A shiver ran up my spine. I've never let my hair go shorter than shoulder length since that shearing I got back in first grade. One day when I was in second or third grade, I overhead a friend of Mom's say in a hushed tone that I'd be real cute if she'd let my hair grow longer. It would round off my thin face and make my nose look shorter, she had said. Mom replied in a cool manner that my nose was perfectly fine, it had character, which was more than she could say about those little pug noses everyone was hankering for. I'd kept on playing with my pug-nosed doll, pretending not to hear Mom and her friend discussing my nose. But ever since that day I insisted on letting my hair grow long, throwing a tantrum if Mom wanted me to have a haircut, even though she said my face was too small and was overwhelmed by all that hair. But moms are supposed to think their kids were pretty; the rest of the world doesn't necessarily agree.

I watched as Pam went on chopping, at first taking small amounts off, but, since my hair refused to return to life, she gathered momentum and began to energetically cut more and more off with bold fast clips. I watched in fascination as my hair fell on the floor. Pam kept an ongoing monologue about how cute I'd look, like an ingenue.

When she was done, all that remained on my head were short, uneven strands, no more than two inches in length. I tried not to let my face register my consternation, but I obviously fell short. I'd say I looked more like a street urchin than an ingenue.

"Don't worry, it'll be fabulous when I'm done. I'll put plenty of gel and spike it up like I do mine. It will be really chic. A new Marika," she said. Then, seeing my face, she twirled my chair around. "Not gonna let you face the mirror until I'm done."

I wasn't sure if she was trying to reassure me or herself, but I wasn't feeling very confident. A part of me wanted it to work, not only for myself, but also so as not to erode her confidence. The multi-level irony didn't escape me, though. Our role reversal was quite jarring. At work I was the knowledgeable one, giving advice. And here I sat meekly while Pam was the competent, reassuring one. No question, I didn't enjoy this turnaround. My makeover was not going well. If Mom was looking down on me right now, which I hoped she wasn't, she'd be shaking her head and muttering "Careful what you wish for, you may get it." But all I'd really wanted was straight hair. Now I'd have given anything to have my thick curls back.

"Ta-da," Pam cried as she twirled my chair so I could face the mirror again.

What I saw was a waifish creature with huge, pool-like worried-looking eyes and barely two-inch long spikey hair. A cross between Mia Farrow and Phoebe's hedgehog head.

"You look adorable," Pam said. "All you need is some eye make-up to make your eyes pop. A pair of fake eyelashes, eye liner, the works. Your eyes are so pretty, you should show 'em up. I can do it if you'd like. We carry all that stuff here. Oh, please let me do it."

I jumped out of my seat. There were limits to what I was willing to go through for my makeover and I thought I'd pretty much reached it with this cut. Next thing, Pam would talk me into adding red highlights to my dark blond hair, and, in my state of mind, I was worried that I'd let her. But just as I was getting ready to go, another thought occurred to me. Why not? Why shouldn't I get the works? I'd gone this far. I should go all the way. I had nothing to lose. Besides, I'd been craving a new look. It was now or never. It felt liberating to throw caution to the wind.

"Do it," I said. "I've always wanted to try fake lashes." I sat back down, my insides quivering, but gave myself over to Pam's ministrations. I even allowed her to pick the lavender eyeshadow I prayed wouldn't look too garish.

When she was done, I barely recognized the vision staring at me in the mirror. I fluttered my thick lashes. My little brooms.

"Don't worry, you'll get used to them," Pam reassured me. "But you look amazing. Doesn't she look amazing?" She turned to the other two hairdressers in the salon. They all agreed that I looked amazing. Unconvinced, I thanked her profusely, paid and tipped her generously, way beyond my normal tipping practice. I felt a pang of guilt at using her, but I dismissed the feeling. Before leaving I reminded her, no one must know of this visit.

"Get a pair of hoop earrings," she called after me. "They'll look perfect with your new look."

I forced a smile as I flew out the door. Once outside, I gasped for air, feeling as if I'd been holding my breath the entire time I was in the salon. I walked down toward the subway station, now and then checking my reflection at the storefront windows, and each time my reflection caught me off guard. In my mind's eye, I still had my long curly mop. My neck and ears felt bare, exposed. I missed my hair.

It was still early afternoon, so I had plenty of time to shop for a pair of hoop earrings as Pam had suggested, something to complete her makeover. But if I didn't rush downtown, I'd miss my visit with Mr. S. On second thought, the way I looked might scare him to death. So I decided to walk on, stopping now and then at the cheap costume jewelry shops. When something caught my eye, I walked in and browsed, yet nothing struck my fancy. Everything seemed cheap and loud, like my hair and eyelashes.

"Love your hair." I turned around and saw a young salesgirl. "Where'd you get it done?"

I told her. "Ask for Pam, she's really good. I'm looking for some earrings to go with this look," I said swallowing my innate shyness. "I'm going to an art opening tonight."

"I've got just the thing," the girl announced brightly and picked up a large pair of rainbow-colored earrings. An ornate candelabra. "These will look cool. Very edgy. That's what you want with artists. You want to be edgy."

I eyed them dubiously. However, when I put them on, I was pleasantly surprised. Perhaps I did look a bit odd. Bizarre and edgy indeed. So totally unlike me. A complete metamorphosis. There was something different about me besides the hair, and I couldn't pinpoint what that difference was. I didn't even *feel* like me. And that, I decided, was a good thing.

# ~CHAPTER SIXTEEN~

Cecil's gallery was located on 82nd Street and 1st Avenue, in one of the toniest parts of the city, albeit a little too far east from where the major art galleries with their A list artists were. Derrick and I emerged from the Lexington Avenue subway and turned east. It was one of those extra humid days, and I now worried, ironically, that instead of my hair mushrooming into a big cloud, it would fall flat as a pancake despite all the gel Pam had spiked it with.

I was pacing up and down the block outside my building when Derrick and I met to go to the gallery. I'd expected Derrick to say something cutting about my appearance. At the same time, I was quite relieved to see him dressed in a light linen jacket, his white shirt collar open. He was not bad looking, even with his dreadlocks. Derrick did sort of a double take when he saw me. His lips twitched ever so slightly.

"A new do?" he asked. I detected a tiny glint in his eyes

"I needed a change. Nothing wrong with wanting to change. I hope I haven't lost *all* of my appeal," I added with a sardonic grin. I was wearing a spaghetti strap dress that accentuated my slim body, at the moment my only good feature. In the past week, I'd adhered to my diet with extra care.

"Actually, I was going to compliment you." He paused and seemed to be searching for the right words. "Very ... striking. And congratulations on an unusual achievement, getting your lashes to be the same length as your hair." He bowed his head slightly.

"You're such a charmer. If you want, I'll take you to my hairdresser. I'm sure he'd like nothing more than to have a go at your fetching dreadlocks."

"Touché." He laughed good naturedly.

It was still light out as we made our way to the gallery, although it was past seven. I loved the long, drawn-out days of July. I remarked to Derrick that it was a bit sad that we'd passed mid-summer and all too soon the days would start getting shorter again.

"True enough. But why not focus on the here and now? It's a gorgeous summer's night and the sky's still a perfect blue," Derrick said.

He was right, of course; I had a hard time focusing on the present.

"Just saying that I hate to think of the long winter nights just around the corner."

"Geez, aren't you a ray of sunshine always focusing on the positive. How *did* you get so cheery?" He said straight faced, but his left eyebrow shot up as he looked down at me.

"Wait, wait, I get it," I said snapping my fingers. "It's called sarcasm, right?"

He shrugged but didn't respond and I decided to change the subject away from my neurosis. If he knew how both my heart and stomach were fluttering at the prospect of my Cecil Project coming to fruition, he'd probably put me on the analyst couch and diagnose me with some sort of disorder.

"Mr. S wants me to spring him out of the hospital on Monday even if it's against medical advice." I used my fingers to put spring in quotation marks. "What do you think of that?"

"Spring him?" He chuckled. "The old man's got a sense of humor. And he might do just as well at home at this point. The way I see it, it's his right to call the shots. Unless he has a fever and is still contagious, of course."

"You're no help. I thought you'd be a stickler for rules, not encouraging a patient to leave against medical advice. Must be the Jamaican in you. Very laid back and all."

"Yeah, mon, that's us. Lounging on the beach, listening to reggae and smoking ganja all day. You nailed it." His mouth turned up on one side, again triggering his dimple.

"I only meant—oh, never mind," I stopped because we'd arrived at the gallery. "Looks like we're early," I whispered as I peered through the window and saw a few people milling about.

"What does it matter?" he said. "Would you rather we'd be late and then you could call it Jamaican time? We're known for not being punctual on account of our laid-back attitude and all."

I decided to ignore his little dig. My attentions were now laser-focused on the task at hand. The anxiety I normally felt at social situations was only slightly lowered by Derrick' presence. Still, my pulse thumped in my ears and the little butterflies were wreaking havoc in my stomach. My feet in their high heels already felt like rebelling after our two-block walk. And the night had barely begun.

"Let's not stand around like awkward teenagers," Derrick said. He opened the door and put his hand on the small of my back, urging me in. I felt an odd little stirring inside me at the feel of his warm hand, and I skipped forward.

My eyes darted around, surveying the scene, wondering where Cecil was. A few people were milling about, and I didn't feel out of place with my spiky hair and broom-like lashes. All the women had on garish makeup and odd clothes, very *avant-garde*. A few were of indeterminable sexuality, which made me feel quite prim. Derrick's dreadlocks weren't out of place, either.

"Oh, look, wine and snacks," he said, motioning to the far end of the gallery. "Come." He put his hand on my back again, coaxing me forward.

I eyed the fattening *hors d'oeuvres* with a mix of yearning and disgust and went directly for the wine, although, upon remembering what happened the last time I drank at Daphne's, I filled my glass only halfway. Derrick meanwhile popped a couple of deep-fried shrimp rolls into his mouth and topped his glass to the brim.

"Shall we admire the art?" he asked. I turned my head away as he licked his fingers.

I followed him and we walked around the gallery. The art was very abstract and most of the paintings were untitled. "Lots of splash and splatter paintings. I guess it's supposedly meant to be irreverent or shocking," he said.

"You have to have an appreciation for this kind of subversive art. Some people probably would find it shocking, though I don't see why," I said, hardly knowing what to make of abstract art. I always felt there was some meaning, and I wasn't getting it.

"Marika, look at you! So ... edgy."

Cecil! I turned around to face him, my ears glowing from the compliment. There he was: tall, reed thin, impeccably groomed in his white shirt and blue blazer, with his blond mane and stubbly little nose, and the scant little chin that lent his face an incomplete look. That velvety, evenly polished skin, as always better moisturized than mine. I was slightly dizzy. He bent down and his lips brushed my cheeks lightly, like gossamer wings.

"You like?" My hand hovered around my hair.

"Oh ,yeah. Shows off your cheekbones." He acknowledged Derrick with a nod. "Glad you could come. I hope you like this kind of counter-culture art form," he said.

"Not sure what's so revolutionary about it. Seems reminiscent of Jackson Pollack," Derrick said.

A little frown formed on Cecil's beautiful face. "Well, all art is derivative, if that's what you're getting at."

"Fair enough. Not much room left for originality," Derrick said, taking a sip of his wine. "Although, to be perfectly frank, I like paintings that are pretty to look at, that make me feel good rather than disturb me. Something that inspires me."

Cecil looked him up and down, clearly assessing, a derisive little smile on his face. "Check it all out, maybe you'll find something inspirational. I hope you don't mind, but I'd like to borrow Marika for a moment."

Derrick bowed his head and I thought I heard him mumble something I couldn't make out in patois. I followed Cecil.

"I want to introduce you to the artist. I think you met him when we ran into each other at the restaurant. And where'd you say you found this character you're with?"

"Work, the new shrink," I said, feeling a little pang of guilt at leaving Derrick behind. But he seemed perfectly relaxed walking around the gallery by himself. Mister Too Cool for School.

"I *need* to make a few sales tonight or else this will be a bust," Cecil whispered to me. "I made promises. He's my first discovery at the gallery. He's banking on me to get known. I actually had to promise a larger commission to get him."

"But, Cecil, no one can predict anything about art sales," I said in a hushed tone, worried already that he might have gotten himself in over his head. "What will you do if you don't make a sale?"

"There you go with your negativity," he said.

"Oh, I'm sure you'll sell," I said quickly, even though I couldn't imagine too many people wanting this sort of art hanging in their living rooms. Too depressing.

"See that couple over there? They're big investors in new artists, real patrons. I better go talk to them. Why don't you wait a few minutes and then join us? Pretend to love the paintings."

My heart sank. I wasn't very good at subterfuge; my face gave me away. I gulped down the remains of my wine and went to get a refill. I popped a stuffed mushroom into my mouth while I was at it. Something to soak up the alcohol. I took a sip and went in search for Cecil and his art patrons. Out of the corner of my eye, I caught sight of Derrick. He was talking to a young woman, and I couldn't help but notice that she was a stunner.

I approached Cecil and the couple. "Hello," I said without waiting for an introduction. "Such interesting, evocative paintings. At once invoking happiness and sadness."

"Marika is a psychotherapist," Cecil said by way of introduction. He never called me a social worker. "She's a director of a clinic."

"A psychologist? Can you read into the artist's psyche when you look at a painting?" asked the short, wizened-looking man with a long goatee. His hefty wife towered over him. I did not try to correct his mistaken belief about my profession.

"I don't think psychologists are any better at understanding people than the rest of us," the woman said. "The beauty of modern art is that we make what we choose of it. But I do see your point." She turned to me. "This particular painting evokes strong emotions, at once happy and sad. I like it indeed."

"Yes, yes. I see what you mean, dear," said the old goat.

"Shall we?" she said, a twinkle in her dark eyes.

"Why don't we go into my office and talk," Cecil pounced. "This young man is a very promising artist, and I wouldn't be surprised if your investment pays off in a very short time. I'll make the introduction afterwards."

"We're not in it to make money. We simply love art and want to support up and coming talent," said Mrs. Goat.

As they moved off, Cecil turned around and said to me *sotto voce*, "Thanks. Don't go anywhere. I'll be back."

I stood glued to the spot for a moment. Was the Cecil Project beginning to pay off? I drained the rest of my wine. As I casually glanced around the gallery, I saw Derrick watching me but then avert his eyes. The gallery seemed dreamlike, illusory, the art just a lot of unfocused fuzzy colors dancing around me. Up until that moment, I hadn't really believed I could pull my project off. That I'd get Cecil interested in me again and I'd be on my way to living on the Upper East Side and shopping regularly at designer stores. Cecil and the life I'd been hankering for was all within my grasp. I felt slightly woozy and went outside for a bit of fresh air. A gust of warm air blasted my face. The smell of rain permeated the air but at least I didn't have to worry about frizzy hair.

I must have lost track of time, because after a while I saw more people leaving than coming and I went back in.

Cecil came up to me. "Sold another painting," he announced. "All told, we sold three."

"Wow, that's amazing," I said.

He cleared his throat. "Are you and Derrick together? I mean, you came together."

"Me and Derrick?" I repeated, like I was shocked at the suggestion. "No! Of course not. You invited him and he's my neighbor, so we took the subway together."

"Well, if you're not leaving with him and want to go out for a drink or something?"

I felt my heart leap a beat. "Why not? For old times' sake, ha-ha."

"Give me a few moments after everyone leaves, just to make sure that everything's okay. I'll let Clara lock up."

He went back to his office, and I tried to make myself useful by gathering some of the used glasses, but I was in the way rather than helpful. Looking out the window, I saw Derrick standing on the sidewalk. Since he had been my unofficial date for the evening, I decided I ought to go out and let him know I was planning to leave with Cecil. However, he was engrossed in a conversation with the stunner I'd spotted him with earlier so he might not even have noticed I was missing. I waved and walked over.

"Looks like you got what you came for," he said, an odd little smile pasted on his face.

"What a strange thing to say," I said. "Cecil did ask me out for a drink, if that's what you're hinting at. Not that I was planning on it. But if you don't mind …."

"Why would I mind? See you Monday." He waved, took his lithesome beauty's arm, and off they went.

I waited outside for Cecil to come and get me, unreasonably annoyed with Derrick. The way he presumed to know what I'd come for, as if he knew me. *But I did get what I came for*, I thought when I saw the leonine head emerge from the gallery. At last things were falling into place for me.

# ~CHAPTER SEVENTEEN~

"Fuck," Cecil muttered as another cab passed right by us and stopped further down the block for someone else. "Getting a taxi on a Saturday night in this city is a fucking pain."

"Let's just take the subway," I said, not liking to see his good mood evaporate. He never used to swear. "Subway's so much faster anyway. And looks like it might start to rain soon."

"Ugh, I hate the subway. It's either jam-packed or full of indigents and junkies," he grumbled. "But you're right, let's go."

We started toward the station, me as usual taking extra little skips and hops to keep up with his long strides. It dawned on me, irrelevantly, that the few times I'd walked with Derrick, he'd moderated his steps to be in synch with mine. But what did it matter? My Project was coming to life. We scrambled down the stairs when we heard the rumbling of an approaching train, and Cecil leaped a couple of steps at a time, urging me to hurry. I made it just in time, thanks to him holding the door for me. The train was nearly empty. Here and there were a couple of homeless men. We ignored them and sat, a little winded.

"Why don't we go to my place?" he suggested. "More relaxing, after the gallery. I need to decompress. Still feeling pumped up from the show. You haven't a clue how much work and anxiety went into doing a show like that."

"I can only imagine. All that pressure to sell," I said, wanting to be empathetic. "And I'd love to see your apartment. Where exactly do you live?" I pretended not to know.

"Gramercy Park, but I've got my eyes set on the upper east side one day soon, I hope. All I need are a few more successful shows." He smiled at the prospect. "I don't want to keep taking my parents' money. You know there are always strings attached and it's time I stand on my own two feet. Besides, the trust fund won't last forever if I keep drawing on it, as my dad keeps reminding me."

I tried to visualize the two of us in one of those white gloved buildings in the most exclusive part of town. I saw myself in high heels, with long flowy hair, in a slinky gown, waiting for guests to arrive for one of our famous cocktail parties. But the vision was rather hazy and wouldn't come into focus.

By the time we got out of the subway station, it had started to rain. Big fat drops were coming down, one drop at a time, and we jogged lightly, Cecil holding a gallery flyer over his beautiful head of hair, my own needing less protection. We made it to his building just before a bolt of lightning illuminated the starless sky, followed quickly by a crash of thunder, and we ducked into the lobby. We scurried into the elevator.

"I think you'll be quite surprised when you see my place," he said, unlocking the door. "My tastes have evolved. I'm not the same man I used to be. Gone is the conservative, traditional furniture and prints. I've acquired a lot of modern, you might say provocative, art."

I shut my eyes in anticipation. My hands were clammy, and my chest felt heavy. When he left me, he'd refused to give me his address. Now he was inviting me to his home so we could resume where we'd left off. I was amazed by my own prowess to make things happen. Mom, I was sure, would be proud of the way I'd taken charge of my destiny.

Once my eyes adjusted to the ambient light in the room, the first thing that smacked me straight in the face were two huge paintings practically covering one entire wall of the living room. Two naked, contorted bodies of uncertain sexuality, painted in a rainbow of colors, were hung on an equally bright purple wall. A giggle threatened to burst out and I gulped it down.

"So?" He gestured at the wall.

"Wow! These paintings are … eh … out there. And I mean it in a good way," I added hastily. "Are they men or women? On top they're certainly well-endowed, yet their vaginas have sprouted penises."

"Exactly. Symbolic, don't you think? Maybe a little subversive. On the other hand, maybe we're all a bit like that, if we allow ourselves to be honest about our sexuality."

I hesitated. He certainly was different than the Cecil I knew. "For sure. We all have masculine and feminine traits," I agreed.

"That, too," he said. "Now, what can I get you to drink?"

I stalled momentarily. I had had enough to drink, although I was feeling quite sober by now. I rubbed my clammy hands on my dress and adjusted the spaghetti straps.

"Would you like something different than a drink?" he asked, raising his eyebrows suggestively.

"Different?" I felt a tightening of my chest. What could he have in mind? He's never done drugs.

"You know." He rolled his eyes and I frowned. "Relax, I was only thinking of pot. I don't do hard drugs."

"Since when?" I asked. "No kidding you've changed. But I can't do any drugs, you know that. We get tested at work and we're probably due soon enough since we haven't had one this year." I hated that I sounded so prissy. "I'll stick to wine."

He raised his hands in resignation. "Fine, fine," he said, and went into his kitchen. I followed

"I see there's one thing that hasn't changed, still a full wine rack," I said eyeing it. The rest of the kitchen was immaculate.

"And you probably still have one opened bottle lingering for weeks at a time in the fridge."

That was fair enough. I smiled. He offered me a glass and I took a rather large gulp, hoping to quell the jittery feeling in my belly. It had been three years since we'd had sex, and our past sex life had been less than fulfilling. Cecil often complained that I was too uptight, a complaint he issued because I wouldn't give him blowjobs, and I usually preferred the missionary position. As for anal sex, I refused to even consider it. "Why would you want to risk having poop on your dick," I'd asked him. He had no answer except to grumble that I was cold and probably frigid, although I'd thought that I was pretty good at faking my orgasms. And I wasn't frigid; I had strong sexual longings. My erotic fantasies, tame or banal as they were, were quite satisfying in my lonely bed. And yet with Cecil I could never get into the moment. Instead, I would hover or float as if I were up in the air looking down upon us writhing on the bed, Cecil groaning, his face slightly contorted, his mouth open. I'd been too timid and insecure to tell him what I needed, and he'd never asked. It had all felt absurd rather than erotic and, in those moments, I thought that people looked darn ridiculous when they were having sex. He'd finish pretty quickly and rush to grab a handful of Kleenex and hand them to me to wipe myself off, while he was dabbing his dick with another handful. He was always concerned about getting drips on his six hundred thread count sheets.

Now I drained the rest of the wine, readying myself for what was to come. Without preamble, he took the glass from my hand, put it on the table, and wrapped his arms around me. His nostrils flared slightly, and I recognized what was to come next. He bent down and kissed me. It was a wet kiss, his tongue intruding, insistent.

"Come, prove to me that *you've* changed," he said, taking me by the hand and leading me into his bedroom. His bed was new, full of fluffy pillows and a downy blanket. "You've said you've reinvented yourself. Come on, don't be shy."

He walked me over to his bed and pushed me gently on it. Perhaps it was all the wine I'd consumed, but I felt my shoulders and body loosen as the tension left my body. I looked up at him, a foolish grin plastered on my face. At last, here was the final proof that he wanted me. "Show you what?" I asked, my cheeks quivering ever so slightly.

He unbuttoned his pants and stood before me in his boxer shorts. I started to haul my dress over my head, but he stopped me.

"Before you take it off, go down on me." He pulled out his semi-erect penis.

I looked up at him. I knew plenty of women who thought giving head was no biggie. Some didn't even think of it as sex exactly, just a thing they did because it gave pleasure. I was not one of those women. Once I tried to practice with a banana and gagged. But now I had to prove myself, make good on the claim that I'd changed. I couldn't let a blowjob come between me and my future happiness.

"Wait," he said. He reached in his bedside table and retrieved a condom and proceeded to pull it on.

I looked at his engorged dick. With a shaking hand I guided his dick into my mouth. The important thing, I told myself, was not to gag, to hold my breath. I started sucking it gingerly, but he took over, thrusting it back and forth, ever deeper and faster. Mercifully, it was over quickly. He groaned and I felt the warm liquid squirt into the condom.

I ran into the bathroom to rinse my mouth even though nothing had spilled into it. I gurgled several times with the Scope I found in his cabinet. When I glanced at my reflection in the mirror, the only thing that took me by surprise was my short spiky hair and heavy lashes. Otherwise I looked the same, although my cheeks were flushed. When I got back to the bedroom, he had already zipped up his pants. He sat on his bed, legs crossed.

"That was great. You were great. You okay?" he asked solicitously. I nodded. "I'm kinda spent, so you don't mind if we don't …."

I shook my head. "Fine. I'm fine," I said quickly. Never mind that I didn't get any pleasure; you can't always get what you want, right? Mick Jagger's a genius.

I left shortly after as he didn't ask me to stay and I wanted my own bed. The rain had stopped, and as I traipsed back home in the humid night, I congratulated myself again. The Cecil Project was well under way, and I was metamorphosizing from a wilting wallflower into someone who's in control of her destiny. Someone no longer repressed. Someone who gives blowjobs.

# ~CHAPTER EIGHTEEN~

As it turned out, I didn't have to 'spring' Mr. S from the hospital. The doctors agreed to discharge him on Tuesday instead of Monday and he conceded that one more day in the hospital wouldn't kill him, although he seemed disappointed at not getting his little adventure. The day of his release, I took off from work so I could bring him home and settle him comfortably in his apartment. He seized my proffered arm as we climbed slowly up the few steps of the stoop. We stopped at the top and waited for him to catch his breath.

"Why'd you stop? Getting old?" he asked, huffing. But even his Yoda grin didn't hide his pale face. A tiny bead of sweat was clinging to the tip of his nose. He took out a hanky and wiped his nose and face. "Of course, this had to be the hottest day of the year," he said.

I couldn't think how we'd make the two flights up the stairs and wished Derrick wasn't at work. I looked inside the lobby, but saw no one. It would have been nice to have made some friends in the building, but this was New York City, the place where you hardly recognized your next-door neighbors, never mind creating meaningful relationships with them. I took a few deep, controlled breaths. He should have moved to an elevator building, but I didn't want him to move now.

"What's the matter? You don't look so good." Mr. S's concern was like a splash of cold water on my face.

*Get your act together*, I commanded myself. "Gramps, do you think you can make it up the stairs, or should I go get help?"

"Not to worry. Nothing wrong with the old ticker; it was the lungs that were sick," he said. "Just a bit out of shape, but slow and steady wins the race. Come on. One step at a time."

\*\*\*

"The first, and most important, thing I want you to know is that being HIV positive is not the same as having AIDS," Derrick said, his voice comforting, almost soothing.

"Fock this bullshit. HIV just means that sooner or later you'll have AIDS," Carmen retorted. She sat with her hands crossed across her chest, glaring at him. The others nodded their heads in agreement.

I exchanged a knowing glance with Derrick. That was my darling group all right, and I was grateful to Derrick for finally joining us to give his little spiel about the wisdom of getting HIV tested. I certainly hadn't made any headway with them over the last few weeks. I wanted him to get a taste of what I put up with every time I tried to bring up the subject. I suppose it was a bit of *schadenfreude* on my part, but I couldn't help taking a *little* pleasure at his apparent discomfort.

He tucked a dreadlock behind his ear and rubbed his eyes with his fingertips. "I know it's a scary disease—"

"No shit," someone interrupted.

"It's very scary, yes. But," he went on, "it's no reason to bury your heads in the sand. Knowing is better than not knowing. And we have new medication—"

Rosie broke up in a derisive laugh. "Yeah, we all heard about the new medication. It makes you sicker'n a dog. Bottom line, there ain't no cure, so what's the point of knowing?"

"That's not exactly correct. While there is no cure right now, the medication can help forestall getting full blown AIDS." Derrick slogged on. "It means that life can be prolonged. Like if you get cancer, chemo may not cure it, but it can make it go into remission. Besides, knowing will make you not share needles or have unprotected sex."

"Which you ain't supposed to do anyway," Cindy chimed in a self-satisfied way.

"As if." Carmen rolled her eyes.

I had to hand it to Derrick, he wasn't backing down easily, and he remained calm. My too-cool-for-school doc. We'd agreed before the group that I'd let him run it, do his thing while I'd intervene only if it was necessary. However, he was doing just fine without my two cents' worth, so I allowed myself to relax and let mind wander. I pondered fleetingly what had happened between him and the woman he left the art gallery with that evening, but it was none of my business.

Instead, my mind drifted back to that night's events. I replayed every single moment and thing that Cecil and I had said to each other, albeit I skipped quickly over the blowjob. At no point did I remember setting a date to meet again, but I'd assumed that it would be just a matter of a day or two before he'd call me. And yet a week had gone by, and I hadn't heard from him. Every time the phone rang at home I jumped out of my skin. I vacillated between sitting around waiting for it to ring and finding excuses to stay out of the house so I wouldn't stare at it in anticipation. I started jogging, which was good for my figure and my mind. And I did join the gym.

When Cecil finally called, he invited me out for a drink and casually told me he was going to the Hamptons for a couple of weeks, because it was August, and *everyone* was leaving the sweltering city in August. The fact that I wasn't leaving didn't occur to him. Although he did say, apologetically, that since he was a guest at someone else's house he couldn't extend me an invitation. I was in the midst of fantasizing about our reunion when I heard my name.

"Something funny?" Derrick's voice interrupted my daydreams.

"Eh, no. I was just thinking ...." I let the sentence trail off.

"Good. Seems like we've got at least one woman who's ready to get tested," he said.

"We do? Who?"

He looked at me and shook his head from side to side as if to say where have you been. "Rosie said she's going to do it."

"Hold on, I didn't say I'd do it like now. Just that I'm gonna *think* on it. That's all, think," Rosie said.

I was surprised and wondered if it had been Carmen or Rosie's mom who'd talked her into it. Chills went up my spine and I shuddered. I wasn't sure *I* was ready for Rosie to get tested.

***

On a Sunday afternoon a week or so after that group, I was lacing up my running shoes, getting ready for my jog, despite the heat and humidity. I needed to let off some steam after leaving Daphne another message. I'd left her several in the last few days and on this last one I lost it and told her she was acting like Mom used to with Dad. Holding on to her anger, not being able to forgive, and I was not going to call her again. The ball was in her court.

I put on a headband and checked my image in the mirror. My thighs were firming up since I started jogging and going to the gym, but there was still getting used to my short hair, I looked like a poodle. However, it was easy to take care of with tons of gel. Just then the phone rang, and I grabbed the receiver, hoping it was Daphne at last.

"Ma-Rika," Rosie's hoarse voice took me by surprise.

"Rosie, what are you doing calling me at home? Where'd you get my number?" I said, shocked at her brazen action.

"Duh, your number's listed." She cackled.

*I'll have to change that.* "So why are you calling? You know you shouldn't be calling me at home, right?"

"Sorry. I know, but I was feeling so ... so down and lonely. I had another fight with my mom, and with Carmen, and I really just need to talk to someone. I'm trying *so* hard not to relapse. Can I talk to you somewhere? Please." Her voice cracked.

"I can't. I just can't do that, Rosie. If I could, I would, but it's not appropriate. Besides, if I do it with you, I'd have to do it with everyone." I paused and waited but she didn't say anything. "Did something happen?"

"Never mind. I'm sorry. You're right I shouldn't have called. Boundaries and all that." She sounded dejected.

For a split second, I saw Phoebe's disapproving red lips. Then I remembered the new powerful me. "Wait," I said. "Where are you?"

"I'm actually in your 'hood."

Right. My number is listed *with* my address. I told her to meet me at the waterfront. "Don't make me regret this," I said before hanging up.

I should have my head examined, I realized as I jogged the couple of blocks to the Hudson River. I spotted her immediately, in her shorts and T-shirt, pacing up and down the riverfront. I waved and crossed the street.

"Let's walk further down. There are a few places we can sit, though this park project is a mess right now," I said.

We walked quietly side by side for a bit before we spotted a bench. Young people in rollerblades whizzed by, along with joggers, but otherwise it was relatively deserted. This riverfront project was supposed to make the place spectacular, but it had run out of funds and stalled. I took off my hair band and fidgeted with it.

"I'm scared. I'm really, really scared, like I never been before." Rosie spoke so softly I wasn't sure she was actually talking to me or just mumbling to herself. "Did I ever tell you that my brother died of AIDS?"

"No, you didn't." I was surprised she hadn't told me about something so important.

"It's not something you advertise. My mom nearly died from grief. He was the apple of her eye. Even though he was messed up just like me."

I wished she'd worn sunglasses so I wouldn't see the pain in her eyes. I looked away at the river.

"She won't survive if I get it, too."

I wracked my brain for something comforting to say, but came up empty.

She picked at a scab on her knee. "Have you ever been so scared you feel it in your bones? It would be so fucking ironic if I get it now when I'm finally trying to get my life back on track."

"I ... I know." The same thought had crossed my mind, how unfair life could be. "I can't imagine how scary it must be, to face this ... this thing." I couldn't even name it, but then the therapist in me kicked into gear. "Don't catastrophize or try to read the future. You can't assume you've got it. Focus on the here and now, one step at a time."

"There you go, trying to make me feel better. I love you Ma-Rika, I really do," she said.

"Sure, until you hate me when I won't give you take-home privileges. Then it's fuck you, Marika," I chuckled.

"No, I'm not joking, and I don't mean it the way you think I do. I really love you."

"Rosie," I said, "you're confusing being grateful with love, that's all. Besides, it's normal to fall in love with your therapist."

"Have it your way, but I just wanted to tell you once and for all that I love you. Before it's too late." She put her elbows on her thighs and rested her chin on her fists; her eyes fixed somewhere on the horizon. It dawned on me that this was the reason she wanted to see me, to make her confession, which I didn't really want to hear.

I looked away. Further up the river, a little sailboat bobbed. The air was shimmering. No one has ever told me they loved me like that, not even Cecil. He only ever told me that he "cared a great deal" for me. It wasn't the same.

The shadows were lengthening as the sun marched closer to the horizon. An ice cream vendor walked past us.

"Hey, how about a Haagen-Dazs?" I asked, suddenly craving something sweet, comforting. To hell with the calories. "Chocolate chocolate chip."

She grinned. "Vanilla for the Black girl, thank you very much."

"Suit yourself, but you don't know what you're missing." I went to buy us ice cream.

\*\*\*

Later that evening, my thoughts crowded with Cecil, Rosie, and Daphne, I decided to go back out. I jogged around my neighborhood blocks over and over until I was weak from exhaustion. I collapsed in my bed, grateful to succumb to sleep.

# ~CHAPTER NINETEEN~

The next couple of weeks were uneventful. Cecil returned from the Hamptons and we had another date, where I got to practice my blowjob technique. Rosie took the HIV test a week later. The days waiting for the results crawled by. Thank goodness I had Gramps to look after, and he kept me busy. While he was getting stronger every day, he still got winded easily and going up and down the stairs was still hard, so I shopped and cleaned for him. I cooked a lot, all kinds of new elaborate recipes to tempt him. He ate ravenously. It seemed to be the only activity where he wasn't impaired. He boasted at how his appetite never wavered, probably a result of being on a starvation diet all those years ago in concentration camps. On the other hand, the more I wanted to cook and feed others, the less I felt like eating.

One Sunday morning I was cooking up a storm for no reason other than needing the distraction. Rosie's test results were due the next day. I was also uneasy about my Cecil Project. It seemed to have stalled again. My goal, after all, was not to become the blowjob queen.

I had stuffed a chicken and was now roasting it in my oven, and I put the finishing touches on the lasagna that was going into Mr. Saperstein's oven.

"What? You invited your whole *mishpucha*?" he asked me when I walked in carrying the large lasagna tray.

"No, my family isn't coming," I said. I'd called Daphne that very morning, again, but got her answering machine, and I hung up. Two months now we haven't talked; a record.

An idea popped into my head. "Maybe I should invite someone to help us eat all this stuff. Otherwise we'll be eating chicken and lasagna for the next month."

"You mean help *me* eat since I've only ever seen you pick," he said. "I know, why not invite that nice shrink, Derrick? He came by to visit me the other afternoon with his cute dog. Most dogs I don't like, but Bruce is nice."

"Actually, I was thinking of inviting my ex-fiancé, Cecil. We've reconnected recently." Mr. S raised his thick eyebrows but didn't reply. "I could invite Derrick, too. There's plenty of food," I said.

I even had the crazy thought of inviting Nathan, he of the incredible proboscis. He *had* been nice to me once I apologized for my abhorrent behavior and I thought I could further make it up to him and assuage my guilt by feeding him. "I may even invite another man, someone I owe a meal to."

"Marika and her *four* eligible bachelors?" Mr. S cackled, stroking his stubbly chin contemplatively.

"Four?" I pretended I didn't get his joke.

He'd taken to not shaving every day and no matter how much I tried to cajole him to, he dismissed me with a wave of his hand. "What's the point of shaving? I think of the time I've wasted shaving. It just grows back. If I add it all up it'd probably be years out of my life spent shaving."

Perhaps he had a point, but I saw his not caring as his way of letting go of life slowly. I didn't want to contemplate that. I was not prepared. No way. So I stayed on his case.

I put the lasagna in the oven and went upstairs to make my phone calls. First, the easy one, Derrick. He readily agreed. "Never turn down a good home cooked meal," he said. I warned him about my cooking, trying to lower his expectations.

I then went to call Cecil. I'd improved my blowjob performance with each time I'd seen him, however I couldn't say he'd gotten better at pleasing me. Yet he seemed to try and after what I considered an appropriate length of time, I faked an orgasm and we both congratulated ourselves on jobs well done. Still, I feared my Project was stalling. Summer was quickly running out and with it loomed the deadline I'd given myself: my thirtieth birthday. And my solution: my exit—should I choose to go through with it.

I had to get to that altar. And the longer the project took, the greater the risk of failure. Bottom line, Cecil and I knew each other and I'd either rekindle his love or not. Unfortunately, he wasn't home, so I left a message on his answering machine about dinner at Mr. Saperstein's apartment.

Nathan likewise didn't answer his phone and I decided maybe it was for the best. I probably couldn't handle the company of three eligible bachelors at one sitting. Even if I *was* only interested in one of them.

Dark, heavy clouds hung low in the sky the whole day, threatening rain, and making the air unusually sticky. Normal for the end of August. However, Mr. S refused to turn on the air conditioner, on account he wasn't going to "fatten the electric company." The humid air melted my gelled hair into limp curls on my head, and my T-shirt clung to my sweaty back. I set the kitchen table for four, in the hope that Cecil would make it, and watched as a few heavy drops of rain splashed onto the windowsill. I was just putting the finishing touches on the salad when Mr. S shuffled around the table, tut-tutting his unhappiness at my having taken off the plastic tablecloth which covered the cotton one underneath.

"You'll get *schmutz* on it, spots," he warned me. "Then what?"

I shrugged. "If it gets dirty, I'll wash it." Here he was, on his last leg and still worried about preserving things. Just like my mother. God forbid you should have to replace anything; that would be such a waste.

Through the window, I saw Derrick, in shorts and a polo shirt, making a dash from across the street, his dog in tow. I frowned. Cecil didn't like dogs. And he'd always been critical of my culinary abilities. Perhaps it would be best if he didn't come.

The doorbell rang and I went to answer. Bruce wagged his tail happily and bounded inside, ignoring me and going straight for Mr. S, who bent down and started rubbing his back and neck.

"A mutual love fest," I said.

"Who doesn't love a dog? Especially Brucie," Derrick said. Obviously, he hadn't met my parents. He handed me a bottle of wine, looked at the table set for four and asked who else was coming.

"Cecil. Maybe," I said, tugging at my shorts. A frown crossed Derrick's brow, but he didn't say anything. "We won't wait for him. He may not be able to make it," I added.

Derrick and Mr. S exchanged hearty handshakes, as if they were old pals. We opened the wine and settled down on the plastic-covered sofa. I'd been unable to convince Mr. S to remove it. The offending plastic cover stuck to my thighs.

"So, are you still seeing that woman from the gallery?" I asked blithely. Gramps looked up. He'd been making funny faces to the dog as if Bruce was a baby.

Derrick grinned. "Eh, we've become friends. She's an up and coming young artist. Very talented. She'll be going places. I'm thinking of buying one of her paintings."

"For sure," I interjected, not really interested in his talented new girlfriend. I wanted to ask him what he intuited about Rosie's test results, but I refrained bringing it up in front of Mr. S, who'd gone back to his baby talk to Bruce.

"And you? Have you succeeded in recapturing your ex-boyfriend?" Derrick asked.

"He was my ex-*fiancé*, not just boyfriend," I corrected him. "And maybe you've got it all wrong. Maybe he's the one after me."

"Lucky ex," he said.

Mr. S coughed and I went to get him some water. Then I left the two men playing with Bruce while I went to the kitchen to finish dinner,

110

declining Derrick's offer of help. I felt very *housefrau*, a homemaker getting ready to feed her men. There was something satisfying in that, even though I wasn't a great cook, and these men weren't really family or even distant relations. But there I was with a mini-pseudo-family, dog and all. And when Derrick came in to see if he could help, he found me swaying and humming along with Tina Turner:

What's love got to do, got to do with it,

Who needs a heart when a heart can be broken,

It may seem to you that I'm acting confused...

He shook his head, laughed, and walked back to the living room. When the doorbell rang and Cecil appeared, a bottle of wine tucked under his arm, I felt an odd twinge of disappointment. I quickly dismissed it as unworthy, just an aversion at probably having to perform oral sex later on. He stood in the doorway, his eyes scanning the room behind me.

"I didn't realize you were having some sort of a get together at the old man's," he whispered to me.

"Oh, no." I hurried to explain. "I've cooked up a storm for Gramps, so we decided to share the feast. It's really only us and Derrick." He stayed standing awkwardly, so I pulled him inside and ran through the introductions.

"Come in, come in," Mr. S said encouragingly. "Glad to meet all of Marika's men." My eyes narrowed and I shot him a look. He ignored me and went on, "I've heard a little about you. You're the one with the art gallery, right?"

I turned to Cecil. "You remember Derrick, our psychiatrist. We came to your gallery opening."

The two shook hands. Brucie yelped and Cecil stepped back. He was definitely not a dog person.

"Don't worry, he never bites," Derrick assured him, and grabbed Bruce's collar. "He's just being friendly."

Bruce was baring his teeth and looking anything but friendly at the moment.

"Did you know that dogs have a sixth sense about people?" I heard Mr. S say when I went to the kitchen to get Derrick a glass of wine.

I rushed back to the living room and handed Cecil the glass. Mr. S was still waxing ecstatic about dogs in general and Brucie in particular.

"Yes, dogs are excellent judges of character; they can sniff untrustworthy people a mile away," he said stroking the dog. Cecil shifted uncomfortably in his chair.

"Since when have you become such a dog lover, Gramps? You've never mentioned wanting a dog," I said. I began to wonder if he was running a fever again, but he looked his old self. My Gramps. I smiled at him affectionately.

"So how did your art opening go? Hopefully the artist was successful," Derrick said. I was grateful to him for switching topic away from dogs.

"It was *amazing*. This artist—I discovered him—is destined for greatness. He garnered *amazing* reviews." Cecil sipped his wine and winced slightly. I wished he wouldn't brag. At the same time, I was sorry I hadn't spent a bit more on a good bottle.

"Funny, the idea that people are *discovered*, as though they haven't been there all along," Derrick said. "Like discovering America."

"Art." Mr. S sighed loudly. "To think that Van Gogh couldn't give his paintings away. And now, he'd be turning in his grave if he saw how much they're selling for. Goes to show we're a fickle bunch when it comes to art. A fickle bunch," he repeated, shaking his head.

"We've entered an age where beauty is in the eye of the beholder, that's for sure," Derrick said.

Cecil cleared his throat. "Not quite, not quite. We still have arbiters of taste. If we didn't, then we'd devolve into an anything goes society."

"The last time I was at the Museum of Modern Art, I saw this white painting titled 'White on White.' So if you ask me, your anything goes is here already," Mr. S said. "Any numbskull can paint white on canvass and call it a masterpiece. Modern art, pshaw."

Derrick's mouth twitched as he bent to pet his dog. My legs were restless, and I felt myself flush. I scrambled up from my seat. "Well, we can't solve that dilemma now, and dinner's ready, so shall we eat?"

"Can I help?" Derrick offered, rising.

"Should I open the bottle I brought?" Cecil asked, getting to his feet, too.

"I'm not supposed to drink," Mr. S said peevishly, "but maybe a tiny bit." He'd already guzzled a glass of wine earlier and his cheeks had an unnatural rosy glow to them.

My head turned from one man to the other. The early comfortable pleasantness of the evening had turned and now the air felt thick with disharmony. All I'd tried to do was feed three men. My mood had soured, too, and now I couldn't wait for the evening to end. And my back ached from bending and standing in high heels.

When it was finally over and Cecil left without coming upstairs to my apartment, I felt a slight relief mingled with disappointment. My Project was faltering and tonight it seemed to have taken a huge step in the wrong direction.

# ~CHAPTER TWENTY~

Derrick was sitting at his desk, his head cradled in his hands, his shoulders slumped.

As soon as I saw his eyes, I felt a gut punch; the air whooshed out of my lungs, leaving me empty. I plunked down at the chair across his desk. "Don't tell me. Please don't tell me," I begged. As if simply not wanting to hear the bad news would make it go away. Like sometimes I wondered what if I'd never had gone into Mr. Wilson's office that day, over ten years ago, when my world was first torn to shreds.

He looked at me, his eyes kind, and bit his lower lip. "I'm afraid Rosie's results aren't good."

I remained silent for a moment, letting the news sink in. "Could ... could it possibly be a lab error? Like, you know, a false positive? She hasn't even been sick, just a cold she hasn't been able to shake."

He shook his head. We both sat quietly, absorbed in our own thoughts. My first was *why Rosie*? Why did everyone I had feelings for die? But I quickly dismissed that worthless thought. This was not about me. It was about poor Rosie, and I couldn't bear the idea of having to deliver this death sentence to her. Then I wondered about Carmen and the rest of my group. Who knew how many of them were infected, having shared needles in the past and, for all I knew, sharing them still. A hard knot formed in my throat and I swallowed.

Derrick's voice interrupted my ruminations. "I've already asked Theresa to buzz me when Rosie gets here."

"But ... but what will we say to her?"

He looked me straight in the eyes. "We tell her the truth. What else is there? And since you're the one she has the strongest relationship with, I think you ought to deliver the news."

"Me?" I felt slightly nauseous. "But you're the doctor. Shouldn't you be the one?"

"If you want me to, fine, but ...." He let the thought trail off. "I'll get into all the medical things she needs to know, or as much as she'll be able to digest right now. Given the shock, I expect she won't be able to hear much more than she's got AIDS. Sadly, in her case, it's past HIV positive."

I slumped in my chair. There was nowhere to hide. I had to do what

I had to do. I felt like a judge about to hand out a death sentence to someone who was innocent of any crime. Derrick's intercom buzzed and I jumped. It was Theresa. Rosie had arrived. It was group day, and they'd soon all be here. I decided on the spur of the moment to cancel group and grabbed the phone to ask Theresa to put a sign up. I was pretty confident they'd be happy about it, like kids when class was canceled.

"You ready?" Derrick asked. I swallowed hard and nodded, even though I wasn't. "Don't worry, I'm sure you'll do just fine. Better than fine," he tried to reassure me.

Rosie walked in, her dark eyes darting from me to Derrick and back again. "Hey, did someone die?" she asked. Her laugh sounded hollow, fake.

"Sit down, Rosie," I said, my voice catching. I pointed to the chair next to me, avoiding eye contact.

"What's going on? C'mon. I been on pins and needles since I took that test."

"Rosie," I began, "we've got your test results." It took all my willpower to look into the dark pools of her eyes. I blinked back the tears that were threatening to spill over. I had to maintain my professional composure. I couldn't cry. "I'm afraid the news isn't what we were hoping for."

"Unfortunately, you've got the AIDS virus," Derrick mercifully chimed in. He stopped for a second before going on. "Now, Rosie, please keep in mind, it's not a death sentence. There are drugs now that'll slow it down." He stopped again and we both waited for a reaction. The quiet before the storm, like waiting for a bomb to explode.

Rosie looked at him and then turned her uncomprehending gaze to me, her mouth slightly agape, showing her bright white teeth. She still had her perfect teeth despite the years of drugs. "What you fucking telling me?" Her voice was flat, devoid of all emotion.

"Rosie." I reached out my hand and touched her arm.

As if the touch of my hand jolted her into reality, she let out a growl, like a little animal who's been kicked. "Noooo. Noooo."

She wrapped her arms around her torso and rocked herself back and forth and stared at me questioningly, like she wanted something from me, like I could fix it. Snot began to gather at the tip of her nose and Derrick reached for the tissue box. She took it and dabbed. I knew the look in her fathomless dark eyes would haunt me for the rest of my days. My eyes darted to Derrick, but he was focused on Rosie. *What now? What do I say to make it better?* That was my job, to make people feel better, but I was clueless. I was powerless. Useless. I sat there quietly, waiting, God knows for what.

114

Finally, Rosie spoke. Her voice was flat, resigned, but her words were anything but. "Fuck this shit. You fuck up your entire life and just when you try to get your shit together, bam, it gets you. The past catches up with you and you can't hide. Ain't that a fucking shame? You know what we all say on the street? That once you try to get off drugs, that's when you get sick. Ain't that the fucking truth?"

"That's just old wives' talk, Rosie, and you can't blame yourself. This is a disease," I started, but she cut me off.

"Don't even try. Don't try to make me feel better. For the past few years you been working your butt off trying to get me to straighten out. You pleaded with me so many times, but I'm a knucklehead. I waited too long. It's my own fucking fault." She blew her nose loudly and grabbed a few more tissues.

Derrick picked up his trashcan and took it over to her. Then he sat on top of his desk, keeping one leg straight on the floor. He glanced at me ,waiting for me to say something.

"It's nobody's fault," I whispered.

"Why don't we sit down tomorrow, when our clinic doctor comes, the three of us, and discuss a treatment plan. The new drugs are quite effective in stalling the disease. It's not a cure, but—"

"Don't bother, Doc. I ain't going to linger on and become like the walking dead. I seen what it did to my brother. The cure was worse than the disease." She regained her composure. "I just knew I had it. I shared needles with him. I just hope to God I didn't give it to Carmen."

Not for the first time, I was amazed by how little I knew about my clients' lives. I saw them daily for years, but didn't really know them. "Let's go to my office so we can talk," I said.

"Nah, I better get home. Give my mom the good news." Her face crumpled and she started wailing. "I can't tell her, I just can't. It's gonna kill her."

Derrick and I looked at each other helplessly.

"Do you want me to go home with you?" I asked, knowing full well I was breaking Phoebe's rules of maintaining strict boundaries, but I didn't care.

I was relieved, however, when she declined my offer. We waited a few moments for her crying to subside. I kept my hand on her shoulder, rubbing her back now and then. Finally, she stopped, wracked by hiccups. She grabbed another handful of tissues and wiped her face and nose and then got up to go. I wanted to run after her, but I let her walk slowly to the door. When she reached it, she paused, her hand on the doorknob. She turned and looked at me.

"I love you, Marika. You been really good to me, but you can't do nothing for me now. This is something I gotta do alone. Face myself and how I fucked up my life and what I done to all those who loved me. You always warned me that you hurt the ones you love. I shoulda listened." A bitter smile crossed her tearstained face. She walked out and closed the door softly behind her.

# CHAPTER TWENTY-ONE

It didn't take long for the reverberations of Rosie's test results to shake the clinic. Despite all our many admonitions about the need for confidentiality, within a week it seemed as if half our clients knew she had AIDS. As much as our clients craved confidentiality, they weren't good at keeping juicy news to themselves. One day a couple of weeks later, right after medication hours, the staff convened to discuss damage control. Even Kumar, who usually found something to laugh about no matter what the situation, was somber. The only one who seemed unfazed by the goings on was Theresa. But, of course, she'd been at the clinic the longest and had probably seen worse. Sitting half reclined on the couch in Derrick's office, she had one foot on the floor, the other, shoeless, was poking into my thigh. I inched a little closer to the other end of the couch, which only made her laugh.

"You should have heard them this week. The women who were on the list to give urine declined fearing contamination in our bathrooms," she said. "I assured them that the bathrooms are disinfected daily and gave them the spiel about how you can't get the virus without exchanging fluids, yadda, yadda, but they're not a trusting bunch." She ended with a throaty laugh.

Kumar looked pensive. "I cannot blame them," he said. "I think there's a lot we don't know yet about this virus and how it's spread. Better safe than sorry, as you Americans say." It was funny the way he reverted to "you Americans" when it suited him.

"Kumar, you're a doctor. You should know better than that. We *know* how the virus spreads," Derrick said.

Kumar stiffened at the rebuke. "I'm only saying that it is early days and new things are discovered every day. Anything is possible."

"We're here to discuss how we can disseminate correct information to our patients and *stop*, not contribute to, the spread of false rumors. That's going to be hard to do if our own staff believes in falsehoods," Derrick said. "Now, I suggest every one of you touch base with each of your patients this week to make sure you go over with them about the *scientific* facts of how HIV spreads."

Dinesh raised his hand as if he was a student in school. "That's a lot of patients to see in a couple of days."

Derrick put his hands on his forehead and rubbed his eyes. I knew exactly how he felt. The staff could sometimes be more challenging than our patients. And although secretly I shared some of Kumar's misgivings, we couldn't give in to our unfounded fears.

I chimed in. "Why don't we just run a few mandatory groups, say, divide the patients into four groups over the next couple of days, according to the times they usually come in for their medication. That way, we can educate them all at once and make sure they all hear the same thing." Derrick sent me a grateful, dimpled smile, which made me flutter. *Ridiculous*, I admonished myself.

"How about we put a sign on the nursing station door? Divide it up to the four hours we're open. On day one, we hold two groups in the first two hours and on the second day, two for the last two hours. Only the working folk get to choose the time they can attend," Theresa said.

We were still working on the logistics when the doorbell buzzed. Derrick picked up the intercom next to his desk. We listened as he tried to calm down whoever it was. He hung up and spoke in a grim tone. "It's Carmen. She's in hysterics, babbling something about Rosie. Let her in, Theresa."

We sat there staring at each other while Theresa dashed out to get Carmen. My stomach churned. Within a minute, Theresa reappeared with Carmen, who was looking more disheveled than usual. Her uncombed hair was long and stringy, as if she hadn't washed in a while, and her tight knit blouse had a long tear running from one armpit down to her waist. Dark lines of mascara, tracing where tears had been, smudged her face.

"Carmen, what's happened?" I said.

"It's Rosie. She don't want to go home. She in a crack house two days now. I can't get her out. She don't listen to me," Carmen said, her accent thicker than usual. "You gotta help me."

"But … but how can we help? What can we do?" I asked. My stomach began to really hurt.

"She listen to you. She always listen to you. You got to come with me and talk to her," Carmen insisted.

"You're upset, Carmen, but we can't go out to crack houses to find every one of our clients when they get high," Derrick told her.

"It's all your focking fault. You pushed her to get tested, you did this." Carmen, forgetting how she'd wanted and pushed Rosie to get tested, dissolved into tears.

"Give us a few minutes. You go talk to Theresa and we'll see what we can do," I said. In my head, I knew Derrick was right, but in my heart, I wasn't so sure, and it confused me. I wasn't used to listening to my heart. I was used to dismissing it.

Theresa ushered Carmen, still sobbing, out of the room. Kumar got up and excused himself, muttering something about all his paperwork. Dinesh quickly followed suit, but not before reassuring us that he'd be at work bright and early in the morning to help with our groups scheme. That left me and Derrick to deal with the situation.

"If you're thinking what I think you're thinking, stop," Derrick said.

"How presumptuous of you." I pretended to mind. "You haven't a clue as to what I'm thinking."

He leaned back in his chair and folded his arms across his chest. "I'm all ears. But do tell me that you're not thinking of dashing out on a wild goose chase to some crack house out in Harlem, where you'll stick out like a sore thumb, in search of Rosie."

My back stiffened a little. He was right. While Harlem was less than ten blocks north of us, there was an invisible border I never crossed. I'd never been very brave. "I wasn't going to dash out, as you put it. I'm going to let Carmen take me to Rosie so I can talk some sense into her. I'm sure Carmen knows her way around Harlem."

"Don't you know by now that you can't talk sense to anyone when they're high? You're not thinking clearly. Besides, a crack house, no matter where it's located, is never a safe place. You do know that, right?" He stopped and gazed at me with his penetrating eyes. I put my hands in my lap to stop them from shaking.

"Look," he went on, "I know you want to help Rosie, that she means a lot to you. And I admire that, but think about it rationally. There's nothing you can do right now. You've got to let her come to her senses."

"But I feel responsible." I got up and paced the room. Finally I stopped and faced him. "Carmen is right in a way. We're both responsible. We meddled in her life, convinced her to take the test and let the chips fall where they may. We didn't consider that she wasn't equipped to deal with the results. As if anyone is." I hoped he didn't notice that my voice quivered ever so slightly.

He cleared his throat. "We are not responsible," he said softly, then went on more adamantly. "It would have been irresponsible of us not to tell them that they needed to get tested, all of them. They've shared needles and probably continue to do so. No point in burying their heads in the sand. You're being too emotional right now."

I laughed out loud. "Ha. That's the last thing anyone has *ever* accused me of being. Anyway, I'm going out with Carmen. Sometimes, you just gotta let your heart lead."

I left him sitting at his desk, an odd look on his face as I dashed out the door and went to get Carmen.

The two of us had never had a very good relationship, mostly due to her being somewhat jealous of Rosie's feelings for me. But when I told her I was going with her to look for Rosie, she jumped up and hugged me.

"You the best, Marika. Rosie always told me you the best." Her toothless grin tugged at me.

I grabbed my jacket, and we left in a hurry. It was early September, a cool day, a harbinger of fall, my favorite season, lurking right around the corner. I could smell its sweet aroma as a few rusty leaves floated down from tree branches. Soon the trees would be covered in vibrant shades of orange and reds. Not long after, Christmas carols would fill the airwaves. And maybe, just maybe, by New Year's Eve, I'd be planning my wedding. I didn't want to think of my alternate plan right now. I had to focus on Rosie. I eyed Carmen, who was just about my height, yet she seemed smaller and vulnerable in a way I hadn't seen before. Tough Carmen, the street urchin who, for years, had made her living selling her body to supply her habit. Now she looked like a scared little bird and my heart felt a twinge of remorse. Maybe I had been too hard on her.

We'd barely gone one block when I heard someone running behind us.

"Waaiiit. Waaiiit." Derrick's long Jamaican vowels were music to my ears. We stopped and waited for him to catch up.

I was tempted to hug him. "You don't have to come. We're quite fine," I said as my shoulders relaxed as if a boulder had been lifted off them.

"Right." He looked at me skeptically. "I know you can take care of yourself, but figured there's strength in numbers—I mean the powers of persuasion, of course."

Carmen's eyes flicked from Derrick to me. She smiled a toothless grin. "You are a good doctor. I'm sorry for what I said before. Now let's go." She turned on her heels and walked on.

Derrick bent down and whispered to me, "I still think it's a crazy idea and I don't feel responsible. But …." he shrugged and we followed Carmen, who was by now half a block ahead of us.

We walked quickly uptown on Lexington Avenue, a crowded street with many bodegas, but as we passed 96th Street, the official start of Harlem, boarded up storefronts began to appear. Shortly past 100th Street, the neighborhood turned markedly rundown. Litter scattered the sidewalks. Old burnt-out buildings stood derelict, monuments to poverty and hopelessness. We let Carmen lead us. She walked fast and turned right a few blocks north. We passed a row of abandoned tenements with broken windows, some covered with torn cardboard paper.

"Are most of these crack houses?" I asked.

Carmen cackled. "You don't got a clue, do you? Some people gotta live here. We don't all got it good like you." There was matter-of-fact bitterness in her tone, without reproach.

*Fair enough*, I thought, and decided to keep my mouth shut. She was right, I didn't have a clue about how she and many others like her lived. On the next block, she stopped and pointed to one of the abandoned buildings. "It's here. I'll go and see if she's there and try to get her outside, so you don't have to come in," she said. "If I don't come out in a few minutes, come up to the second floor."

I was touched. She was actually trying to protect us. How could I have been so wrong about her? We waited. Derrick passed the time kicking a stone he found as if it was a soccer ball. My legs were restless; I paced back and forth, checking my watch every few seconds.

"It's been five minutes," I said.

"There's no reason for both of us to go up there. Why don't you wait here?" Derrick said. "I'm less of a threat, me and my dreads." He smiled weakly.

My mouth was suddenly dry, and I felt a tightening in my chest. He was right, there was no reason, except it was Rosie. "The point is that she relates to me best, so I'm going with you," I said.

We climbed up the stoop and pushed open the front door with its broken windowpane. It was dark inside, and I wondered when the last time was that anyone had lived here; it was hard to believe that at one time this ghost house had been full of life. I followed Derrick slowly up the creaky stairs. He stopped on the second floor. Two apartment doors were closed, and, down the hall, a third had been ripped off. We heard sounds emanating from that room. He motioned to me with a finger to his lips to be quiet.

"We don't want to run into a drug deal," he whispered as he cautiously advanced. We stopped at the entrance.

A putrid smell accosted my nostrils as my eyes adjusted to the gloomy darkness of the room. On the floor was Rosie, cradled in the arms of Carmen, who was making "there, there" comforting sounds. If there had been other people, they must have taken off, leaving the detritus of their existence behind. The floor was littered with drug paraphernalia: cookers, needles, plastic cups, and junk. We walked over, and Carmen looked up at us, a pleading look haunting her eyes.

"She dead. She dead. She dead," she wailed over and over again.

I rushed over and kneeled down beside them. I'd never seen a dead body except in movies or on TV. Both my parents had been closed casket as Jewish custom dictated. Rosie looked like she was asleep, except for the dried white foam around her lips. She seemed almost peaceful. I wanted to believe that she *was* at peace at last, but I wasn't much of a believer in an afterlife. "Dead is dead," my mom used to say. I got up quickly and felt dizzy. I was momentarily unsteady on my feet and would have fallen had Derrick not grabbed my arm. I steadied myself and put my hand on Carmen's shoulder. She looked up at me with full eyes.

"She didn't want to listen to me. What can I do? I tried and tried," she moaned.

Derrick bent down and put his fingers on Rosie's neck. He straightened and shook his head. "She's dead. She's probably been dead for a while. Rigor mortis is beginning to set in. Has anyone called an ambulance?"

"No. I came back, and everyone was gone. Those fockers probably ran out as soon as she died," Carmen fumed.

"Well, we have to call an ambulance. They'll need to do an autopsy," he said. "So, somebody needs to make that call, we have to inform her family, and someone should stay with her." I was grateful he didn't say 'the body'.

His words roused me to action. "Come on, Carmen. I'll go make the call. Could you call her mom or, better still, go to her? Do you want me to go with you?" I asked, hoping she'd decline my offer. It was hard enough finding Rosie dead, but to witness her mom's broken heart was more than I was ready for.

"Her family is family to me, too. We been knowing each other for a long time. I'll go." Carmen struggled to her feet and tugged at her short skirt. "Don't leave her alone, Doc," she said before she left.

Derrick said he thought he'd noticed a pay phone back on Lexington. I took one more glance at Rosie, once so full of life, lying now lifeless on the floor, and ran down the stairs and out of the building. My lungs were bursting, as if I'd been holding my breath for a long time, and now, outside, I steadied myself against a nearby tree and inhaled deeply of the sweet cool air. Air that Rosie would never breathe again.

I jogged down the street in search of a pay phone. But as fast as I ran, I couldn't shake the thoughts that followed me. That Rosie would have been alive today if I hadn't meddled in her life and persuaded her to get tested. Her death was partly on my hands. I also thought, yet again, that nothing but pain comes from love.

# CHAPTER TWENTY-TWO

"Want to grab a bite to eat later tonight?" Derrick asked me before we went home that afternoon. After the ambulance had taken Rosie to the hospital for an autopsy.

I declined, avoiding his eyes. I couldn't shake the feeling that he and I were guilty of a crime, co-conspirators of sorts. When I got home, I popped in for a quick check-in with Mr. S. Thankfully, he seemed to be in fine spirits, and doing relatively well, considering his age and everything. I didn't feel much like talking to him. I'd invested too much in my relationship with him and thought I should start distancing myself. After all, he wasn't long for this world, either, and I'd just about had my bellyful of death.

As soon as I walked into my apartment, I ran to the phone and dialed Daphne's number. I had an uncontrollable urge to hear her voice. To know that I still had someone out there who knew me from when I was a child. Someone securely grounded on terra firma, who could affirm that I wasn't alone in the world. But the phone rang and rang and when the answering machine came on, I choked and hung up. What was there to say? That I needed her? She'd told me that she no longer wanted to be my crutch. She'd told me to stay away.

I walked around my living room in circles, rubbing my arms with my hands and hugging my shaking body. Finally, I went to the kitchen and started to fix myself a salad. I couldn't remember when I'd eaten last. My hands were shaking as I chopped away. I tried to distract myself by putting on some music, but Rosie's dark eyes kept dancing in my mind's eye, haunting me. I couldn't find a song to match my mood. It was only then I remembered that I was supposed to go over to Cecil's that night. He probably wanted a blowjob. It'd been a week since the last one, although of late he hadn't shown that much enthusiasm for that. *Oh, well, we do what we must,* I told myself. I rinsed my hands, grabbed my light jacket, and ran out the door.

It started to rain as I walked up Fifth Avenue before cutting across 16th Street to Park. It was a thin, soft, mist-like drizzle, not unpleasant, and I let it moisten my face and short hair, which had grown out from its spiky length and now flopped over my face in soft, unruly curls. I quickened my pace.

The days were getting shorter and were a constant reminder that the Cecil Project was running out of time. Thoughts of my exit weren't as exhilarating any more, but I wasn't ready to back down.

Cecil was back in my life, albeit in a rather tenuous way. Any time I tried to talk about our future, he became evasive or changed the subject altogether. As I rounded the corner to Gramercy Park, I took stock of my situation. Right now, for all practical purposes, I had virtually no one. Daphne was still my sister, and, in a pinch, I knew I could rely on her no matter how angry she was at me. But we'd grown apart and I felt barely attached to her and her family. Mr. S, my adopted gramps, was not long for this world. Although I hoped he'd stick around for another decade, I didn't know too many people who lived into their nineties. None, as a matter of fact. That left Cecil. True, he never was nor ever would be the love of my life, and sometimes I barely liked him, but he felt like an old friend. And he had some good qualities. I felt warmly towards him and reassured myself that we'd make a good enough couple. He was driven, ambitious, had good taste, and stood to inherit loads of money. Life could be worse than being Mrs. Cecil Goldstein. At least he wasn't like Derrick who didn't believe in marriage or even monogamy. I needed to make it happen, I decided as I punched the buzzer for his apartment.

"Hey, you were supposed to be here an hour ago. What happened?" he greeted me at the door with a frown on.

"Were you worried?"

"Actually, yes. Not like you to be late. And dinner is getting spoiled, keeping it warm in the oven." He was such a foodie.

I walked into his immaculate kitchen where the table was laid out for two. The revolting smell of fish accosted me. I felt bile creep up my throat and I swallowed. Why couldn't he remember that I hated fish?

"Rosie died," I blurted out.

"Rosie?" He took the plates from the oven and set them on the table, then reached for the white wine bottle and corkscrew. "This is a really good Chardonnay."

"Rosie. My patient," I said. "She overdosed. Today. We found her dead in a crack house." My throat constricted and, to my surprise, I burst out crying.

"But your patients O.D. all the time. I would think you'd be used to that by now. And what were you doing in a crack house?" He poured the wine and handed me a glass.

I refused the wine. "It's a long story. Anyway, I can't really talk about it, it's confidential." I sniffed.

"Confidential? If she's dead, does it matter? Here, drink it. You need it." He shoved the glass into my hand. "You can't cry every time one of

your patients dies. Come on," he added, his voice softening, "let's eat."
I looked at my plate with distaste.

"Your job is too depressing," he went on. "You should look for a new one. Work with people who actually improve. What do you call them? The 'worried well'. Otherwise you'll never see the brighter side of life."

"Let's see, the brighter side. Someone could ask me to marry him and maybe I wouldn't have to work at all, ha-ha-ha," I said. He took a swallow of wine and arched his perfect eyebrows. I put on my Barbra Streisand voice and continued. "Where I come from, when two people … well, sort of love each other, dot, dot, dot."

"Don't tell me, one of them says why don't we get married." He rolled his eyes and smiled.

I kept my Streisand imitation going. "Yeah, and sometimes it's even the man."

"Look, you're not Funny Girl and I'm not Nicky what's-his-name. I thought we agreed to keep things casual for now. What's the rush?" He got up and started clearing the table.

"Sure, it's easy for you guys. There's always time, it's never a rush. But if you want kids, and you said you did, *my* clock is ticking. Tick tock, tick tock."

"I never heard you say you wanted kids. If I remember, it was a bone of contention. Anyway, it's barely been two months since we reconnected, so I think it's way too soon to talk of a wedding and kids. Why don't you just relax? You've got to learn to relax. Enjoy life, live in the moment." He pulled me up by my arm. "Come on," he said and led me to the couch. "I've got just the thing for you, wait."

He left me on the couch and went to his bedroom. Our conversation left me feeing a tiny bit hopeful. He hadn't said yes, but neither had he dismissed the idea out of hand. I just needed to be more patient, like he said, calm down. My head buzzed with magical thoughts when Cecil came prancing back, his face flushed. He waved his hand in the air.

"Guess what I've got?" he said, brandishing in his fingers what looked like a hand-rolled cigarette.

My eyes must have popped out of my head. Pot? Yes, he'd brought it out once before, but we hadn't used. We had never used drugs. We'd make fun at how straitlaced we were, nerds. That was one of the few things we had in common.

"But Cecil …."

"But what? Come on. I thought you'd changed, that you were less uptight or judgmental." He challenged me.

"I *have* changed. I'd love some pot," I lied. "Honestly. But you know I can't. They test us at work and if we fail, it's curtains. They don't give us a second shot, it's poof, *hasta la vista*."

"A few tokes won't get you fired. Anyway, what're the chances that you'll get a drug test in the next couple of weeks? Probably zero to none. Come on, loosen up. You're depressed and this will help."

"I don't know. It's really risky. Why don't you go ahead? I don't mind if you smoke."

"Oh, you're a barrel of laughs, as always. You're as high strung as ever." He plopped down next to me and lit his joint. Inhaling deeply, he closed his eyes and leaned his head back on the couch. I ruffled his hair playfully, but he flung my hand away.

I was uptight. He was right. Always worried about the worst-case scenario, like my parents had trained me. Why couldn't I relax? Let go of all the worries, the constant nagging fears. It would be nice to unwind. Chill. Help me forget Rosie lying dead, white crust on the corners of her mouth. Her big brown eyes accusing me. Besides, remembering my exit strategy emboldened me.

I raised my hand and plucked the joint from him. "Give a girl a chance," I said. I puckered my lips and puffed.

He snorted laughter. "You gotta *inhale*, not puff. See." He took a drag and handed it back to me.

I put the joint to my lips and inhaled as deeply as I could. The back of my throat and lungs burned and I choked, coughing. "Where'd you get it?" I asked.

"In what universe do you live? I'm in the art world; how hard do you think it is to get pot? I could buy anything I want, easily." He sounded proud.

I took a few more drags; it didn't burn as much and I barely coughed. I wasn't feeling high, or anything, but I noticed that I was no longer worried about work. *Que sera sera*, whatever will be, will be. They hadn't done any drug tests this year and I figured they probably wouldn't until around the holidays, their favorite testing time. Besides, a few puffs wouldn't stay in my system very long; it's mostly stored in body fat and, luckily, I didn't have much of that. So there was really nothing to worry about.

Cecil got up and started shedding his clothes. From his cassette player, a bluesy, desperate-sounding Annie Lennox wafted through the haze with her ode to masochistic desire.

"Some of them want to abuse you, some of them want to be abused," Cecil sang, gyrating his pelvis towards me, his penis erect.

"Everybody's looking for something," I sang along.

And when shoved his dick into my mouth, I thought nothing of it.

"Some of them want to use you ...."

126

"I don't like funerals," Derrick whispered as he inched a tad closer to me in the pew, as if that would in some way make the experience less painful. He looked handsome in a suit and tie; too bad he didn't feel the need to dress like that for work.

"Like anybody does like funerals," I said. I still felt ill when I thought of my parents' funerals.

"Some people actually like them. My grandma likes to go to funerals. She enjoys the ritual, says it makes her feel close to God and prepares her for her own death." He chuckled.

"Maybe she also feels she's won some contest, surviving her old friends. Like Mr. S. He gets a kick out of reading the obituaries and seeing names of people he knew," I said.

I shuddered at the thought. I couldn't imagine outliving everyone I knew. The loneliness of having no one left. I made a mental note to call my sister again as soon as I got home. I was pretty angry at her, but I missed her.

We were sitting at the back row of the church at Rosie's funeral, a week after her death. The closed casket was displayed on the chancel, richly adorned by a large flower arrangement and an ornate fabric. Very different to my parents' simple pine boxes. I imagined the reason for the casket being closed was probably her family not wanting anyone to see how thin she'd gotten. I started thinking about what my funeral would be like, but quickly dismissed the visuals.

It was upsetting to see the hall mostly empty, except for a handful of people. Family, no doubt. I had hoped that the rest of the staff would come, but my two counselors, who were desperately studying for their upcoming exams, had to get to school and Theresa had to stay behind to medicate patients. I tried not to think of my parents' funeral. It had been over a decade and much of the day had been wiped out from my memory. I couldn't remember the car ride to the cemetery, the platitudes people offered, even the eulogies. All was lost in the haze of time. I'd always envisioned in my mind's eye my mom lying in her closed coffin, strangely curled on her side in a fetal position, though, of course, I hadn't really seen her. I also remembered my heels getting stuck in the damp cemetery ground and Daphne getting unrelenting hiccups. I shoved those disturbing images back into the recesses of my mind and watched as people gathered in the church.

I noticed Rosie's mom, a deaconess at the church, sitting in the front pew surrounded by what I imagined were her other children and family members. She was a striking figure in her dark suit and rather dazzling hat with multitudes of silk flowers on top. When she turned around to look behind her, I saw resolve written on her tortured face, maybe even pride. All to cover the searing pain she must have felt. The unbearable death of a child, her second one.

Right behind Rosie's mom sat Carmen. Mercifully, she was dressed in a sedate black dress and her usually greasy hair had a nice clean sheen to it. When she turned around, I smiled at her and she waved and grinned toothlessly at me. It was sad, however, that none of Rosie's so-called friends from the clinic were there. Not one of the group members, other than Carmen, had come and I wondered how soon they would forget her. I said something to that effect to Derrick. He wondered if they were using the sadness as an excuse to get high. I wanted to think better of them, that they just couldn't deal with her death as it was too close to their own reality.

"Look at how sad Rosie's mom is. I met her once; she came for a session with Rosie. She had been so angry and disappointed at her daughter who she thought had had such potential and blew it. That session devolved into a brawl," I said, remembering the hurled accusations, the insults. And all because they loved and disappointed each other. All that hurt and misery that went with all that love.

"And now she'll say only good things about her daughter, about what an angel she was," he said.

"But that's how people are," I said. "We must leave our dead in peace."

The proceedings started with the minister's arrival at the podium while a choir of about fifteen singers assembled behind him. He started with a prayer for the departed. I tried to follow, but quickly allowed my mind to roam to other things.

In the midst of death, I took stock of my own life. Despite the current state of affairs between me and Daphne, my Project had shown some promise in the week since I'd talked to Cecil about marriage. We'd spent more time together. Last weekend he'd surprised me by taking me out to see *Biloxi Blues* on Broadway. I'd wanted to see *A Chorus Line* again, but he scoffed at that. "Who wants to see a play about a bunch of kids who are basically losers?" But that was Cecil. If he'd become a bit more self-centered in the years since we'd broken up, what of it? I understood that people become like that when they're not in relationships. I hadn't brought up marriage again, but I could tell he was warming up to the idea; he'd casually mentioned one day, after we'd had sex, that he'd told his parents about me. Perhaps it was because he was getting used to having regular blowjobs, which I gathered I was getting better at. Taking a toke or two helped. Anyway, it thrilled me that his parents wanted to see me.

His parents, especially his mother, had never been great admirer of mine and used to make me feel that my humble origins were not quite what they'd hoped for in a daughter-in-law. The little digs they'd throw my way, like that time I had placed the napkin on the wrong side of the table. "How was it that your parents hadn't taught you anything about correct table setting," his mother had asked.

My fantasy of how Cecil's parents would now embrace me as one would a prodigal daughter was interrupted by the choir breaking into "Amazing Grace." I thought of Rosie and how she'd smile knowingly whenever we talked about religion, even though she knew I wasn't a believer. I, on the other hand, couldn't understand how she could believe, given all the things she'd endured. But I had to acknowledge that the song was comforting and almost wished that we had the tradition of singing hymns at funerals.

"Amazing Grace" over, the choir picked up tempo, and for the next half hour the mood in the church turned celebratory as everyone rose to their feet and sang loudly—and in tune. Derrick got into it, too. But I didn't know the songs so chose to listen with admiration.

Afterwards, the mourners lined up to shake the bereaved family's hands and offer condolences. I walked over to Rosie's mother hesitantly, unsure if she'd remember me from our meeting of a couple of years ago.

She embraced me to her amble bosom. "I know you tried to help her," she said. "And you know Rosie loved you very much. It was always Marika said this and Marika said that."

I choked at the unexpected emotional outpouring. How often had Rosie and I wrestled over things? How often had she gotten mad at me, sworn at me, and told me off? And how often had we sat in my office and talked like friends, not as therapist and client? And now she was no more. My heart felt literally heavy, as if it weighed suddenly more than I could bear.

Derrick said a few kind words to Rosie's mom, and then, with his hand on my back, he moved me along. "Let's go get a cup of coffee," he said. "I feel the need and there's no point in going back to work. I'm sure Theresa's locked up by now."

"As long as it's your decision," I said. "So when Phoebe hears that we closed the clinic early she won't take it out on me."

We headed south towards the 125th Street station. He navigated, and a block north of our destination we passed by Sylvia's Restaurant. Derrick said it was a Harlem institution and that he'd always meant to check it out. It was just past the lunch hour and the crowd was thinning out. I was faintly aware that he fit in while I probably stuck out, but it didn't bother me. We were motioned to sit at any of the available tables and we found one in a dark corner. A young waitress came by and placed menus on our table.

I took a look at the menu and recoiled. All that greasy fried food. Then I saw the chicken livers sautéed in onions, a dish Mom used to make. My favorite, before I lost my appetite. Diet be damned, I decided, and ordered it. This was in Rosie's honor. She used to tease me about my weight and cautioned me that most men preferred their woman with a little meat on their bones. I figured if she was "up there" somewhere, looking down on us, seeing me eat would put a smile on her face.

When the aromatic livers sizzling with onions arrived, Derrick made a face. He hated liver, he said, a staple at his boarding school in Jamaica. I smiled. It tasted of my childhood. I asked him to tell me about boarding school because I'd never known anyone who had gone to one and because I wanted to talk about anything to distract myself from Rosie. He started telling me about how vicious some of the teachers were, the canings, and about the older kids, who were called the prefects, who were especially cruel to the younger ones. I listened with fascination; it was such a different world than the one I grew up in, where my parents were there to soothe and protect us from all our little hardships, despite Mom's illness and Dad's preoccupation with it. I let myself be pleasantly carried away by Derrick's singsong accent as he told his tales. As I listened, I savored my food and ate every morsel of it. It was the tastiest meal I'd had since before my parents died.

# ~CHAPTER TWENTY-FOUR~

That night I called Daphne again. She didn't pick up. I left her a somewhat bitter message again. True, I hadn't been an easy or maybe very supportive sister since our parents' death, and true, I'd embarrassed her and her Gerald that evening with Nathan, and true, I'd said some harsh things to her that night. But she was still my only blood relation, my sister, and I didn't think what I'd done merited being shut out of her life. It had been over two months since we spoke.

The whole thing riled me, keeping me awake all night. The next day, Saturday, without any further thought, I boarded the train to Westchester. I'd had enough of her punishment. It brought back too many memories of Mom and the way she'd stay angry and shut us out for days on end when we upset her. One time she didn't talk to me for almost two weeks. I couldn't recollect what my crime had been, but I couldn't imagine anything warranting that. I was only in fourth grade when she decided to leave me out in the cold for that length of time. It was the longest two weeks I could remember. Two weeks in which I had to talk to Mom via Daphne or Dad. It was only after I overheard Dad intercede in my behalf, plead with Mom to start talking to me, that she relented. Who would have thought that Daphne, who never failed to criticize me for being too influenced by Mom, would take after her? Meanwhile, I found myself to be like Dad, apologizing over and over into an answering machine.

I'd done my best since Mom's death to keep her with me, to keep her alive, by remembering mostly the good in her. And there were so many wonderful things to remember. The way she loved and instilled in me the same adoration for all things cultural: literature, the theater, the ballet. The way she loved clothes, good fabrics, fashion that was figure flattering and stood the test of time, not trendy. But most of all I remembered the way she loved me—when she wasn't angry—effusively, hugs and kisses in abundance.

What I chose to forget, or at least not to dwell on, was the angry, depressed Mom. The one who'd wake up in a black mood and take her fury out on all of us, especially Dad. The walking on tiptoes on such days so as not to cause any further rage. The Mom whose moods could fluctuate from happy to sad to almost catatonic in a short span. We'd watch helplessly as she'd turn from a loving woman to a disgruntled, frustrated person whom no one could please. I tried hard to not remember that person. I went through my life pretending that the person who tried to take her life that day in the bathtub was not really my mom at all, but rather someone whose body was overtaken by some ghosts or demons.

I got off the train and started walking the mile and a half to Daphne's house. It was one of those perfectly crisp fall days, a few cumulous clouds in the horizon. Only a couple of weeks into September and the trees were already touched with crimson, yellows, and orange, all the colors that reminded me of the cozy days soon to come. Here and there I heard shouts of kids playing in their backyards; a silent transistor radio had been left in someone's front yard, perhaps abandoned in a rush to get back indoors. I passed by a kid on a tricycle, his little chunky legs pumping furiously. It was all very calming and bucolic compared to the cacophonous sounds of the city.

I wondered about the lives lived inside the fine-looking homes. I knew they all had their share of sorrow and heartache. And yet it was hard to believe that the people inside these houses weren't ensconced with their perfect families, living their perfect lives. I let myself get carried away with some fantasy of being married to Cecil and living in one of these splendiferous houses. My fantasy fizzled when I tried to visualize us having kids. Somehow even I, with my fervent imagination, couldn't picture our creation, our children. I assured myself that that was probably the case for most people. No one, after all, could possibly imagine their kids before they had them.

My heart quickened as I got closer and spotted Daphne's house. It's silly, I chided myself. After all, Daph and I had never had any major arguments that lasted more than a week or two. Of course, it was usually I who made the first move to reconcile, but she was eight years older and I'd been taught from a young age that that in itself was meaningful. She was older, looked out for me, and therefore deserved my respect. And, if I was honest with myself, most of our tiffs were probably more my doing than hers. So I'd learned to swallow my pride, as I was about to do again.

Walking up the driveway, I was struck by how shuttered the house seemed. All the blinds of the front windows were down. That was unusual. I knocked on the front door and waited. The house was silent. I put my ear to the door; no sounds emanated from inside. I tried to think what their schedule was for Saturdays. But other than running around with mundane chores, nothing came to mind. Perhaps Davey was playing sports on Saturdays, soccer, was it? I wished I could peek into their garage, but the little windows were too high up. I walked to the back of the house and peeped through the slight opening in the white curtain of the kitchen window. All looked fine, albeit from the little I could see the kitchen looked spotless, lacking the usual dishes drying on the counter by the window.

I walked back to the front and sat on the stoop, shoulders hunched, bringing my legs close to my body. A feeling of unease descended on me. Perhaps they'd all gone somewhere for the day and there was nothing to this. I wondered where they could be, overcome by a wave of panic. They rarely all went out to the same place on Saturdays, what with the kids having different schedules. And the super clean kitchen?

I don't know how long I sat there, hunched over. I shivered slightly; my body felt stiff and I got up and stretched. I started pacing up and down the driveway, looking furtively down the street in the hope of seeing one of their cars, checking my watch every couple of minutes. A woman across the street waved to me. I recognized her. Judy was one of Daphne's neighbors and good friend. I crossed the street.

"Hey," she said. "What are you doing here? You know that they're away, right?" She looked at me with concern in her eyes.

"Away? When? Where?" I was too astounded to try and save face and pretend I knew. "Where did they go? The kids have school," I protested.

She looked at me strangely. I suppose she was wondering how it was I didn't know my sister's whereabouts. "Daphne's firm has had her working in California for the past month. She usually comes home on weekends, but Gerald flew out there with the kids for a few days. I think they're contemplating moving there."

I hit my forehead with my hand. "Silly me, of course. I totally forgot. Daph did mention something about it last time we spoke, but it wasn't a done deal and I forgot about it," I said, glancing at her nervously. "Did … did she tell you that they're moving for sure?"

"No, not for sure. But they're considering it," she said. "Do you want to come in, freshen up before you go back to the city? You still live there, right?"

"Oh no, thanks, I'm fine. I was actually visiting a friend in Scarsdale, so decided to stop on over here," I lied, even though I didn't have an overnight bag with me. "Well, I better get to the train station and catch the next train." I waved and turned to go, choking back tears.

"Are you sure you don't want us to drive you to the station? Clouds are gathering," Judy called after me.

I turned around and waved to her again. She was a good soul, but I didn't want her to see me dissolve into tears. I didn't want her pity. The wind had picked up a bit and the trees were shedding their leaves in the gusts. I should have worn a warmer jacket, but by the time I got back to the city the winds had died down and it felt milder. I remembered the morning I came back from Daphne's after our blow-up. It had rained in the early morning that Sunday, the day I'd rushed Mr. S to the hospital. It seemed like such a long time ago, but it was really only little over a couple of months.

I hailed a taxi. I wasn't sure where I wanted to go. Often on Saturday afternoons I liked to visit museums, not because I needed to prove that I was cultured, but because I really enjoyed the vibes at museums. They were so relaxing. Especially the semi-stodgy Met. Suddenly I knew where I needed to be: I had the urge to see Gramps. I stopped at the corner deli and got him some Hostess Ding Dongs. Gramps and his sweet tooth.

I found him in bed, reading a book.

This alarmed me. "Why are you in bed at this hour? It's barely four o'clock.," I said.

He waved his hand with unconcern. "When you get to be my age, you can live by your own clock," he said and shrugged. "I felt like going to bed. Besides, does it matter which room I sit in? I get tired of one room and move to another. That's all."

I put my hands on my waist and exhaled. "Gramps, don't give me that. You were the one who told me not to ever let my standards get lax. Why, until recently, you always wore a tie in the house."

He shrugged again. "No fool like an old fool. Let that be a lesson to you."

"Oh, come on." I felt myself close to tears again. "Look what I've got you." I waved the brown paper bag in the air. "Ding-dong, ding-dong," I sang.

"All right. But only if you join me. None of that eating a few crumbs and calling it a meal."

I left him to get up and went to the kitchen to put the kettle on. It dawned on me that in the past couple of years I'd spent more time with my adopted Gramps than my own family. At least more time drinking tea and eating pastries. His sink, normally spotlessly clean, had a few dishes in it and I quickly rinsed them off and put them in the dishwasher. I started to worry. What would happen if he couldn't take care of himself? The idea of putting him in a nursing home was repugnant to me, and I doubted that he'd even be willing to go. I decided to shove the idea to the same area of my brain where all unwelcome ideas were stored. No doubt it would pop up when the rest of them tended to: in the middle of the night.

He shuffled into the kitchen. "No, don't use these, they're chipped. Use the good china." He opened the sideboard in the living room and took out cups and saucers.

"What's the occasion?"

"Us having tea is the only occasion we need. It's foolish to save finer things only for so-called special occasions. What for? You end up having lived your life and using them what, ten, twenty times? What's the point of that? From now on, we will use only my finest china, *every day*," he announced.

"And what about these?" I pointed with a smile at the plastic covered furniture.

"Off with them. Come help me, right now."

I poured the tea and let it steep in the cups, one teabag in each, and then went to help him yank the plastic off his furniture.

We bundled the covers up and put them in a pile by the door. I'd take them out to the trash later.

"What caused this change of heart?" I asked once we were seated at the table. It was nice not to have the plastic squeaking under my butt.

"It's taken me this long to realize that it's ridiculous to try and make things last. And for what? At the end nothing lasts, including us. We weren't meant to last. Things are made for us to enjoy, to use. Otherwise, there's no point in having them," he said.

"It's just that we want to keep things with us as long as possible. Things, people, you know," I mumbled.

"Girlie, there's a saying in Yiddish that may be lost in translation, but it means something like wisdom lags behind. In other words, it often comes late, too late. Don't let that happen to you. Wise up now, live to the fullest and in the moment. And don't forget to love, because without that, life lacks joy."

I'd wanted to tell him about Daphne and how she totally shut me out of her life because of something I'd done, not even telling me that she might be moving to California. And I wanted to tell him about Rosie and how I'd failed her and because of that she died. About how love hurt too much. But I hesitated, not wanting to worry him.

He tweaked my cheek and gave me his Yoda smile. "You look like the sky has fallen. Don't take everything so hard, *meydale*. All things pass. And the last time I looked the sky hasn't fallen yet."

# ~CHAPTER TWENTY-FIVE~

Gramps was right as usual. The sky didn't fall. Yet I felt as if my world was closing in on me. Daphne was out of my life for the moment, Rosie was gone forever, and I was now constantly worried about Gramps. I called Cecil, got his answering machine, and hung up. Now where was he? I'd told him before I went to Daphne's that I might stay the night there; he said he hadn't any plans for the evening. I was too antsy to stay at home and left my apartment to go for a walk.

The cool evening air was refreshing after Gramps' somewhat oppressive apartment with his old furniture even though everything was finally free of its plastic wrapping. His furniture was a constant reminder of my parents' home. Even the smell.

I started walking aimlessly southeast towards Washington Square. It was almost dark and the buildings were lit up inside, although, being a Saturday evening, many of the apartment windows were dark; people were out having fun. Soon enough it would be Halloween and I looked forward to the Village parade, always a treat to watch, even if I didn't dress up and participate. I walked slowly, enjoying the sights I was used to. I'd forgotten again how much I belonged in this city and how calming it was to feel the vibrant life humming all around me no matter that I stood at its fringe. Even if I often felt apart, in some ways we were all in this thing together. And I only felt it in the city. I found myself in the heart of the Village with its cafes and outside tables. Soon people would take shelter from the cold and move indoors, and the tables would be taken in. The cafe windows would mist over and form little rivulets from the steamy heat generated inside, but for now people were still sitting out, albeit a little huddled.

My stomach rumbled and I remembered that other than a Ding Dong cupcake I'd had nothing to eat since breakfast. I'd tended to avoid going alone to restaurants, especially on a Saturday night, but now I saw a tiny row of tables meant for one or two. A few were unoccupied, and I took a seat without even asking. A waitress hurried past me with a tray of steaming food. On her return, I stopped her and ordered a glass of house wine and a salad. When the wine arrived, I took a sip. It tasted fantastic. I could feel its warmth slowly spread down my insides. I tried not to think of Daphne and the way she'd frozen me out of her life. I tried not to think of Rosie, dead. I tried not to think of Gramps.

I leaned back in my chair and waited for my salad, people-watching. I pretended not to care that I was alone, pretended I was some heroine in a novel. A young, beautiful woman, drinking wine alone in a Village bistro. What could be more romantic than that? I forgot how much fun it was to people watch. There was an old woman walking her dog. That made me think of Derrick's dog. Perhaps once Cecil and I moved in together I'd convince him to get a dog, although he was definitely not a dog person. There was a couple walking, holding hands; the man looked like Derrick. I chuckled. It was as if I had conjured him up by thinking of him. But, yes, there was no mistaking his dreadlocks; it was him. And the young woman looked familiar, too. Of course, she was the stunner he'd met at the gallery. He was laughing and had his hand on her back. I turned my head. I didn't want to see anymore.

My salad arrived, but suddenly I wasn't hungry anymore. I took a few bites, paid, and left. I walked briskly towards Gramercy Park. I thought of stopping by a payphone to call and make sure Cecil was home but didn't see one on the way, so I kept on. Worst case scenario would be burning up some calories with my walk. Always a good thing. Thankfully, he was home when I got there and seemed pleased to see me.

"Thought you were staying at your sister's," he greeted me.

I exhaled. "Hmm, she forgot to tell me they were in California, perhaps moving there for good. Must have skipped her mind, what with being a hotshot lawyer and a busy mom."

"Cynicism becomes you," he remarked with a short laugh. Unexpectedly he hugged me; a stiff, little hug. "Come on, let's party a little, chase the gloom away. I got a nice bottle of wine, and then we may move to something a little more potent. I scored some really good weed."

"What's the occasion?" I asked. He rarely showed much concern with my moods. He usually didn't even notice them.

"Sold another painting. Why don't you put on a CD? Been replacing all my old tapes," he called from the kitchen.

I browsed through his new collection. AC/DC, Metallica, Van Halen. We didn't have the same taste in music and hard rock especially set my teeth on edge with its aggressive vocals and distorted electric guitars. But, what the heck, it had already been an odd day, so a little more couldn't hurt. I put on Van Halen and took the glass of wine that he offered. I drank greedily as the deafening music slammed through the apartment. The sound waves thrummed through my body and soon we got up and danced, swaying and gyrating to the music.

Someone banged on the door and yelled. "Hey, lower the fucking music."

That set us giggling uncontrollably. So that's what people meant when they said they partied. Cecil lowered the volume.

"Wait 'til you get a whiff of this shit," he said and produced a joint. He lit it and inhaled deeply before offering it to me.

I hesitated for just a split second as visions of Rosie's dead body popped into my head. Rosie's beautiful sad eyes. Perhaps I shouldn't have felt sorry for her. She'd had her share of partying, more than I ever had.

"Come on," Cecil egged me on. "The dead are dead; life is for the living."

He was right. So many of those I loved were dead and there was nothing to be done about them. And as for Daphne, she'd have a conniption if she saw me now, drinking and dabbling in drugs. But so what? She'd shut me out of her life, wiped me off like I didn't exist anymore.

Cecil was absolutely right. Life was for the living and it was about time I stopped watching from the sidelines. I snatched the offered joint, inhaled deeply, and waited for the haze to envelope me. Waited for that buzz Rosie'd often described to me, the moment when you no longer cared about anything.

***

"Hold your pee this morning," Theresa greeted me a week or so later as soon I walked into the clinic.

I stopped in my tracks. "What?"

"We got Phoebe's directive this morning. Staff urine tests today. Hope you been good," she chortled.

"You know me, straight as an arrow," I shot back, my heart beating faster.

"Ha, tell me something I don't know. So," she said to my receding back, "let's you and I do it right after I'm done medicating, 'cause by then I won't be able to hold it."

I closed the door to my office and collapsed into the chair. This was not happening. I gasped for air. This was not happening. Not happening. I repeated those two words like a mantra. But it was. I was going to be fired for not passing a drug test. Humiliated before everyone. Everyone. Not just staff, but all the clients would soon find out that Marika, their counselor and the clinic supervisor, was a junkie. I could see them laughing, telling jokes at my expense. I flushed at the thought. And it would do no good to deny the results, to tell them I'd only used pot a couple of times. They would no more believe me than I believed them when they denied their use.

I wondered irrelevantly if this was poetic justice. I could see myself becoming virtually unemployable, because Phoebe would never give me a reference. What would become of me then? And Daphne? She'd never forgive me this trespass. Her sister a drug addict, such a disgrace. And, of course, Cecil. What would he say? He was the one who gave me the pot, but would he be able to overcome the fact that I'd now be a disgraced woman who'd destroyed her career and would be mooching off him?

My stomach churned and I rocked myself back and forth in my chair. How unlucky could I get? Of course, I wasn't a drug addict and I never intended to continue to use pot. I didn't even care for it that much, especially the way I felt afterwards, parched and headachy. If only I'd resisted Cecil and his foisting it on me. If only I had a couple of weeks to clean my system. Perhaps I could claim that I was suddenly feeling ill and go home. Yes, that was it, stay home a couple of weeks and clean my system by drinking gallons of water. I often heard the clients say that does the trick. I held my head in my hands to stop the thoughts from buzzing around and around.

A knock on my door brought me back to the here and now. It was Carmen reminding me that the women were waiting for me in the group room. Since Rosie died, Carmen had taken a leading role in group. My stomach was cramping, and I had to rush to the bathroom.

"You okay? You don't look so good," she said.

I told her to assume the leadership position and start the group, and I ran to use the toilet. I looked at myself in the mirror as I rinsed my hands. I hated the vision that stared back at me. The big, worried-looking eyes, my pale lips and skin. Did I look like I'd used drugs just a few days ago? I dismissed the paranoid thought and forced myself to face my thorny group.

I had nothing to worry about where they were concerned. There was Carmen upbraiding Cindy for not taking the group seriously, while the rest of them listened in silence as she proceeded to tell them about Rosie's last few days, perhaps adding a little extra drama and embellishment. To hear Carmen tell it, this was no overdose. No, Rosie didn't want to go on living with that shameful disease and continue to hurt those who loved her; nor did she want to suffer the agony of a slow death. Rosie was courageous, Carmen said. I sat back and listened as the other women chimed in with sympathy. If I hadn't been so worried about my upcoming drug test, I would have congratulated myself on the group finally bonding, even if it had taken Rosie's death for that to happen.

After group, walking back to my office, Carmen caught up with me and wrapped her arms around me. "I know you miss her almost as much as I do. She always love you and I was jealous. I so sorry." She sniffed.

I felt tears well up, not because of Carmen's newfound goodwill towards me, but rather because I understood that I'd misjudged her, I'd been too harsh. She'd loved Rosie unconditionally. She'd been brave and was now suffering for it. She put me to shame. I invited her to come and talk to me whenever she wanted, and we agreed to have a session later in the week, even though I wasn't her counselor.

Soon thereafter Theresa buzzed to let me know that she'd closed up the medication and was ready for the drug test. I felt a tightening in my chest and asked her to wait a minute as I was in the middle of something. I then dashed over to see Derrick. His door was open, and I found him at his desk writing in a chart.

He raised his head and set his pen down. "What's up?"

I stood hesitantly at the door. "I … I'm not feeling very well. I think I need to go home now. It's my stomach, some bug or something. I'm feeling feverish."

His eyebrows furrowed and he motioned for me to sit. He got up, and closed the door behind me, then sat on his desk and leaned in closer, peering at me. "Do you think you have a fever?" He looked as if at any moment he'd put his hand on my forehead the way my parents used to do when I was sick.

"No, no. It's probably just a slight fever, but my head and stomach hurt. I think it's best I get out of here. I may be contagious." My words tumbled out. And I wasn't lying. By this point, I'd talked myself into really feeling ill.

"Sure. And stay out until you feel a hundred percent better," he said.

I got up quickly and headed for the door, but I wasn't quick enough. He added, "Could you just do the drug test before you go? It won't take but a minute and Phoebe was pretty adamant about everyone doing it today. You know how she is; she won't let it go."

I looked at him, my eyes wide in disbelief. A questioning look crossed his face. I muttered something about that suspicious Phoebe and left to get Theresa.

We walked to the bathroom with our little empty bottles in our hands. My hands were sweating, and beads of perspiration formed on my forehead; my heart pounded wildly. I had a crazy thought to tell Theresa the truth and throw myself at her mercy, ask her if she'd pee into my bottle, too, but some sliver of dignity stopped me from doing it. I went into the stall, hiked up my skirt, put the bottle between my shaking thighs, and let my drug-laced urine flow.

# CHAPTER TWENTY-SIX

I stayed home for the next three days. I didn't even have to fake being sick. I really felt ill. I was feverish and couldn't eat much, and what I did eat, I couldn't keep down. My chest felt like there was a brick on it, while my heart raced wildly every time I thought of what had happened. Which was most of the time. Cecil had gone out of town on a business trip, and the couple of times I'd talked to him, he'd sounded unconcerned.

"You're making too much out of it," he tried to calm me down. "You'll get another job. Maybe it will be for the best. Get a job with higher functioning clientele, like I've been telling you, and you won't need to take these stupid drug tests."

I knew he was trying to be encouraging, and yet I wished he could have been a bit more sympathetic. But sympathy had never been his strong suit. I remembered the time his dad had had a bout with cancer and how unemotional he'd been about it, rarely going to visit. Perhaps the fact that he had a difficult relationship with his father had something to do with it, but still. That was Cecil. He seemed to use up all his emotional supply for his mom and art. None of that was news to me; it just made me feel lonely. Lonelier than I'd felt since I started the Cecil Project.

On my three days' hiatus I stayed mostly in bed, except for quick check-ins with Mr. S. He seemed diminished since his illness, but he was holding his own, clinging on to life. He even went out to get *me* some chicken soup. When he showed up at my door with the steaming, aromatic tonic, on the second day of my sick leave, I teared up. No grandpa could have been more caring. I wanted to tell him what had happened, but I couldn't risk it. I didn't want to lose his respect. I kept mum. But he could see right through me.

"Whatever it is you think is so bad, it's probably only half as bad as you think," he said, setting the container of soup on my tiny kitchen table. "Nothing homemade chicken soup can't cure," he added with a cackle.

"Sure, but that's not homemade, is it?"

"Sure it is. Homemade at the deli."

"Oh, Gramps, you're the greatest." I gave him a hug. He put his frail arms around me and patted me on the head.

"Listen, I know something's upsetting you and you probably think it's the end of the world. However, I've seen the end of a world—at least it was the end of the world for millions. But then we picked up our ratty bones and started over again. So, eat your soup, go to bed, and in the morning everything will look brighter." He patted the top of my head.

"I don't know what kept you going through your hell." I dabbed at my eyes with a used Kleenex.

"That thing with feathers," he said, his eyes staring at something in the distance. I couldn't see what he was seeing.

"The thing with what?"

"Emily Dickenson. You know. That poem, 'hope is that thing with feathers.' That's what kept us going. Those who lost hope were the walking dead. We called them *Muselmann*. Now go eat your soup. And remember, as long as you're alive, you can choose hope."

I still didn't quite get the feathers thing. But I finished my soup, probably the first hearty meal I'd eaten in two days and turned on the TV. I spent my afternoons watching back-to- back soaps, starting with *All My Children* and ending with *General Hospital*. It was a mind-numbing relief to immerse myself in the painful lives of other people and to take some perverse pleasure at their misery. They called it *schadenfreude,* and I guessed I wasn't the only one to experience it, so I didn't have to feel guilty about it.

I was beginning to experience my daily soaps withdrawal moments after the last one aired, when my phone rang. I expected it was Cecil and wasn't sure I was up to listening to his daily account of his successful dealings, but I picked it up. After all, he was my hope for a future. The only thing I had right now.

"Hello," I said, forcing some energy into my greeting.

"Hi," Daphne's voice came through the receiver. I detected a slight hesitancy in her hello.

There was a momentary silence at both our ends. Finally, she broke it. "I called you at work and was told that you were home sick. You okay?"

"It's nothing serious. Just a tummy bug. I'm much better now." I tried to sound friendly, but I could hear the chill in my voice. I trembled with hurt feelings.

"Sorry to hear you're not well." That's my sister, always polite yet a little cool. I said nothing, for what was there to say. "I heard from my neighbor Judy that you came by when we were away. A lot's been going on, I guess, and I haven't been very communicative." She stopped and waited. I waited, too. She went on. "Look, I may have overreacted with my silent treatment. I just had a lot going on. I guess I had a good teacher in Mom, ha-ha. But I was wondering if you wanted to meet up tomorrow—that is, if you're feeling up to it. I'm going to be in the city. I'll catch you up on everything."

I'd already decided that I'd avoid work for three days and go back on the fourth, when the drug test results were expected. I couldn't hack the thought of going in before then and trying to carry on as if all was fine. The actual idea of me counseling anyone right now about drug use made me want to puke. The hypocrisy didn't escape me. It was best to stay home until D-Day. Go in, face Phoebe, gather my stuff, and try to leave with some shred of dignity.

I told Daphne I expected to be home the next day, and we agreed that she'd come over at lunchtime. Knowing her, she'd probably bring bags of food with her. But then again, maybe Daphne, too, had changed. Perhaps I didn't know her as well as I thought I did.

***

The minute I saw my sister's face, I knew something was awfully wrong. Daphne and I could tell each other's mood from hello. Her body appeared to have gotten smaller as she stood at my doorway, shoulders sagging, lips pinched together. She faked a smile and greeted me with a gushy hellos. It didn't erase the pained expression in her eyes, nor hide the puffy, splotchy face.

We hugged, tentatively at first, then lingered a few seconds in each other's arms. I invited her in and assured her I didn't have anything contagious. Which, of course, was true.

"Your place is a mess," she commented casually. "Not criticizing. It's just not like you."

"Haven't had the energy to do much," I said. That at least wasn't a lie. I let things pile up and didn't care. My sink was filled with unwashed dishes, mostly mugs and a few plates, including Mr. S's take-out soup container. Even my bed, which gets made first thing each morning, remained undone. I'd begun to understand why people didn't bother to make their beds. What was the point? It just got messed up again each night.

"Got us some sushi. I know you like it," she said, hauling out some containers from a plastic bag. Daphne didn't care for sushi. This must have been her peace offering.

I wished I had something for her. "Daph, I know I acted hideously and said some horrible things," I began.

"Oh, let's not talk about that," she interrupted. "We both said harsh things, some of them even true, but it's water under the bridge. Let's just move on."

The therapist in me wanted to dissect and analyze everything we said, perhaps ad nauseam, but my lawyerly sister preferred to stick to facts not emotions, so I let it go. I put a couple of place mats on the table, my own chop sticks, and plates.

"Water or Diet Coke?" I asked.

"Water's fine," she said. "I got us some miso soup, good for the digestion."

I brought out soup bowls and she ladled.

"How are the kids?" I decided to start on a safe topic.

Daphne put down her spoon and covered her face with her hands briefly before pulling them away. When she looked up, she seemed in full command of herself. "The kids are fine, for the moment."

"What do you mean, for the moment?" I gripped the table.

"I mean they're fine because they don't quite understand what's going on." She swallowed hard.

"What *is* going on? Come on, you're scaring me."

She gulped some water and set the glass down. "Gerald and I split up. At least for now," she said in a detached, matter of fact way.

"What are you talking about? You two are the most in love couple I know, no matter what happened in the past."

"Well, even people in love do stupid things. And as you know and reminded me not long ago, Gerald has had a proclivity. I should have known better the first time he screwed around."

"Don't tell me. He didn't." I gasped.

"He did all right. Yep, he did it again."

"Oh, Daph." I dropped my spoon in the soup and it splattered.

I got up and went to hug her, but she put her hands out to stop me. "Don't. Don't be kind, or sweet, or even sympathetic. That'll just make me bawl. And I can't cry. I just can't. If I start, I won't stop." But her face showed a weakening in resolve even as she spoke. Her chin and lower lip gave a little quiver. She raised her chin and took another sip of water. "Wish you had something stronger for a change."

"No, you don't," I muttered.

She laughed ruefully. "Yeah, good thing I don't like alcohol, or I might turn to drink, ha-ha-ha."

"Tell me what happened."

"It's really quite prosaic. Banal. I had suspected he'd been seeing someone from work a couple of months ago, but he denied it when I confronted him, feeding me some cockamamie story about a research project he was working on. Then I intercepted a bill for a piece of jewelry he bought a while back, obviously not intended for me. Gold *hoop* earrings. You'd think he'd know my taste by now."

"Maybe he wanted to expand your sense of fashion. Men like

144

women with hoop earrings," I offered, remembering my own makeover project.

"Right." She rolled her eyes. "Of course, after my cross examination he folded and admitted the whole ridiculous story. How it all started innocently enough, how ...." Her face crumpled. Then she shook her head, as if admonishing herself and remained dry-eyed.

The one thing I knew how to do, given my profession, was to keep my mouth shut and listen. So I did.

"Of all the clichés. It's a new nurse. It would be almost laughable if it wasn't so contemptible. When I found out, I took an assignment in L.A. just to get away from him. Then a couple of weeks ago I discovered I was pregnant. Only a fool lets history repeat itself," she said bitterly.

"Stop it. You're no fool."

"Says she who thinks that only fools fall in love," she said with a smirk. "But I'll tell you what. In the past couple of months, I started thinking that maybe you had it right all along. That maybe it's best not to worry so much about love, marry for more practical reasons, maybe for friendship. You may have won that argument. And don't tell me 'I told you so.'"

I gulped. I wasn't sure I wanted Daphne to be like me. "I would never say that. Besides, you don't mean it. You're just upset."

"No, I do mean it." She banged her hand on the table. I winced. I wasn't used to seeing Daphne angry. "Look, what's falling in love got me? We were *sooo* much in love. How you can cheat on someone you love is beside me."

We were quiet for a few minutes, each of us deep in our own thoughts. For some reason, I had always wanted Daphne to dissuade me from my own belief, as much as I fought her when she tried. I didn't want to co-opt her to *my* way of thinking.

I cleared my throat. "You know, Daph, that cheating on your mate doesn't necessarily mean the love is gone," I said quietly. I was thinking of Rosie and Carmen. They'd cheated, but still loved each other. "It's complicated."

She looked at me with narrowed eyes. "Don't give me your psychobabble. I don't see how you can *intentionally* hurt someone you love. And if you do, then you're sick."

"All I'm saying is there are all kinds of reasons people do what they do, that's all. I'm just saying that maybe you two should seek therapy."

"Whatever. Right now, I can't stand being in the same room with him. I've sent him packing to his parents, or a hotel, or wherever. For all I know, he's shacked up with *her*. Playing doctor and nurse together."

Then the floodgates opened, and all the anger and bravado spilled into sadness. I went over and put my arms around her, the way she used to do to me when I cried. I rocked her like that for a while. This was my sister, my rock. My heart ached for her.

"Now I've got the hiccups," she said. "I hate that."

I poured her another glass of water and then cleared our half-eaten lunch. Later I'd take the leftovers to Mr. S.

"Let's go for a walk," I suggested.

"I thought you were sick. What's wrong with you anyway?"

"Told you, some sort of stomach bug, but I'm much better and will go back to work tomorrow," I said as I went to get my jacket. This was no time to burden her with my problems. "Let's go to Washington Square," I said as we walked down the stairs.

The air was slightly nippy, but it was sunny and a late afternoon September sun warmed the air. Kids were streaming out of the school near my house, laughing and shouting, seemingly without a care in the world. I envied them, though I knew they had their own childhood problems and that their days in the sun wouldn't last very long. We walked in companionable silence. My worry for Daphne had earlier pushed down my own problems, which now threatened to resurface, but I shoved them away.

"Mr. S said something yesterday that reminded me of what Mom used to say. That nothing is as bad as we think it is; that at least no one is threatening to shove us into ovens," I said.

"Yes, until she decided to off herself one day." Daphne sounded bitter.

"That was her depression," I said quietly. "We don't know what she went through, so we really oughtn't judge."

"I guess so. Still, you don't kill yourself and leave two kids. You just don't." Daphne's eyes were pools of fury. "You've got to stop idolizing her. And you can't keep her alive by trying to be like her. Let her go." She sounded tired.

We got to the park and sat on a bench, our faces turned to the sun that would soon disappear behind the buildings. We watched mothers and nannies pushing strollers, older kids playing in the playground, shrieking and laughing. A happy cacophony of sounds.

"So, what next?" I ventured. "Does he want a divorce? More importantly, what do you want?"

"Oh, no, he certainly doesn't want a divorce. They're making me a partner at the firm and I'll make more money than him. As for me, I don't know. I can't think clearly right now. I sent the kids to his parents for a couple of days so I could think. He's been apoplectic with me flying out to L.A. weekly. 'How can you deprive the kids of their mom?'" she imitated him, her mouth turned downward. "But it was okay for him to go screwing around and come home way past their bedtime."

146

"Yes," I agreed.

That's how the world worked. Men left women to deal with the kids. It was a given. I wished I had some words of wisdom to offer, but none came to me, despite being a therapist.

"Anyway, let's change the subject. What about you? Any new tiny-nosed men in your life?" She gave me a look and we both giggled. Then our laughter exploded, a crescendo of barely suppressed hysteria, the letting go of tension, which had build-up around my shoulders and neck. We laughed so hard we ended up on the verge of tears.

# ~CHAPTER TWENTY-SEVEN~

When Daphne left for Grand Central Station, I went home, showered for the first time in three days, and washed my hair. At least I'd meet Phoebe and my sentence with some semblance of dignity. I couldn't think of the aftermath; my mind couldn't visualize life without the clinic.

I was drying off my hair, which now made me resemble a Yorkshire terrier, when my doorbell rang. It was an odd hour for anyone to come over and I hoped it wasn't Daphne returning for some horrible reason. I put on my sweats and ran to get it. I heard a dog bark. Looking through the peephole, I was surprised to see Derrick's emerald eyes. For some reason, it brought back the first time I'd seen them, also through a peephole, at work. I yanked the towel off my head and ran my hands through my hair before opening the door.

He looked at me and apologized. "I should have called, but I was walking Bruce here and decided to pop by on an impulse."

Bruce wagged his tail and sniffed around me. I was thrilled that the dog was happy to see me. "No problem. Come on in. I was about to make tea, would you like some? I'm feeling much better and plan on returning to work tomorrow." I hurried through my words.

He declined my offer for a drink. "I can't stay long, but there's something I needed to talk to you about," he said, looking down, avoiding my eyes.

"Sure, sure. Here, sit." I offered the sofa while I sat opposite on my stiff-backed upholstered chair. It was uncomfortable, but it kept my back upright.

He sat down and patted his dog. Bruce looked at him and then me with sad eyes, as if he knew something, and I began to feel uneasy. Derrick coughed. "The thing is," he started, and cleared his throat. He raised his head and finally met my eyes. "The thing is that we got the results of the drug tests today."

An involuntary whimper escaped my lips and my hands shot up to cover my mouth. I swallowed hard. "I … I can explain. I know it'll sound lame, but I really can." But even as I said it, I knew I really couldn't. What would be my excuse? I was trying to please my boyfriend in a desperate attempt to rekindle our relationship, so I did drugs because he pressured me. It sounded like the sorriest excuse I'd ever heard, and I've heard plenty.

He raised his hand to stop me. "Before you say anything, let me finish."

I gasped for air, but my lungs felt like there wasn't enough oxygen in the room; I got up and opened the window. A burst of cool evening air blew in and I inhaled deeply. I returned to my seat and raised my knees up to my chest.

He waited for me to settle, his eyes alert. "As you obviously know, your test came back positive for pot. Do you want to tell me about it?"

"Will it matter?" I asked. Historically, any positive test at work meant immediate dismissal.

"Maybe not, but I'd still like to know." His voice was measured, almost kind.

"I really only used a couple of times, maybe three or four. It all started after Rosie died. I ... I lost it. I couldn't deal with her death. I could never deal with death." I babbled on incoherently. "Then I was with my boyfriend and, well, things got a little out of control and ... and I used." I blinked, hoping to forestall tears. *I must not cry. Whatever happens, I must not cry in front of Derrick.*

"We could probably test for quantity, but I don't think that would make a difference. I already talked to Phoebe." He stopped and cleared his throat again. "You're aware of the policy. However, I managed to persuade her that not only is it too harsh, but also inappropriate for a substance abuse treatment facility not to offer rehabilitation to the staff. After all, we're the ones who supposedly understand the issues and we ought to be more compassionate in how we deal with this amongst our own staff."

I looked at him, uncomprehending. I still couldn't find my voice, nor would I have known what to say if I had.

"It was surprisingly easy to convince her that there are other ways to deal with this besides outright firing you." He leaned back on the couch, as if he was relieved at having delivered the worst of the bad news.

"What ... what does that mean exactly?" My voice quivered.

"It means that you're being put on a month-long furlough without pay. And the expectation is that you'll get some treatment yourself, even if it's only going to a twelve-steps program. When you return, you'll be put on a three months' probationary period. You'll be given drug tests weekly during that time." He rattled all that off fast, rat-tat-tat.

I was stunned into silence.

"Well?"

"I ... I don't know what to say. Or how to thank you enough. I know if it was up to Phoebe, I'd have gotten the boot faster than we kick any of our clients out, we give them so many lapses."

"It's one of the arguments I used with her. We can't have one standard for our clients and a different one for staff. And, again, she surprised me at how open she was. She almost seemed relieved at this solution."

I had a hard time believing that and said so.

"I also reminded her that ,as medical director, I should have the final say." He stood up and picked up Bruce.

"I … I really don't know how to thank you," I stuttered.

"You can thank me when the month is up and you can tell me that you haven't used and …." He stopped and gave me a wan smile. "Well, you know the score, don't you?"

I felt my ears burning and I hung my head in shame. "Wait," I called when he opened the door. "The rest of the staff, do they …?"

"Total confidentiality. Your secret is safe. I'll tell them that you're on a medical leave for a month, but since you left the day we did the drug test, some of them may put two and two together." He shrugged. "I wouldn't worry about that right now if I were you. I'd focus on how you got here instead. Walk good, Marika." At my quizzical look, he added, "That means 'take care' where I come from."

It was only after he left that I noticed big circles of sweat had formed around my armpits. I could only hope he hadn't noticed them. However, that was the least of my worries. I raced to the phone to call Cecil. He wasn't home, but that was the story of our relationship: he never was there when I needed him. I picked up the receiver and dialed Daphne, but I hung up before it started ringing. I remembered what she'd revealed to me earlier that day. It felt like ages ago. The last thing Daph needed was to be burdened with *my* problems, especially since I'd caused them myself.

I paced around my apartment, frenzied thoughts racing through my mind. A tiny bit of relief pricked through the dread; I had gotten off relatively easy. I'd expected to be fired and I was still employed. Uppermost on my mind was how would I explain my month-long layoff to my clients, let alone the staff and everyone else. I was grateful for once that my parents weren't alive to see my shame.

I went into the kitchen and started opening and closing the cupboards and drawers in search of comfort food. I needed desperately to fill my stomach, which had long since digested the few pieces of sushi I'd had with Daphne. I'd given the rest to Gramps. All I could find was a can of Campbell's chicken soup, some popcorn, and, in the fridge, a head of lettuce and a tomato. I took out the lettuce and the single tomato and slammed the fridge door shut. I rinsed the lettuce aggressively under the running faucet and moved on to the tomato. On inspection, it was way past ripe. I threw it into the sink and it splattered all over the counter and my sweatshirt. I stomped my feet and screamed. How could I have fucked up my life this way?

Everything that had gone wrong in my life was my own doing. It all started with the misbegotten Cecil Project. The way I charged through single-mindedly with the idea that I'd do whatever it took to nab him. Even the fight I had with Daphne was because my head was buried so far up my *tush* I couldn't see a guy's worth beyond his nose. Then I had carelessly risked my job by getting a hair cut from a client, Pam, a haircut I wouldn't have needed to begin with if I hadn't tried to straighten my hair to attract Cecil. And then, of course, the sex. Doing all those things I found distasteful to please him, to show him I'd changed, and using pot to make the experience bearable. All the while not thinking at all, throwing caution to the wind, damn the consequences.

I had no one to blame but myself.

# ~CHAPTER TWENTY-EIGHT~

After staying up until the wee hours of the night, I woke the following morning with a throbbing headache. It was a chilly, damp-looking day; the trees outside the windows were wet and fewer leaves were hanging on to the branches, colorful though they were. The kind of day I normally would have loved to stay at home, but now that I had no work to go to, I longed to be there. I wandered from room to room, aimlessly. I assumed that by now Derrick would have told the staff of my mysterious illness that would keep me home for a month. If I was in college, I could have claimed to have mono. But I wasn't in college anymore. In the next few days, all the patients would be told, and I imagined the rumors would start flying. Most of them could probably not care less about my absence, with the minor exception of a few of my own clients. Rosie would have cared, but Rosie was no more.

I skipped the shower and dragged myself to the kitchen. There was no reason to change out of my pajamas, other than to switch them out for a pair of sweats. I thought of the stories of people who live alone and don't work, who stop showering, shaving, waxing or even combing their hair. I could let my hair grow into a big puffy cloud and no one would notice. I'd save on all those damned expensive hair products. That would be a good thing; I reminded myself that I'd have no salary coming in for the month. I was furloughed, not on vacation, and economies would have to be made. Good thing I wasn't a big eater. However, I'd have to eventually go out to the market; I barely had enough coffee for the next couple of days and the freezer held only a few slices of bread.

I put coffee into my recently acquired French press and waited for the water to boil. As soon as it did, I poured the hot water, stirred, let it brew just a couple of minutes before pressing down on the plunger. I poured myself a cup and added the milk. The milk curdled and I poured it down the drain. Now I'd have to go out into the wet morning and get a few essentials, for while I was used to going with little food, I couldn't do without my coffee. I decided to shower after all, and put on a pair of jeans and sweatshirt, because to stop by and check on Mr. S, I'd have to look halfway decent or raise his suspicions.

He was still in his bathrobe when I knocked on his door. "Still not feeling well?" he asked when he opened it. "Come, I'm making coffee."

I wasn't going to tell him anything, but as soon as I entered his apartment the whole story came tumbling out of me. He looked at me kindly and scratched his head of thinning hair. "The thing is that by the time you get wise to the world, you're too long in the tooth to do much about it."

He set the steaming mugs on his kitchen table and proceeded to butter toast. "Here," he put a plate with two slices of rye toast in front of me. "Eat!"

He sounded just like my parents. Eat! A lump formed in my throat, but I took a bite and chewed on it slowly, if only to please him. He sat and slathered apricot jam on his toast. "Did I tell you already that when you look back on all of this, you'll realize it wasn't the catastrophe you thought it was at the time?"

I nodded my head for yes, although I didn't believe a word of it.

"Well, it's true. As a matter of fact, something good may come out of all of this. I can feel it in my old bones. And I trust these old bones better than I trust the news. My bones tell the weather pretty good, too." His Yoda smile made me feel a little better.

I finished my coffee and a slice of the toast and put my raincoat back on. "Don't forget to get Ding Dongs," he called after me. "Life is just a little bit better with Ding Dongs."

It was late morning by the time I had finished my grocery shopping and straightened up my and Mr. S's apartment, which was actually spotlessly clean. There was still the whole afternoon of day one to get through, and the only things I had on my to do list was tell Cecil and Daphne about my new circumstance. I supposed I could get away with not saying anything to them; they didn't really need to know, so I held off. In any case, they were both, unlike me, busy at work.

I picked up the Yellow Pages and rifled through them in search for AA meetings. It was interesting that the name the organization chose placed them practically on the first page. Clever people. I put the Pages down and walked around the room. I wasn't an alcoholic and using pot a few times did not make me a drug addict. And yet. Here I was facing dire consequences due to my stupidity and use of a drug. There was no getting around it. If I wanted my job, I had to show proof that I was getting some sort of treatment and the most readily available option was AA. I wouldn't have to talk, just go, I reassured myself as I dialed their local number with shaking fingers to get times and places of meetings. As it happened, there was a meeting every evening at six o'clock, nearby. It would at least be in a part of town where I needn't worry about running into any of my clients; that would be too much to bear.

I set out to make my mom's chicken soup. It was a cliché, but her chicken soup cured all. It was certainly excellent for colds, but just as good at ministering for the soul. Soon the kitchen started smelling of soup, and in my mind's eye I was transported back in time to childhood. Friday evenings. The smell of chicken soup permeated our whole house, mingling with an aroma of chocolate Babka cake in the oven. I closed my eyes and saw us all sitting around the white-clothed dining table. Mom would light the candles even though we weren't religious, just slightly observant Jews. She said lighting the Shabbat candles was her way of a weekly visitation with her dead family. Three watchful, worried pairs of eyes would follow her movements closely as she walked the fine line between being dragged down into the dark rabbit hole or buoyed by the candle lights. On the good Friday evenings, we laughed at Dad's silly jokes and ate and sometimes even sang. On the bad Fridays, we sat quietly, my stomach clenched, as I tried to gulp down the soup so Mom wouldn't get angry at my lack of appetite. We never knew what kind of Friday it would turn out to be.

I shook the memories loose and ladled out the soup. It came out just like Mom's, clear and light golden yellow with little circles of glistening fat, bright carrots swimming in the broth, jostling with the celery and aromatic verdant dill. I hadn't bothered making noodles to go with it, and I could see Mom clucking her tongue as I heaped on vegetables and chicken. Then, feeling uncomfortably stuffed, I set aside some for Mr. S, cleaned up, and went to put on a sweater over my T-shirt and jeans. There was no postponing the inevitable; I had to get to that meeting.

The rain had stopped, but still I put on my raincoat and hat, if only to cover my face somewhat, just in case I ran into anyone who might recognize me. I walked briskly down the few blocks to the church where the meeting was held in the basement. I was never comfortable upon entering a church, but now I was positively shaking. I stood outside for a few moments, watching as others walked in, men and women, young and old, some in work clothes, others dressed casual like me, and still others scruffy looking as if they'd slept in their clothes for days. An elderly man with an unkempt beard and a long greasy ponytail stopped and asked if I was going in; he held the door open for me. I murmured my thanks, lowered my gaze, and I walked through.

"First time?" he asked, following on my heels.

I nodded my head, keeping it down.

"You've come to the right place. Don't be shy. We all had our first time." He chuckled. "Welcome to the club."

I waited for him to pass me by as I scanned the room. A few dozen hard-backed chairs were lined in rows on one side, as if they were set for a lecture. I'd expected a smaller venue, perhaps a dozen or so people sitting in a circle, something cozy, like my women's group, and I shuffled my feet, unsure where to sit. Most of the people were congregating by the coffee urn set up on a table against one wall, chatting and laughing like it was some kind of social club gathering. Finally, after some hesitation, I chose a seat in the back, in a row occupied by one other fierce-looking young woman with a nose ring and very long hair. Shortly thereafter, the meeting was called to order by the man who'd talked to me outside. He made several announcements about various meetings and then read something from what they called the Big Book and then opened the meeting, encouraging one and all to share their stories.

I shrank further into my chair, but I needn't have worried. Very quickly, a few people raised their hands, and one man was called upon to talk. This wasn't like a classroom where the teacher forced you to talk. How I used to dread being put on the spot; my face would burn every time my name was called. But here, one by one, people stood up, without any prodding, to tell their tales of woe. They talked of how their lives were ruined, how they lost families, careers, health, how they reached their bottoms and still kept on with their addictions. One by one, they ended their stories with some sort of achieved redemption, even if only temporary, brought about by having admitted their powerlessness in the face of their addiction and by accepting a higher power.

Obviously, none of it was new to me. After a while, the stories all had a note of familiarity. Having been raised in a home where the idea of a God was almost mocked with bitterness, the notion of accepting and submitting to a higher power was objectionable to me. The way I saw it, I was my own higher power. I had to make choices about my life and accept the fact that many of my decisions of late had been bad ones. Starting with my Cecil Project. Yes, my project might have been nearing its successful completion, but it was the way I'd gone about it, losing myself and making too many compromises along the way. I'd acted in unacceptable and even disgraceful ways. Sitting there listening to all their stories, I felt a new-found respect for their struggles. I was humbled.

I left as soon as the meeting ended, not lingering to mingle. A small group had already formed outside the church, and I saw the young woman with the nose ring. She waved at me to come over. I waved back with a smile and walked on, but she dashed after me.

"I'm Jo. I noticed that you weren't that into all that higher power bullshit in there," she said, to my surprise. I hadn't thought my face registered my feelings. She wore a hoodie and put it up now as it was beginning to drizzle again. "What poison brings you here?"

"Actually, I'm only here—" I realized that if I told her the truth of my situation I'd come across as if I was in denial. So I told her that my drug of choice was pot.

"Mine, too, preferably laced with cocaine, ha-ha. To be honest with you, I don't really see the harm in it, but what can you do, it's illegal, so ...." She shrugged her shoulders. "Now I gotta pee in a cup once a month for my probation officer. Such an asshole."

I murmured in sympathy and quickened my step.

"Wanna go to this club downtown? They have some really good shit there. I'm a little short on cash though," she said.

"But what about your drug test?"

"Heck, I just gave one up, so I got at least three weeks to party. Cocaine doesn't stay in your system long." She laughed a husky little laugh.

I begged off, claiming that my test was the next day.

"Well, maybe I'll see you at the next meeting. Good luck," she yelled after me.

I quickened my steps as if I was afraid that someone else might come and try to offer me drugs. I needed to get myself back on track.

# CHAPTER TWENTY-NINE

First thing I did when I got home was call Cecil even though I fretted over what his response would be. He sounded hoarse when he picked up the phone.

"Are you getting a cold?" I asked.

"I fell asleep, that's all. Kinda late to call. Is everything all right?"

"Sorry I woke you," I said. "But it's only a little after nine, not past your usual bedtime."

"I'm tired and I have a very early wake up tomorrow. I called earlier to tell you that I'm flying out first thing in the morning. Going to Dallas for a few days."

"Dallas? What's in Dallas?"

"Meeting an artist and checking out some galleries. Anyway, what's up?"

"You'll never guess where I've been tonight." I paused, but it didn't seem as if he was going to attempt a guess. "An AA meeting. You know, Alcoholics Anonymous."

"What for? Don't tell me, you finished a bottle of wine in three days and now you think you're an alcoholic?" He chuckled.

I told him about my furlough. If I was hoping to hear remorse, an acknowledgment for his role in it, for pressuring me to use pot, I was quickly disabused of that notion.

"See, you still got your job. Think of it as a month off. Relax and enjoy yourself," he said, not unkindly. "I think you need this time off. You've been so on edge."

"A month off without pay is not exactly a relaxing idea," I grumbled.

"Look, if you need some cash to tide you over, let me know. But, honestly, don't take it too hard. Smoking a joint now and then doesn't make you a junkie." He paused, then added as an afterthought, "Seriously, relax. It's not the end of the world. Maybe it's for the best. Look for a job where you won't have to take drug tests."

I didn't want another job, but I didn't get into it with him. I wished him a successful trip. He promised to take me out for a nice meal when he got back, told me again to relax, and we hung up.

The rest of that first week of my probationary month crawled by in a daze of inactivity. I woke up at all hours of the night and watched late night movies and ate fat free ice cream pops. In the mornings, groggy from lack of sleep, I'd shuffle around and make my breakfast of three quarters of a cup of Farina or oatmeal and coffee. I settled in to watch more TV, switching back and forth from *The Today Show* to *Good Morning America*, depending on who was on. When the game shows came on, I turned off the television until the start of the afternoon soaps. I tried to stay active with walks and visits to Mr. S. Now and then I roused myself to cook the two of us a decent meal, mostly because Gramps had to stay healthy. The worst time of the day was during that lull in the afternoon after the last of the soaps were over. It was too early to eat and too late to be otherwise productive. Sometimes I called Daphne, but she'd usually just be getting home from work and feeling rushed to get dinner ready for her brood. She was still living apart from Gerald and didn't really want to talk about it. After dinner, I'd go to one of the AA meetings, making the rounds so as not to go to the same one twice. Surprisingly it wasn't hard to do. It seems there was no shortage of addicts—or meetings—in the city.

Theresa had called me a couple of times, but seemed to lose interest when I told her I had mono. "Too much kissing with Cecil," she teased.

She gave me tidbits of gossip from work, but I really didn't want to hear any of it. It made me sick to my stomach. Especially when she told me how well she was getting along with Derrick, and that even Kumar and Dinesh seemed to have stepped up, seeing most of my clients. None of them missed me.

One afternoon, I took a walk after my soaps and ran into Derrick walking Bruce. I wanted to duck out of sight somewhere—my hair had gone unwashed the entire week and had reached that horrible in-between stage—but he saw me and waved me down. Bruce wagged his tail in recognition.

"How's it going?" he asked, his forehead furrowed with concern.

I shrugged. "As well as can be expected. I'm going to AA meetings daily. I've got the signed paper."

He smiled, his dimple showing. "No worries, I trust you."

"Don't be too sure. If I didn't have to, I probably wouldn't go. Anyway, how's work?" I changed the subject.

"Everything's fine, but you're missed."

"Right." I twisted my mouth. "Especially by Kumar and Dinesh, who must be thrilled I'm not on their case about charts."

"Seriously, they expressed concern, and the clients miss you, too. The other day, Carmen stopped by my office. When she heard you were out for the month, she wanted to make sure you weren't dying. She actually cried."

"Ha, Carmen of all people. She hated me," I said. "In some strange way, it took Rosie's death for her to see me in a different light. And me her. Go figure." I scratched my head.

"We're all counting on you coming back recharged and ready to take the helm."

"For sure," I said. I waved and crossed the street back to my apartment and my solo dinner.

My run-in with Derrick left me a bit more buoyant. I bounded up the stairs to my apartment, fixed a plate of chicken for Mr. S, and gobbled down my dinner, half a chicken breast and a cucumber salad. On my way out to the meeting, I stopped by to see Mr. S. I dismissed his pallid complexion as the result of lack of sunshine. Tomorrow I'd take him out for a walk, but now I had to rush to my dratted meeting. I wanted to make sure I didn't get there late as I had the other day, when I snuck in and felt everyone's eyes on me.

That night, the meeting I chose was near Cecil's place on Gramercy Park, so on my way back, I decided to stop and say hello. He'd been due back from Dallas that afternoon. I was slightly annoyed that he hadn't called me yet but figured he must have been very busy. For all I knew, the trip might not have been the success he'd hoped for and he was brooding in his apartment, nursing his wounds. I even thought I might take real pity on him and not wait for him to ask for it, but willingly offer a blowjob. Given my self-imposed isolation of the past week, I was even looking forward to it. I longed for human contact in any form.

It was a cloudless early October crystal-clear night; nonetheless, no stars were visible in the city sky. They never were. The early evening breeze had died down as it tended to do after sunset. Everything was still. Despite all that had happened, I couldn't blame Cecil for my drug use. It had been my choice. He hadn't forced me. I'd made the decision. He was self-involved, but given the stress of running a new gallery, it was understandable. Deep down, he was a good man, and he cared for me, in his Cecilian way. In December, shortly after Thanksgiving, I would turn thirty and I still held out hope that he'd pop the question for my birthday. Men did that on birthdays, holidays, and other special occasions. And I decided that even if he didn't, I'd give him a little more time. I'd decided to move my exit date further down the line, at least until after the new year. I allowed myself to get carried away by the proposal fantasy again. Being a married woman, living the life. Not a care in the world—or at least no financial cares. Perhaps even become a mom one day. I wanted to have those options.

It was then that the thought occurred to me. Why wait for Cecil to pop the question? Why not finish the Project the way I started it, by taking control of my destiny and ask *him* to marry me, and not in jest? I

159

had nothing to lose even if he turned me down, except perhaps re-set my exit date. The risk was worth the reward. My resolve hardened and my temples pulsed. When I reached the park, I slowed down and decided to take a stroll around it to rehearse what I was actually going to say. The proposal. It had to be serious, not a Barbra Streisand imitation, yet I also needed to inject some levity into it, just in case. Keep it light enough so as not to totally lose my dignity should he say no. A difficult balancing act.

I completed one loop around the park and still the perfect script refused to come to me. I gave up and turned the corner to his building. It wouldn't matter anyway. The appropriate words would materialize at the right moment; they usually do. The important thing was for Cecil to see the new me, a self-assertive woman of independence. Gone was the old clingy, insecure Marika, who only liked the missionary position.

As luck would have it, someone was coming out of the building as I got there, so I got into the elevator without having to buzz his apartment. I wanted this to be a total surprise. I pressed the button for the fifth floor. My palms were sweaty, and I wiped them on my jacket. My hands shook as I fussed with my hair and clothes, wishing I'd changed into something sexier, but it was too late now. I closed my eyes, inhaled a few deep breaths, and waited for the elevator to stop. I stood outside his door a moment to still my pumping heart before knocking, at first hesitantly, then again more forcefully. I heard muffled sounds, then the door opened. But it wasn't Cecil who greeted me. It was that young artist he'd discovered and whose art show was the night Cecil and I reconnected. The night of my first blowjob.

"Marika, right? I'm Clive," he said, offering his hand. He was dressed in sweatpants, bottoms only. His hairless chest glistened as if he'd just exerted himself. "Cec, it's Marika," he called.

Cecil emerged from the bedroom, looking disheveled. The top button on his jeans was undone. He was tugging a sweater over his messy hair. His face went ashen when he saw me. My eyes darted from one to the other, uncomprehending.

"Marika. I … I …."

"Please, why don't you come in?" Clive offered genially. "I'll make us coffee or, better still, we could probably all use something stronger." He made it sound as if we'd be cozy, the three of us having a drink, maybe even cocoa, on a nice cool autumn evening. I wondered if he'd even put a log in the fire.

I stood frozen for a second, when something finally clicked in my brain. I whirled around and ran down the hall. I didn't wait for the elevator but scrambled down the stairs. I heard Cecil call after me, but I didn't stop. I didn't stop running until I was outside his building and halfway up the street. I bent over and sucked in the night air. Bile came up my throat and I forced myself to swallow it back down.

When I arrived home, I crept up the stairs, just in case Mr. S was listening for my footsteps as he sometimes did. But once home, I was at a loss. Without turning the lights on, I crashed on the couch and stared out the window. The anticipated tears refused to flow. I shivered and wrapped the throw around my body, yet I still shivered uncontrollably. I remembered reading in a schoolbook that one can have a delayed reaction to shock. At one point, I thought I'd throw up, but all I got was dry heaves.

I was unaware of the passage of time except that at one point I saw Derrick leave his building again with his dog and a while later return. His last walk before bedtime.

The ringing phone startled me. I didn't wait to hear who the caller was and disconnected the answering machine. A part of me wished for the caller to be Cecil, apologizing and offering some perfectly plausible explanation for what I'd seen. But I didn't want to know that it wasn't him, that he didn't care enough to call and offer an explanation or apology. In any case, I was too numb to talk to anyone. My mind was blank, empty. I couldn't think, and I didn't want to feel. Finally, somewhere in the middle of the night, I got up and went to take a bath. I soaked in the hot tub until the water began to cool, with one thought looping around my brain over and over again: the Cecil Project had been a dismal and total failure.

# ~CHAPTER THIRTY~

What a fool I'd been. A nearly thirty-year-old woman who had let herself run away with a childish notion derived from watching too many movies. I'd convinced myself that Cecil, the man who had dumped me once before, would still care for me and want to marry me. That he probably never wanted to marry me hadn't dawned on me, fool that I was. He'd dumped me the first time around not because I wasn't mature enough, or too clingy, or didn't like to give him blowjobs. He'd dumped me because he didn't love me. He wasn't drawn to a woman like me because he wasn't drawn to women. The reason he'd proposed the first time was so I'd be his cover, so he could stay in the closet.

I had plenty of time during the long night to nurse my shame and to finally come to the understanding of why my Project had failed so miserably. It was weirdly comforting to know that it wasn't because I'd made the wrong logistical moves, that there was no 'if only' here. It wouldn't have mattered if my hair was long or short or straight or curly, if I'd been prettier or wittier or sexually more adventurous.

I woke up the next day engulfed by shame and humiliation. Shame at what a fool I'd been. The reckless spending on a new wardrobe, the pretense of enjoying sexual acts I hated. He must have seen right through me. I flushed at the thought. Even if he was interested in women, he wouldn't have been attracted to someone groveling at his feet. Nothing was wrong with Cecil other than his inability to let the world know who he was. What was wrong was *me*. Sad, lonely Marika with my pitiable job, waiting for someone to rescue me. I was the delusional one living on a fantasy. And that's what it was: a fantasy. How pathetic to be dreaming of being whisked off by a rich prince and living happily ever after. I deserved exactly what I'd gotten.

An ache and nausea roiled my insides. I found some sleeping pills and went back to bed. I disconnected my phone and slept on and off until the next day. I must have gotten out of bed every now and again to go to the bathroom, but I didn't recall. Eventually, I walked down to the corner shop to get take-out food and carried it over to Mr. S.

He opened his door and looked at me. His eyes widened and his mouth fell slightly open.

"Marika?" he said in a hushed voice. "Something wrong?"

"No. Probably that bug I had has come back," I said. My voice sounded odd: raspy and cracked, like I hadn't spoken for a few days.

"I started to worry. You didn't answer your phone yesterday," he said.

"Sorry, I took it off the hook so I could sleep undisturbed." That, at least, was not a lie.

"Come inside. I'll make you some tea," he said when I handed him the bag.

"No, no. I don't want to infect you with whatever I've got." I retreated from the door. "I'll check in with you tomorrow."

"You know you can talk to me. About anything," he said. He tipped his head sideways, a worried look on his deeply wrinkled face.

"I'm fine, really. I just need to sleep this off," I said and dragged myself up the stairs.

Once in my apartment, I crawled back into bed and curled into a ball. A ball of shame. Mom would have been so embarrassed by me. She'd taught me better than this. Yes, she'd instilled in me the idea that to have a fulfilled life one must be married. She'd also taught me right from wrong and that it was wrong to forget your dignity. That was the most enduring lesson she had learned in life: they can take away everything but not your dignity. To humiliate yourself meant that you had no self-worth. For once, I was happy that she wasn't alive to see what I'd become. A lonely, pathetic woman, ill-equipped to cope with life, with few friends and with little prospect of ever forming a romantic relationship. Husband and children, those were not to be my lot in life. I remembered studying in psychology how we're wired to connect, it's a human need and without it we shrivel and even die. The few people I'd felt connected to, Rosie, Gramps, well, one was dead and the other very old. What was it that was broken in me that I found it so hard to connect to people?

\*\*\*

I woke up to the sunlight coming through a crack in the curtains. My throat felt parched and sore. Perhaps I was coming down with something after all. In old novels, heroines would often take sick to their beds after a love affair gone wrong and die from a broken heart. Except I couldn't even claim that. What Cecil and I had couldn't be called a love affair, more like an affair of convenience. They didn't make movies about that.

There was a bottle of water by my bedside and I drank greedily from it. I debated getting up and taking a shower; I suspected that I probably smelled. But there was nothing to get up for. The whole day stretched in front of me, filled with nothing to do. No one would notice if I showered or not.

My stomach rumbled and I realized I hadn't eaten in the last two days. I felt my stomach, it was flat, almost concave. At least one good thing had come out of this mess: I'd lost what little fat I'd had. If I lost any more, I might disappear. That would take care of my exit plan. Then it dawned on me, my exit plan. Why wait to execute it? There would be no wedding, no Cecil, no anything, just the drudgery that was my life. I felt at one with Mom. I understood why she'd done it. And how easy it would be. I wasn't hungry anyway. I could just lie here until it was over. I felt warm and fuzzy at the thought.

I lay my head back on my pillow and contemplated how relaxed I felt. I shut my eyes and put my arm over my head to better keep the sunlight out.

*** 

I woke to persistent banging on my door. A familiar man's sing-song voice was calling my name. It took a moment to realize that the banging was real and not one of the dreams and that I was alive. I threw off my blanket and put on my robe. It felt heavy on my limbs and when I started walking towards the door, my legs buckled under me. I felt dizzy and grabbed hold of the little side table in the hallway.

"Coming," I croaked. I fumbled with the chain and finally opened the door.

Four eyes looked at me, wide with bewilderment.

"Vat is dis?" Mr. S exclaimed. When he was excited, his accent got thicker. I held back a giggle.

"Jesus, Marika, why haven't you been answering your phone?" Derrick said. "We've been trying to reach you for days."

He probably went on, but that was the last I heard before I fainted.

*** 

When I came to again, I was lying on my couch. My stomach was filled with all kinds of sharp pain and my head was pounding, pulsing with irregular beats. My mouth tasted pungent, sulfurous, and I could feel acid shooting up my esophagus. I shivered even though I was covered with a throw. When I raised my head, I felt dizzy again and let it fall back on the pillow. I noticed a glass of orange juice on the coffee table next to me. I reached out with a shaking hand and lifted it to my mouth and drank it eagerly.

Lying back again, I heard clanging sounds from my kitchen. The clatter of dishes. Someone was singing softly, *no woman no cry*. It was a melodious, honeyed voice, definitely not Gramps. A moment later Derrick's face peered from the kitchen door. A crooked smile appeared on his face, with the usual dimple, and he spoke very gently.

"How are you feeling?" he asked.

"Fine. Well, still a little dizzy. But what made you come here?"

He came over and stood by my bed. "Mr. Saperstein called me. He said the last time he saw you, you looked pretty bad, and then he hadn't seen or heard from you in two days and was getting concerned. You weren't picking up the phone. He knocked on your door yesterday, but you didn't answer."

I wanted to die of shame, again. "I … I'd taken a sleeping pill."

"Hmm." He looked at me suspiciously.

"No, really. Maybe I took two, I don't remember." I closed my eyes. I couldn't confess that I'd wanted to die; he'd be appalled. So I bent the truth a little bit—okay, a big bit. "It's not that I tried to off myself or anything like that. It's just that I haven't eaten for the past couple of days."

"I suspected as much. You weigh about as much as a little pullet. Not that you were big to begin with," he said.

I realized he must have carried me to the sofa. "I just slept and drank water. I didn't have the energy to eat."

"Well, you'll have to introduce food slowly. I'm heating up some chicken soup I brought. A certain old man told me you like chicken soup."

"I do like chicken soup," I said and lay my head back down. I'd forgotten just how much I loved chicken soup.

"I understand it's nutritious for body and mind and you need both."

He went back to the kitchen, and I eased myself up into a seated position. The orange juice must have done the trick, for I was no longer feeling dizzy. I swung my feet down into their slippers and, wrapping the throw around me, stood. Slowly, like an old woman, I walked into the kitchen.

Derrick placed the heated soup in a bowl on the table with a spoon and sat down across from me and watched as I sipped the warm life-affirming broth and noodles. The warmth spread inside me as the soft, salty noodles swam in my stomach. We didn't talk until I finished.

He folded his arms and extended his legs. "So, do you want to talk about it?"

"You sound like a shrink."

"Occupational hazard. And since I already sound like one, can I venture a guess? Love affair gone wrong? With that Cecil of yours?"

"Something like that. Only it wasn't really a love affair. It was all a big lie gone wrong, as I guess all lies do, eventually. Exploded in my face. Can't really blame Cecil."

"Hmm." He picked up the plate, got up and put it in the sink. "It usually takes two to carry on a lie." He came back and sat down again. "Look, I don't know how to say this diplomatically, so I'll just say it."

I held my breath, not sure I wanted to hear whatever it was he was going to tell me about myself. About what an idiot I'd been and how obvious it was.

"I've noticed your eating habits. You're verging on anorexia. Stands to reason that you got worse while you were going through this."

"I … I was always a small eater. Used to drive my mom crazy," I said.

"Whatever it is you're going through, you're not alone. People care about you, despite what you think. Even Kumar asks about you every day."

I was surprised to hear the crack in his voice, as though he was fighting back emotions. Kindness was hard to digest, and tears filled my eyes. I didn't even have the energy to blink them back. I just let them fall.

# CHAPTER THIRTY-ONE

Over the next couple of days, I was hungry all the time. I rested and cooked, and for a change I gobbled down whatever I prepared and didn't foist it all on Mr. S. Every time I brought him something to eat, he said he'd only eat it if I sat down and ate with him. I didn't need much encouragement. We ate and talked, and I tried not to count how many calories were going down into my stomach with each mouthful. I also started jogging again along the Hudson, the nippy air bolstering me.

Derrick called a few times to check in on me, reminding me that in two weeks my furlough would be over and not to get too used to this life of leisure. My pulse quickened at the thought of going back to work. I realized I loved my job more than I knew, despite all the challenges, the difficulties with Phoebe, the daunting clients. It was my little community: the good, the bad, and the ugly.

One day, I called Daphne. What she'd been going through was much worse than my imagined Project going awry. Her whole world had collapsed around her and she was facing a life-changing dilemma. We talked and after I told her the whole story of my failed Cecil Project, I asked if I could come and stay with her for a few days. To my surprise, she reserved judgment and was amazingly sympathetic. The next day I packed a small suitcase and headed out, after first asking Derrick if he'd check in on Mr. S.

On the way out, I stopped to tell Gramps that I'd be gone for up to a week so that he wouldn't freak out if he didn't see me.

He greeted me at the door wearing his shirt and tie and looking perky. "Look at you," I said, raising my eyebrows. "Haven't seen you all dolled up in a while. I thought you decided dressing up wasn't important. What's the occasion?"

He raised his shoulders. "Your shrink invited me to have supper this evening. And I'm feeling chipper."

"Stop calling him *my* shrink. He's not," I protested.

"Maybe he should be."

"I don't need a shrink, if that's what you're getting at. I've just had a tough few weeks. That's all." I quickly changed the subject. I had a train to catch. "Good to see you feeling so frisky, Gramps."

"It's always better before the end," he said, smiling his Yoda smile.

"Stop that! I'll see you in a few days. I'm going to Daphne's. I'll get us some Ding Dongs or, better yet, *rugalach* when I get back and we'll have us a little party."

"Have a good time." He waved. "I prefer *rugalach*," he called after me.

***

"So?" My sister widened her eyes after I gave her all the gory details of how things had ended between me and Cecil. "Didn't you ever suspect *anything* about his, you know, sexuality?"

"No." I said. We were having a heart-to-heart, but there were certain things, like my recent sexual activities, that I wasn't ready to divulge, even to her. "I was a virgin when I met him, so I didn't have a frame of reference or comparisons to make. I just thought for the longest time that something was wrong with *me*, that I was frigid or something." I still worried about that.

"Yes, we're taught to blame ourselves first." Daphne sipped her tea.

We were sitting in the guest bedroom, just as we had been a few months ago when we'd had our terrible fight. Now we had a new-found reason to bond: misery. Both of us had been let down by the men in our lives, although Daphne had much more to lose. I, on the other hand, couldn't claim a loss of something I never had in the first place. But letting go of one's fantasy is still a loss.

"Do you think we learned that from Mom? Blaming ourselves for everything?" I asked hesitantly. Daphne always got edgy when I brought up Mom.

She bit her lips and exhaled. "What I learned from Mom, sadly, was how *not* to behave. How not to be a mom or a wife."

"Boy, you really have it in for her. What did she ever do to you? She wasn't perfect, but who is?"

She lowered her gaze. "I don't have it in for her. I loved her. But I was always scared of her, even when I was a kid. I feared not knowing what mood she'd be in. Her quick switches from being cheerful and loving one moment to angry and detached the next. We always walked on eggshells." Daphne sounded bitter.

"Still, we shouldn't judge her." If there was one thing my job had taught me, it was not to judge unless you've walked in someone else's shoes. "Mom was ripped apart from her family, spent her youth in a slave labor camp. We're clueless about the hell she'd gone through."

Something fluttered across her eyes before Daphne spoke. "Maybe I've been too harsh on her. The way she made us all unhappy." She

168

paused for a long time before going on. "Dad and I shielded you for years about her first suicide attempt. You were so young you wouldn't have understood."

I still felt the pain every time I thought about that. That Mom chose to leave us.

"Poor Dad," Daphne went on. "He was dull and quiet, but all he ever wanted was to make her happy. Remember how she used to quote that ridiculous saying 'when poverty knocks on your door, love flies out the window'? She hurt him badly."

I lowered my head. "D'ya think she loved him?"

"Mom married Dad because she was twenty, without a family, lost. And here came this American soldier, her savior, her knight in shining armor. He was crazy about her, but I don't think she ever loved him in that way. And, at the end, it turned out he wasn't such a good provider. He must have disappointed her."

I giggled and mimicked Mom's accented English. "It is just as easy to fall in love *mit* a rich man than a poor *von*."

Daphne cackled. "Right. See, Rika, marriage without love doesn't make you happy after all. She was wrong."

"Dinesh at work thinks we Americans make too much out of love being necessary for marriage. You fell in love; how's that working for you now?"

"I know I'm not going to change the way you were brainwashed by Mom. But look at how your coldhearted attempt to get Cecil turned out." She shoved another piece of cake into her mouth, and I resisted temptation to tell her that she'd been gaining a lot of weight. My own relationship with food wasn't the healthiest, so who was I to counsel her?

I closed my eyes and clenched my jaw as Daphne's words slammed into my heart. And yet. "The way I see it, yes, it was an ill-conceived project, but just think, if I'd been really in love with Cecil, I'd be devastated right now. As it is, I'm mostly upset because I'm still single and lonely. But at least my heart isn't broken. Only my pride."

Daphne got up and picked up our empty mugs. Her face was haunted, adding depth to her dark eyes. "Fine, have it your way. Have a loveless and lonely life just so you don't get hurt. If you can call it a life." She sounded tired. There were dark rings under her eyes. I hated Gerald for doing this to her.

"What are you going to do?" I asked in a hushed tone. We hadn't talked yet about her unwanted pregnancy. Or, at least, I assumed it was unwanted.

She sat back down again and glanced at me sideways. "Gerald agreed to come with me to couples counseling. He admitted that he's got a problem. And … and I also owned up to the fact that I'm not that easy sometimes."

I could hardly believe what I was hearing. She was ready to take him back, forgive his trespasses, again. I swallowed hard. It was her choice and there was nothing I could do about it. Besides, who was I to give advice about relationships? "And the baby?" I finally asked.

"Whether we stay together or not, I'm going to keep it. Not because I don't believe in abortions, but at my age, this may be my last chance of having another child." Her voice broke slightly, and she flicked away the tear that threatened to fall. "I may not be the best mom in the world, but I'd love to have another child."

I reached out and touched her hand. "You're a great mom. And I understand." But I really didn't.

She clutched my hand tight, her head slightly bowed, dark hair falling around her face. The mists of seeing Daphne as a pillar of strength cleared, and I could see her objectively. She was every bit as vulnerable as me. I slid over to where she sat on the sofa and flung my arms around her.

"Tomorrow's Sunday. How about we take the kids and go somewhere? Maybe drive into the city and see a musical or something," I said.

She straightened up, tall again, and I backed off. "Actually, I meant to tell you, but I'm taking them to see their dad, and then there's a birthday party, so you'll have to amuse yourself."

She was back to being Daphne, the elder sister in control, and I was back to being Marika, with too much time on my hands, at a loss of what to do with myself.

The next morning shortly after breakfast, Daphne and the kids left. I called Mr. S, but he didn't answer. It was the second day that he hadn't picked up his phone, and this time I dialed Derrick to ask if he could check up on him. Derrick's phone rang and, like Mr. S, his machine didn't pick up. That was mildly worrying. I told myself that Gramps had probably gone down to get his own pastry and that Derrick was out walking Bruce. Or maybe he'd taken Mr. S out for a coffee. Or maybe he was out with his girlfriend, the stunner. The possibilities were many, and I decided not to worry about anything. I'd take a walk.

A cool, brisk wind whipped my face, but the sun shone bright as only an autumn sun can, warming my body as I walked, pumping my arms. I walked for a while without any purpose or direction and yet I wasn't completely surprised when I ended up again at the neighborhood where I grew up. I crossed the street and leaned on a large elm planted long ago next to the sidewalk opposite our old house. I watched my old home as if I expected to see Mom and Dad at the window. It was a small two-bedroom Cape Cod in a neighborhood that had been regentrified. Although at the time we lived there, it was crouching on the wrong side of town. It had been repainted in dark grey and the shutters were now red. It used to be white with black shutters.

Time slides away and I'm once again ten years old. I see the ghosts of all of us when we were sad. Mom's haunted eyes devoid of energy or life. I see Dad following her, always vigilant after her bathtub incident. Quiet, gentle Dad, trying to suffuse some levity into our existence with his unfunny jokes and little pranks. And I see myself, an urchin with billowing hair, shadowing Mom everywhere she went. But piercing these visions are other ghosts of us when we were happy, or at least pretending to be. Mom dressing up in her favorite outfit—a simple silk dress, black, of course, with an open neck and a plain row of pearls—as my parents got ready to go to someone's Bar or Bat Mitzvah. Mom in high heels so she could reach Dad's shoulders. I'd thought Mom was the most beautiful woman in the world, despite the permanent furrow of her brow.

This was the first time since her death I was able to conjure her face as she was, clearly, without the haze of time. Oh, my mother. She was beautiful, she was sad, and at times she tried so hard to be happy. I didn't ever really know her, no more than any child can truly know their mother. But if there was one thing I did know, it was that, despite her being my mom and loving us, she'd tried to kill herself. Love hadn't cured whatever ailed her. And the loss of my parents still hurt. It was the unfortunate side effect of loving.

# CHAPTER THIRTY-TWO

"Did you hear the ambulance last night?"

Kenneth, my neighbor from across the hall, opened his door a crack as I jabbed my key into the lock the next day. He must have been waiting to waylay me on my return from my week at Daphne's. To my knowledge, he wasn't friendly with his other neighbors any more than he was with me, but somehow, he knew everything about our lives. We were as cordial as any New Yorkers were upon running into each other on the stairs.

"What ambulance? I was away for a few days," I said, as if he didn't know.

"Poor Mr. Saperstein. I'm afraid they were too late." He shook his head.

"Mr. Saperstein? Too late for what?" I blinked. A wave of terror looped through my chest and sloshed down to my gut. My heart started thumping so hard I was afraid it would jump out of my chest.

"I gather you were friends." He shook his head again. "He told me once that you were like a daughter to him. Anyway, he passed away last evening. Just like that. Poof." He snapped his fingers. "His nephew's here now. Honestly can't be too upset; he lived a long life. And a quick death, that's what we all want. Say, you okay?"

I felt bile shoot up from my stomach into my throat. "Fine. I'm fine. I just have to do something," I managed to say, shoving the door open and slamming it behind me.

I made it to the bathroom in the nick of time before heaving the egg sandwich I'd eaten on the train. After the last of my breakfast came up, and all that remained were dry heaves, I slumped on the cold bathroom floor and leaned my head against the wall. I'm not sure how long I sat there, unaware of the passage of time, until the doorbell jarred me.

It took a moment before it registered that the man standing in my doorway was Mr. S's absentee nephew, Andrew. He stood, looking uncomfortable, shifting his weight from one leg to the other, fidgeting with an envelope in his hand. He seemed quite a bit older than in the photo in Mr. S's apartment

"Marika, right? Apartment 4-B." His eyes shifted from me to the door as if he needed to make sure he was in the right apartment. "Your neighbor just informed me that you were home."

I nodded.

"Uncle Shmuel spoke so highly of you. You reminded him of the daughter he lost. And … and you were very kind, bringing him food and crossword puzzles, and … and taking care of him, more than I had," he went on.

I felt like smacking him and lowered my gaze to the floor so that he wouldn't see the fury in my eyes. But in the end, I'd failed Gramps, too. I wasn't there. I felt like a fake. "I … it wasn't kindness. I … I just liked him."

His cheeks went pink. "I wish I'd been more attentive, but he didn't want to move to be near us in Pennsylvania. He was stubborn that way. Independent." He let the thought dangle. I understood he'd have to deal with his own guilt, and it was best not to judge.

"Anyway," he went on, "he didn't want a funeral, so he'll be buried tomorrow at ten in the morning, next to my aunt, his beloved Esther. In Brooklyn."

I nodded again. My mouth was dry. What was there to say?

He cleared his throat. "I found this letter in his desk. It's addressed to you."

He handed me the envelope. He turned to go before I thanked him. "I'm sorry for your loss," I added the old cliche.

He turned around. "I'm sorry for *your* loss. It may be as great than mine."

I shut the door behind me and faced my empty apartment. My suitcase was still on the floor in the hallway and the apartment had that special smell of a place that's been shuttered for a while. Stagnant. I shoved the suitcase to the side and went to wash my face. It was only then that I noticed that I was gripping Gramps' letter in my hand. I put it gently on my kitchen table, as if it were a delicate object. I decided not to open it for now; seeing his handwriting would be enough to dissolve me into a puddle and I didn't want to cry anymore. Instead, I climbed into bed even though it was barely noon. I wanted to do nothing. Absolutely nothing. Not think, not feel. Especially not feel that ache around my heart. I shut my eyes, my mind, and my feelings. Nothing.

\*\*\*

When I came out of my heavy slumber, disturbed by something, I didn't immediately know where I was, expecting to be still at Daphne's. I lay huddled underneath the covers, curled up against the cold air. It was the ringing phone that had woken me and, as I reached for it, I remembered everything. It was dark outside; at this time of year, night begins to fall early. I looked at my alarm clock to learn it was only half past six. *I should pull down the blinds*, I thought, as I turned on my table lamp and reached for the phone.

"Hey." Derrick's deep melodious voice reminded me, suddenly and strangely, of my father, only with an accent. Perhaps I'd dreamed of my father.

"Hi," I croaked. My throat felt like I'd swallowed sand.

"I wanted to call you when Mr. S got sick, but you didn't leave your number, and I didn't know your sister's last name." There was no trace of an accusation in his tone, just the facts. "I'm so sorry that you had to find out about his death this way."

"Don't be too kind," I whispered. I couldn't take kindness right now. "I deserted him. I knew he was ill, but I had to take care of me first. Selfish. I really didn't want him to be all alone when … when …."

"He wasn't." Derrick stopped me. "He called me that morning. He hadn't been feeling well and I went over. He was very weak, and his breathing was shallow. It was congestive heart failure. As you know, he refused to go to the hospital. He knew he was dying and asked me to call his nephew. He even joked that he'd timed his death just right because he didn't want to upset you too much. Said you didn't handle death well. He smiled when he talked about you."

I heard a howl. It started in my gut and escaped before I could stop it. I put my fist in my mouth, but it was too late; the floodgates had opened. It was embarrassing to lose control in front of him. Derrick was quiet. He let me cry until I ran out of tears and gained control of myself.

"I'm sorry," I said. "It's not like he was family or anything, but I felt like he was. He was the perfect Gramps, and I can't believe I won't be taking crosswords and eating Ding Dongs with him. Ever again." My face crumpled and I took a deep breath.

"He was your Gramps, without the genes. It's really all about the love you had for each other."

*And how was that supposed to make me feel any better now that he's gone?* I shoved the thought down inside my chest where hopefully it wouldn't disturb me. "Are you going to the cemetery tomorrow?" I asked. Then I remembered, he was working.

"Yes, I notified Phoebe and told Theresa not to count on me in the morning. She can do the medication and the other two can manage unsupervised," he said. "You're going, right?"

His question surprised me, caught me off guard. I hadn't planned on going. What was the point? I wasn't religious, and neither was Mr. S. He'd scoffed at all things religious. It wasn't as if I could say my farewell, he was gone already. Dead is dead, as my dad used to say. But I couldn't very well not go now since Derrick was. We agreed to take the subway together to Brooklyn.

***

"*Adonai natan, Adonai lakach, yei shem Adonai m'vorach*
God has given, God has taken way, blessed be the name of God,"
intoned the young rabbi Andrew must have found yesterday.

It was a cold grey day, appropriate for a funeral, and heavy clouds
hung overhead. Far out on the horizon I could see the rain, and I
buttoned the top button of my coat with my gloved hands. I was
standing close to Derrick and could smell his cologne—or perhaps it
was aftershave—something vaguely spicy. The warmth of his body
drifted toward me.

We were a tiny gathering: the two of us, the nephew, the rabbi, and
the funeral director. Gramps had often vacillated between bemoaning
the fact that he was the last one of his friends left standing so no one
would be at his funeral and enjoying the idea that he'd outlived them
all. I guessed he wouldn't know now that there weren't enough male
mourners to say the *Kaddish*, the prayer for the deceased. Andrew didn't
know anyone locally, and the rabbi hadn't been notified to bring men
along.

The rabbi approached Andrew with a small pocketknife and made
a slight tear in his blue tie. Then he offered us each a little torn black
ribbon with a tiny safety pin. I attached mine to my coat's lapel and
Derrick did the same with his. Our heads bowed as we stared at the
closed casket. I didn't want to think of his frail body in it. "Ashes to
ashes, dust to dust," we repeated after the rabbi, each taking a handful
of dirt with our hands and tossing it over the casket as it was lowered
into its final resting place.

Death was ugly. Stupid. Frightening. There was absolutely nothing
that could be done to give it meaning or make it purposeful or easier to
endure. And the more one loved, the worse the pain of loss. The way
I'd chosen to deal with this conundrum was to ignore it for as long as I
could. The less you love, the less you lose.

# ~CHAPTER THIRTY-THREE~

We made a dash to a café Derrick knew before big, fat drops started coming down. We were somewhere in Brooklyn, a few stops from the cemetery, a borough I'm not familiar with, having never strayed from Manhattan unless I had to. He opened the door and waited for me to enter first. It struck me that this was the second time Derrick and I'd broken bread after a funeral. I hoped it wasn't going to become a habit.

The smell of strong coffee assaulted my senses, spicy and nutty all at once, making my stomach rumble. It was that odd hour, too late for breakfast and too early for lunch, and the little café was mostly deserted. A tall, slim woman with a tidy afro waved at us from behind the counter, pointing to all the empty tables. She glanced at Derrick with something I couldn't quite read on her face. Disapproval? Perhaps of me.

I took off my coat and sat down at the chair Derrick pulled out for me in his usual courtly manner. The tables were tiny in this small joint and I was acutely aware of the limited space between us. My shoulder brushed against his upper arm when I sat down and briefly my knee bumped against his under the table before I quickly moved it. I was also aware that my hair, which had been held in place with a plastic headband in an attempt to tame it, now had escaped and wild curls draped around my face and along my forehead. But there was nothing I could do about it. I leaned back in my chair and looked at him. I'd known Derrick for a few months now, worked with him daily, so why I suddenly felt my senses heightened at his presence was something I didn't want to think about. I turned my attention to the room.

It was a humble place, no muss no fuss. On the wall behind the bar was a string of small flags, each of which consisted of a gold saltire cross, divided into four sections of greens and blacks.

Derrick followed my eyes. "It's the Jamaican flag," he explained. "This place has the best patties outside Jamaica." He waved his hand and the tall woman with the afro, exuding sensuality, sauntered over to our table.

"What'll you have?" She didn't carry a little pad or a pen.

"Coffee?" He looked at me questioningly and I nodded yes. "And what kinds of patties you have today?"

"The usual," she answered with a strong lilt, elongating her vowels. "Beef, Ital, chicken."

"Beef or veggies?" He asked me. "They're all delicious."

I decided on veggies; less fattening. Even though I was no longer as restrictive as I had been before I fainted, some standards had to be maintained.

"You come here often?" I asked.

"Not really. I did for a while. I knew someone who lived nearby and she introduced me to this place."

I wondered if it was that girl from the gallery I'd seen him with. "Your girlfriend? The one you met at the gallery?" His eyes narrowed as they bored into me questioningly. I raised my palms up. "I've seen you two together a couple of times."

He laughed. "I guess you put two and two together and came up with the wrong number. We did see each other, but I wouldn't have called her my girlfriend."

"That's right. I forgot. You don't believe in any sort of long-lasting relationships."

He threw his head back and laughed, and his maddening dimple appeared in his cheek. "Did I say that? I must have been talking about Jamaican men in general. And I guess all generalities are lies."

The waitress brought us our order and I dropped his unsatisfactory explanation. It didn't matter, because after the Cecil debacle, I'd decided it might be wise to stay away from all men for a while, work on myself. She settled the basket with the patties in the center of the table and put small plates in front of each of us. No utensils apparently were needed. "I'll bring the coffee," she said as she sashayed off.

Derrick offered me the fragrant basket first, holding it in a decorous manner, while I debated which golden yellow pastry to select. "I think this one's the veggie," he pointed to one of the turnovers. He took another one.

I sniffed at the strong spices emanating from the pastry as the waitress returned with our coffees. She set mine roughly and some spilled on the saucer, but she moved away without apologizing. I took a sip of the piping hot coffee, black, and nibbled on the pastry edges. Derrick dumped three spoonsful of sugar in his cup, followed by lots of cream. I grimaced. He stirred his coffee while admiring his turnover for a moment before taking a hearty bite.

"Mmm. Taste of home," he said, his mouth full. "Go on." He encouraged me with his elbow. "What doesn't kill fattens."

I took a small bite. An explosion of flavors filled in my mouth. A combination of allspice, curry, and peppers, jostled one another for my attention; they had it. "This is *not* my mom's boiled chicken, that's for sure," I said when I came up for air. My tongue was delighted at the mix of heat and butter.

"Ha," he said. "Wait 'til you get a taste of bulla cake. Although that may be an acquired taste."

We stopped talking, giving ourselves over to enjoying the patties.

"Have another one," he urged. I hesitated. I was sure that a pound of butter must have gone into that flaky crust.

"Not still dieting, I hope," he said. I raised my eyebrows and shoulders ever so slowly. "Here, try the beef. You won't regret it."

I took the offered little golden package and closed my eyes as I took a bite. Heavenly.

For another few moments, we were silent, and I became aware of his eyes resting on my face. He finished the last of his third patty and licked his thumb and forefinger. The thundershower had passed, and weak sunlight filtered through from the window behind him, creating a halo around his dreadlocks.

He leaned back and patted his flat stomach. "That'll do 'til the next meal. What next?"

"Next? You mean what do we generally do after we bury our dead?"

"I think I know what you do. You sit Shiva, but only for immediate family, right?"

"Poor Gramps, no one will sit Shiva for him." I bent my head. It dawned on me suddenly that no one would sit Shiva for me, either, now that my prospects for marriage were shattered.

"I don't think it matters to the dead; it only matters to those of us left behind. You can do whatever you want to commemorate the departed." He looked at his watch and exhaled. "Too late for me to go to work, but let's take the train back." Without waiting for my reply, he waved to the waitress. I made to get my wallet out, but he pushed my hand down with his warm palm. "Patties are on me."

We left the café and walked back to the subway. We jumped on the first train going to Manhattan and sat quietly in the half empty car, each of us buried deep in thoughts, although my mind resisted thinking of anything. Not of Gramps. Nor of the pledge I'd made to myself about my exit. Suddenly the idea of being the cause of more pain for my sister was unbearable. Selfish. Besides, I didn't think I could go through with starving myself again.

At the stop before ours, Derrick motioned to me to get off. I followed him up the platform.

"Let's just walk a bit," he said. The sun was playing hide and seek amongst the fluffy white and gray clouds, but the air had warmed up enough that I unbuttoned my coat. We walked toward Washington Square Park. It was deserted except for a few derelicts and women with strollers scattered here and there, out taking advantage of the sporadic appearance of the sun. We strolled aimlessly, side by side. I felt the palm of his hand on my back, ever so lightly, and yet it sent an alert throughout my body. I stiffened slightly. *Don't fall in love,* I reminded myself, *especially not with a guy who's not into marriage.* His hand moved, edging me towards a bench exposed to the sun. He took out a hanky and put it on the bench, which remarkably was dry.

"Looks like it didn't rain here," I said, wiping my hand on the seat.

We sat down close enough that our arms touched. I crossed my legs, laced my hands around my knees, and watched a young woman bending and making faces and cooing sounds at her infant in the stroller. The child smiled and clapped its hands merrily. Strangely, this little moment brought me back to a party I'd attended in college shortly after my parents died. I remembered how it had hit me then that I was likely the only person in the room whose both parents were dead. That feeling of being utterly alone, utterly lonely has never left me. Now, looking at that sweet connection between mother and child brought it back full force. That, and that Gramps was gone, too. And then. to my horror, tears streamed down my cheeks, flowing and flowing, against my will.

"I'm sorry. I don't know what's come over me," I said, my voice ragged. I fished in my purse for a tissue.

"Someone you loved just died, that's what's come over you," he said, his voice and eyes kind. He placed his hand on my arm tenderly. "Want to talk about it?"

I felt an ache in the vicinity of my heart. That's what it feels like to have a broken heart. I'm not unfamiliar with that feeling although I tried to numb myself to it.

"I don't want to unload on you," I said.

"You're not. I asked for it. And remember my profession," he added with a crooked grin.

And just like that, the words came gushing out I told him the story of how my mom had killed herself. I couldn't understand how, despite a mother's love being the most unimaginable, unconditional, fiercest, and purest love of all, she had been willing to abandon us. He kept quiet, nodding his head now and then.

"Have you ever felt utterly, perfectly lonely? So lonely that you think you could actually die? Well, I have. And that's thanks to having someone you love abandon you."

He seemed about to say something, but didn't. He looked like he was grappling with something. "How so?" he finally asked.

"Don't you see? Loneliness awaits us all at the end, like it did for Mr. S. The end is always bad. The more you love, the more pain and suffering you'll get."

His eyes met mine and he shook his head so that his dreadlocks danced. "But you can't refrain from all the good things that come from love only because you're afraid that one day they'll be gone."

"I don't see why not. I don't see the point of it. Love makes us miserable more often than not, and it never lasts. You said as much. too. You're the shrink. Tell me, why is love so great?"

"Because if someone you're with accepts you the way you are and completes you, really sees your soul, that's the only time when you're truly not alone. It is possibly the *only* cure for loneliness."

I looked at him doubtfully.

"I didn't say that all love lasts. Maybe you're right, maybe most doesn't. But what else is there?"

"Really?"

"Have you heard the story of Kafka and the little girl?"

I flicked away a curl from my eye. "Kafka? Let me guess. He said that love is absurd."

Derrick stretched his legs and swung his arm to the back of the bench. I felt it resting lightly on my shoulders. I tilted my head backwards so that it rested on his arm and opened my eyes toward the warming afternoon sun.

"The story goes that Kafka meets a little girl in the park where he walked daily. The little girl had lost her doll and was crying. He offers to help her find the doll, but obviously he can't. They arrange to meet the next day. He goes home and composes a letter to read to the little girl. In it, Kafka wrote as if he was the doll and tells the girl not to mourn, that the doll has gone on a trip to see the world and have adventure."

"Nice man, that Kafka," I interjected.

He nudged me to be quiet. "Anyway, this was the beginning of many letters Kafka wrote of the doll's adventures to comfort the little girl. When Kafka finally had to leave, he brought a new doll to the little girl. It was obviously a different doll, but he explained to the little girl that the doll had traveled, and it had changed her."

"And?"

"In the last letter, he explained to the little girl that everything that you love, you will eventually lose, but, in the end, love will return in a different form."

I raised my head and looked at him, not quite comprehending.

He smiled down at me. His arm was still on my shoulders, warming it. "Grief and loss are universal, for young and old, and the only way toward healing is to look for love again in whatever form it comes."

# ~CHAPTER THIRTY-FOUR~

The light had changed to that deep golden color that came with the sun low in the horizon, covering the clouds in orange and purple hues, and, with it, the winds picked up. We left the bench and started for our separate homes, walking briskly, for the air had gotten cooler and was threatening rain again. At the entrance to my building, we stopped. Derrick put his hand on my shoulder and asked if I was going to be okay. I was on the verge of brushing off his concern in my usual caustic 'I'm perfectly fine' way, but something, perhaps his hand on my shoulder, stopped me.

"I haven't been okay for a while and may take a while to be. But maybe that's okay?" I said.

"It is," he said. "You're exactly where you should be right now. Don't overthink so much, just let yourself feel. I'll check in with you later."

The very idea of it made me woozy. I felt too full of emotions, simmering, boiling over emotions I didn't want to feel. I took two stairs at a time as I hurried straight up to my apartment past Gramps'. Images of him intruded into my mind: his Yoda smile, the way he relished his pastry, the way he *loved* me.

I went into my kitchen to make myself something to drink. My stomach was still digesting the two glorious patties I had eaten earlier, and I reminded myself that I'd had enough food for one day. I put the kettle on, while visions danced in my head of all the cups of tea I'd shared with Gramps. Again I felt that ache in my heart. The kettle boiled and I dunked my teabag in the cup twice quickly and saved it for another use. I sat at the kitchen table, warming my hands on the mug when my eyes fell on the letter Gramps had written to me. I picked it up and examined the envelope, front and back, as if it was a relic to be treasured. Finally, with shaking fingers, I opened it slowly, careful not to tear it. The note had been written on good stationary with his name embossed on it. Mr. Samuel Saperstein, Esq. With strong, bold strokes he had written:

*Dearest Marika,*
*Thank you for infusing the last few years of my life with friendship, joy, and love. I did not have much of that after my dear*

*Esther died. I am only sorry you did not get a chance to meet her.*

*But, more than anything, I'm grateful that you allowed me into your life. That you did not let an old man live his last years loveless. Grief is an inescapable part of life, but love is the balm that makes it all worthwhile. That someone cares enough to bring you Ding Dongs, or, better still crossword puzzles, when you really need them. That is love. And for that I thank you.*

*This small sum is not payback, it's only a tiny token of appreciation from an old man. Do NOT, under any circumstances, use it wisely. Splurge!*

*Affectionately yours,*

*Gramps*

Tears were streaming down my cheeks and snot dangled from my nose as I folded the letter around the enclosed check and put them carefully back in the envelope. I wiped my face and put the envelop in my bedside drawer. When I went to call Daphne, I saw that the answering machine's light was blinking. I pushed the button and recoiled at the sound of Cecil's voice.

"Hey, I ... I hope you're okay. I really want to talk to you, to explain everything. Please call me. Eh, love ya. Oh, it's me, Cecil," he added, as if I wouldn't recognize his voice.

I pressed the erase button. How dare he sign off with love? How meaningless. I dialed Daphne.

"Hello," her voice sounded chipper, brighter than it had been in a while. Then she modulated her tone. "How are you doing, hon?"

"I've never cried so much in my life, so don't be kind to me, 'cause it'll open the faucets again," I cautioned. "Just when I think I've run dry, the spigots open up."

"Poor you. I'm so, so sorry about Mr. S. You're going to miss him, I know," she murmured. "Actually, I think it's a good thing that you're letting yourself cry. Hey, you're the one who should know that it's good to let it out."

"Sure, throw my own words back at me." I chuckled, and changed the subject. "You're sounding very chirpy. What's up?"

"Not sure I'm chirpy, but I'm feeling cautiously optimistic. Gerald and I have had a few productive couples therapy sessions. Fingers crossed."

"I'm really happy for you," I said, keeping my misgivings to myself.

"Let's meet for dinner in the city before you start working again," she proposed. "You looking forward to it or dreading it?"

"A bit of both, but mostly looking forward to it," I said. We agreed to meet the following day for lunch.

\*\*\*

The metallic clanking of garbage cans woke me up at the crack of dawn. This was the last day of my enforced furlough and my ability to sleep late was foiled; tomorrow, the first of November, it was back to the grind. I lay in bed for a while listening to the muted footsteps of people walking under my window, rushing to work. My first thought was that this being Halloween I should bring a special sugary treat to Gramps, then it hit me. No Gramps. A wave of weariness passed over me, leftover from all the crying of the previous day. I wanted to let go of all that heaviness, of all that had happened to me in the past few weeks with Rosie, Cecil, Gramps. I got up and went into the bathroom, showered, washed my hair, and tamed it with product. It was at the stage where I needed to make a decision: cut it all off again or go long. I was not up to making decisions.

As I waited for the water to boil for my coffee, I decided to let go of the heaviness, to do something special on that day. Treat myself, and for no particular reason. It wasn't even my birthday, although that would come in a few short weeks. I poured myself a cup of coffee and carried it into the bedroom. Opening my closet, the first thing that caught my eye was the neon green dress I'd bought during my foolish Cecil Project makeover. Too ridiculous for words, and not *only* the dress. I yanked it off the hanger and tossed it on my bed. Later, I'd clear my closets and take things to Goodwill. Someone ought to have that dress, but it wouldn't be me. It was never right for me.

I pulled out a pair of black slacks and topped if off with a black turtleneck; my uniform. It was almost but not quite cold enough for boots, so I put on a pair of loafers, my only flats. Studying my pale face in the mirror, I smudged some blush on my freckled cheeks, and brushed on a little mascara. I was going to the Metropolitan Museum. I grabbed a grey blazer, which was as much concession to 'color' as I was willing to make, and off I went, skipping past Gramps' apartment as fast as I could.

Yesterday's clouds had dispersed, conceding the sky to the sun. It was an unusually balmy day and I basked in it, knowing that it wouldn't last long. I'd forgotten how much I loved walking around in museums, especially the Metropolitan. I bought a ticket for a 'pay what you wish' dollar, which I knew Daphne wouldn't approve of, and went directly to the Impressionist wing. I expected it to be mostly empty and was surprised at all the groups of school kids harnessed into sitting on the floor, forced to listen to lectures about art. Some seemed attentive, mesmerized, while others' eyes were glazed over. I wondered what would happen to those kids as they grew up. Would they live up to their potential, would they make the most of their lives, or would they just muddle through, take the wrong path, as I'd done?

I made my way past one group of children walking around with drawing pads and pencils and went into another gallery. An early twentieth century painting of a young mother sewing, with a little girl leaning on her knee, caught my eye. The painting depicted the mother's attention taken up by her sewing, while the child, leaning on her mom's lap, is gazing out of the picture toward the viewer. It's as if the two aren't involved with each other and yet they seem so connected. They looked so perfect: together yet apart.

For a moment, I'm seven again. I'm sitting very still on my mom's lap while she combs my curls, telling me how beautiful my hair is. "Much prettier than limp straight hair," she says. "You're the lucky one."

I'm startled by the realization that my mom was no older at that time than the young woman in the painting, and that when I was born, she was much younger than I am now. But for years I'd expected Mom to be my flawless, heroic mom, and *only* my mom. I'd forgotten that she was a woman before she became my mom. That she was both my mom as well as a flawed and, at times, desperately unhappy woman. I didn't need to create this mythic mom. I could love her with all her failings, just as she loved me despite mine. Her suicide did not diminish her love for me. It was only a result of her lack of love for herself.

I kept on strolling from gallery to gallery, observing the kids as much as the paintings. When the teachers finally announced lunch, I, too, scurried out to meet my sister at our agreed upon restaurant.

As it happened, the restaurant where we met was a small Viennese establishment our parents used to take us to whenever we went to visit the city's museums. It was especially known for the authentic Viennese pastries Mom had loved to indulge in. The place was just starting to fill up, so I chose a table in the corner with a view of the door so I could spot Daphne when she came in. I normally would have waited for her to join me before I sat at a table, feeling conspicuous when alone in a restaurant, but I ordered a glass of wine and sat back, savoring one of my favorite activities: people watching. Four young men in suits sat nearby, indulging in office gossip, and it was with some regret that I had to turn my attention to Daphne when she arrived.

"Guess what," she started as soon as she sat down. She took tickets out of her purse and waved them in the air. "I scored tickets to see *La Cage aux Folles* for your birthday treat. *House seats.* Gerald agreed to babysit the kids. The Saturday after your birthday. It'll be you and me kiddo."

"Must mean that Gerald's changing," I ventured.

"He's trying, and so am I. The therapist said that if we work at doing so, we can make a success of it. So, yes, we're both trying."

"I'm really happy for you, Daph. Truly. You deserve happiness. And your therapist is right. We can change, if we want to." We were quiet for a moment before I went on with something that just occurred to me. "I'm thinking of getting a dog."

She raised her thick eyebrows. "You? A dog?"

"Actually, I always kind of wanted a dog as a kid, don't you remember? It was Dad who didn't like dogs and wouldn't allow it. Mr. S told me that dogs open your heart and I think I'm ready for that. I need to find an attachment. Something to love."

"Wow," she marveled. "You sound, I don't know, different."

I raised my shoulders and grinned. "Not sure how much someone *can* change. But maybe I don't have to live with all the angst all the time. Maybe I can relax a little and just take things as they come."

Daphne looked pensive. "Yeah, people can change. Now let's eat. And I mean let's really eat."

I laughed as I ordered a burger, with a salad instead of chips. But I wouldn't eat the bun. There was a limit to how much change I was ready for.

# CHAPTER THIRTY-FIVE

When I returned home after my lunch with Daphne, I saw a Volvo station wagon with a Pennsylvania license plate parked outside my building. I walked up the stairs and stopped at Mr. S's apartment. The door was slightly ajar. The knowledge that Gramps wasn't there was still a sharp pain in my chest. I inhaled deeply and exhaled slowly.

"Anybody home?" I called.

"Come in, come in."

I recognized Andrew's voice and walked in gingerly. The furniture had tags on them.

Andrew came out from the bedroom. "Hi, so glad you stopped by. We're getting ready to clear the place so we can put it on the market. Most of the stuff is earmarked for Goodwill, but if there's anything you'd like, please feel free to take it."

I looked around and swallowed hard. All those years of saving the furniture with plastic on it, and to what end? So that they could be given away to Goodwill in good condition?

"My uncle would probably be *kvelling*, proud of how good this stuff is," Andrew said as if he'd read my mind.

"Yeah, I was just thinking the very same thing," I said. "Thanks, but there's nothing here really—" Then I spotted the photo on the mantle of a young girl, maybe five or six, swinging in midair, held by two strong hands. The face of the person holding her hands isn't visible, only that the hands are holding on tight. Her stocky little legs are in mid-air and her two blonde braids are sticking out of her head like wings, and her face is lit by a wide grin. She'd always reminded me of myself when I was that age.

"I was wondering," I started, pointing hesitantly at the photograph. "I know she's your cousin, but if you have other photos of her, I was wondering if I could have this one."

"Oh yes, little Rachel, or Rochale." He looked at me and at the photo. "Sure, you can have it."

"Thanks." I didn't know why I wanted this picture of a little girl I'd never known, but I grabbed it before he could change his mind. I looked around the apartment and for a second almost expected Gramps to appear in his kitchen, kettle in hand, wearing his Yoda smile. An involuntary sigh from deep within escaped my mouth, but I realized I'll always have those wonderful memories of him. They were mine to keep. Just like I'd always have his love. That would only die with me.

"Well, I better leave you to it," I said, turning to go.

"Thank you again for being so kind to my uncle. And please don't be a stranger. We'd love to have you visit us." He said it in the way such things are often said, knowing full well it would never happen.

Clutching the photo to my chest, I climbed the stairs. I walked in and scouted my apartment, and finally rested the photograph on my living room bookshelf. The little girl taking flight, being held up by loving hands. The photo had captured a perfect, happy, fleeting moment. It was a reminder that happiness could only be attained in moments. I went to the phone. If I was to get my happy moments, it was time to close the door on the unhappy ones.

I picked up the receiver and dialed Cecil's gallery number. He'd still be at work, unless he'd left early to get dressed for the Halloween parade, assuming he'd be going.

"Marika, so glad you called me back," he sounded sincerely pleased to hear me. "I've really wanted to talk to you."

"I'm not sure we have much to say to each other," I said, my voice cold and businesslike.

"Well, I do. I have quite a bit to say. Please?"

I'd never heard Cecil like that. Where was the cool, arrogant Cecil I'd fooled myself into wanting to marry? He said he was leaving work soon, and I agreed to meet him at a pub near my house. *Let him come to me.*

The pub was more crowded than it would normally have been at such an early hour. I figured everyone was getting into the Halloween spirit. I managed to grab a tiny, rickety table near the front. Every time the door opened, I got a whiff of cool wind in my face, but at least I'd be able to see Cecil upon arrival. For some reason, I thought it would put me at an advantage to see him first. When a youth with a riotous head of red hair came to get my drink order, I was on the verge of asking for a glass of wine, but decided it was best to lay off the stuff. Given my history, even a small amount of alcohol clouded my judgment. I asked for Perrier with a twist of lime. He squinted his eyes at me in disapproval before turning around and wiggling his tight ass as he went to get my drink.

A group of young men in lots of leather walked in and headed straight for the bar. I shifted slightly in my chair, still uncomfortable being alone at a bar, and was relieved when the next time the door opened it was a group of women students from the nearby university. They were immediately followed by Cecil and his unmistakable leonine head. His rectangular features, minus chin, seemed fuzzy and sketchy, as if they'd been eroded by ceaseless dissatisfaction. I could almost imagine what he'd look like as an older man, after the demise of his youthful beauty, and I felt a little sad for him.

I waved my hand, and he came right over. "Glad to see you. I was worried you would stand me up," he said, bending down and giving my cheek a dry little kiss.

The same young red haired man approached us, and Cecil ordered a gin and tonic. I stuck to my Perrier. "What? Giving up all your horrible vices?" he teased.

"Not really. I still like to shop," I retorted. Then I turned to the business at hand. "So, what did you want to talk to me about?" He looked startled. "I mean, let's not pretend that we're two old friends sharing a drink, okay? 'Cause we're really not." I smiled to soften my words.

"I thought we were friends," he started and stopped as his gin and tonic arrived. He lifted his tumbler, took a long drink, and grimaced. "Horrible swill. I should have specified the gin."

I wanted to laugh. I guessed he hadn't changed much if at this moment he was still focused on his liquor. "Why don't you order another?" I said.

"It's okay, this'll do. As you said, we're not here for pleasure."

"That we're not."

He cleared his throat. "I just need to explain things to you. That I never meant to hurt you is a given. I'm sorry that everything happened the way it did. Please believe that." He stopped.

I looked down at my hands. They were still. I was awash in calmness, but I found it hard to look at him, remembering the things he'd made me do. The drink gave me something to occupy my hands while I waited for him to continue with his confessional.

"I always felt that I was a little different, I thought that's what you liked about me. You know, for years I didn't really admit to myself that I was gay. I felt attraction for men, but I was also sometimes attracted to women. I was attracted to you. Prior to you, I hadn't had any sexual experiences and I convinced myself that I was straight, or *maybe* bi-sexual. Until … until a short time before we broke up. Which was, by the way, why I broke up with you three years ago."

"Why weren't you honest with me then? You let me think it was all my fault. That there was something wrong with *me*. I had to mature, you said. I was too clingy. And I believed you, I really did." Anger bubbled up inside me. I took a deep breath and exhaled. "Although you weren't totally wrong on that count."

"Don't you think I wanted to be honest? I wish I had been, but I just couldn't. I couldn't come out of the closet. As a matter of fact, I still haven't, not officially, and not to my parents." His eyes glistened and he blinked. "When we met again, by happenstance, and I realized you still wanted me, I thought it was a way out for me. I thought maybe we could marry so that I could please my parents, and you, and that you and I, we'd be a family, of sorts. Have kids, be a family," he repeated.

"Lovely," I said. "You, me, and your male lovers. Perfect recipe for happiness, like the British Bloomsbury group. Except I think there were a few suicides in that bunch."

"Look, I deserve your scorn, but people marry for all sorts of reasons. Love's just one of them. And, honestly, I never felt that you loved me in that way. I thought you wanted marriage for security more than anything else, that you needed me for your own reasons. So, from that perspective, we weren't that different."

"You're right." I felt humbled, and my anger dissipated. "We used each other. But I would have tried my best to be a good wife. And I would have been faithful. At least I wouldn't have gone into it planning on being *unfaithful*."

"No, you wouldn't have." He gulped the rest of his drink. "And for that I am truly sorry. I did love you, in my own way. Although I know it's not the way one ought to love a spouse. I know that sometimes I was unkind to you, but mostly it was because I was angry at myself, so I lashed out at you. You deserved better than that."

"I guess we both did." As I said that, I felt a weight lift off, a lightness of being. I no longer hated or resented him. I didn't have to carry the anger with me.

The bar was humming as the happy hour crowd got louder. "What will you do now? About your boyfriend, I mean," I asked, partly out of curiosity, but mostly because I realized that I really did care for Cecil.

"I don't know. We want to be together, but I'm not ready to come out of the closet to my parents. They'll never accept me that way. Never." He sounded so sad.

"Never is a long time," I said. I was thinking that I'd never thought I'd change, that I'd want to embrace love into my life. But now I couldn't wait for that special feeling to hit me. I was ready for the real thing pain and all.

"Maybe you're right, but I'm not holding my breath."

I looked around at the merrymakers. "Are you going to the Halloween parade?"

"Nah. Not this year."

Something about his stooped shoulders made my heart warm to him. I put my hand on his. I'd always admired his beautiful fingers. He looked up, his eyes brimming again.

There was nothing left to say, and I stood to leave. "Hey, we'll always have New York." I smiled.

He saluted me. "Here's looking at you, kid."

# CHAPTER THIRTY-SIX

It was just before the alarm rang, not quite six o'clock, when I awoke the next morning. Little doubts gnawed at me, dampening the excitement of the day ahead. I sprung out of bed and went to pull up the blinds. Foggy dew blanketed the window. It was going to be a cold day for my return from exile, the prodigal's return to work. My body was pulsating with exquisite anticipation mingled with apprehension. I made my bed and jumped into the shower. All out of hair product I simply gathered my unruly mop with a band and let the halo form around it. After a little vacillation, I put on a crisp white blouse, my black pencil skirt, black tights, and boots. My power shoulder-padded blazer completed my uniform. I grabbed a yogurt and apple from the fridge and went out in good time to walk, not run, to the subway.

My body was tingling, alert, as I breathed in the cold morning air. Every fiber of my being was hyper awake, as if I'd had caffeine infused into my veins, although I hadn't had my morning cup of coffee. The autumn sun seemed too bright, the sky too blue; even the people on subway sounded louder than normal. After the usual amount of jostling, the train stopped and I was heaved out at my station by the throngs. I remembered the day I'd seen Cecil on my way to work and the fall I took trying to catch him. I shook my head to get rid of that image and focused on the tasks that awaited me at work. My neglected clients, the staff, and, of course, there'd be Phoebe to deal with. I would have to face them all. What was it that my mom used to say? Something about always having to face the music.

I stopped to get my regular cup of coffee even though my stomach was jumpy enough without it. Near the clinic, I saw a small group of women hanging outside. I inhaled deeply and approached them.

"Oh, Marrrika, you back?" Carmen squealed with delight. "We miss you."

"Are you going to do the group again? It wasn't good without you, and Kumar cancelled it half the time," Cindy said with her usual dourness.

"We been meeting on our own when they canceled the group," someone else said.

"I hope you haven't been hanging outside the clinic. No loitering, you know," I blurted out, and immediately regretted it. "I'm really happy that you've been meeting, wherever. That's the whole point for the group, for you to support each other. But, yes, I'll be doing it again, as soon as possible," I promised, their excitement rubbing off on me.

"We may have to kick Dorie out. She been using and talking trash," Carmen said.

I took another deep breath. No, I wasn't in Kansas anymore and this wasn't Oz, or whatever, this was what it was: a mental health clinic with many broken people. I reassured them that I'd try to meet with them individually within the next few days, and pushed the buzzer for Theresa to let me in.

A rancid, musty smell greeted me when I entered the gloomy waiting room. Funny how I'd gotten so used to it that I hadn't smelled it anymore. The puke green walls and torn linoleum floors made me queasy. That our patients had to wait here daily for their treatment was a shame. Maybe I could talk Phoebe into loosening the purse strings and splurging on a little paint job and new linoleum.

Theresa's dark hair appeared at the nursing station window. "And she's back," she announced.

Passing through the waiting room, I saw one or two unfamiliar faces in the crowd waiting for their medication. Derrick hadn't mentioned admitting new clients, but, then again, I hadn't even thought to ask.

She buzzed me in and I stopped at her office door. "Not much has changed, has it," I said. "I actually missed this joint."

"What? The chaos? The patients? Or us?" She cackled.

"Yes, all of it."

"Well, good, 'cause it's all been waiting for you. As well as charts galore. Next month we have the Joint Commission inspection, so fasten your seatbelt." Good old Theresa, nothing was to be taken too seriously.

I raised my shoulders. "It is what it is."

"Wow, you've turned philosophical or what?" She chuckled. "Anyway, how are you?" She looked straight into my eyes.

"I'm good. Never felt better in my life." I knew that eventually I'd have to tell her the real reason for my sick leave, but it could wait. I just wanted to get to my office and start the day before having to face everyone with all their questions about my month off. And there was the dreaded back-to-work interview with Phoebe to get through.

On the way to my office, I popped my head into Kumar's and Dinesh's cubicles. I was surprised to see them sitting at their desks, heads down, writing in charts.

"Marika." Dinesh rose when he saw me. I thought he was going to offer me his hand, but they remained limp by his sides. "I am so happy you are back." His face split in a wide smile, before a little frown appeared. "You are okay, right? You look very fine."

"I am fine, Dinesh. It's good to be back, and good to see you."

"Welcome back, boss. Your hair looks different, you changed it. No more blow dry," Kumar said, his head tilted to the side, inspecting my gathered curls with awe. "We are having an inspection next month. We have been working hard on the charts. See?" He pointed proudly to the open charts on his desk.

Yes, they had my back after all.

Derrick's door was shut, so I went to my office and unlocked the door. A fresh, earthy odor hit me. On my desk was a bouquet of yellow chrysanthemums, held together by a string, plonked into a coffeepot serving as a makeshift vase. I assumed the flowers were from the staff as there was no card attached. What an unusual choice. These yellow flowers symbolized friendship and cheerfulness, not a trait I was associated with. I stuck my nose into the bouquet and inhaled their herby, rather than sweet, aroma. But to me they smelled sweeter than any flower.

I settled at my desk and eyed my overflowing in-box. In my pre-furlough days, I'd been in the habit of leaving things to linger there for a long time, the idea being that eventually whatever was pressing would be dealt with, and all the other items would either have resolved themselves or would no longer need resolution. But today I set out to address all the problems. I was thus occupied in completing a form sent to us from the Joint Commission when Derrick appeared in my doorway.

"Hey, who's your admirer?" he asked, nodding towards the flowers.

"I thought it was from the staff," I said, slightly disappointed that they weren't from him.

He tugged at his dreadlocks. "Eh, we should have thought of it. Sorry. But no. Unless they went behind my back."

"Maybe I have a secret admirer," I wiggled my eyebrows up and down.

He smiled. "How're you settling in?"

"Having fun with my in-box, ha-ha."

"Well, don't get too comfy with it. I was on the phone with Phoebe and she asked that you come see her as soon as you got here." I felt the familiar fluttering in my stomach. "Now, don't tie yourself into knots," he said, as if he could see my insides. "She may be a pill, but she liked you enough not to fire you."

"And I have you to thank for that." I felt my face flush. "Truly, I don't think I thanked you properly for that. And for other things." I was thinking of Gramps and how kind and helpful Derrick had been.

"You can thank me by going out to dinner with me tonight."

I gulped. "Sure, but not a date; we're not allowed to date."

He stuck his hands into his jeans pockets. "We'll call it a business meeting, okay?"

\*\*\*

I stood outside Phoebe's door and inhaled. Oddly, though, my pulse wasn't racing as it normally did before a meeting with the old bat Standing there, I realized that even if she had fired me, or if she did so in the future, I would survive. I'd survived the death of my parents, of Gramps, and of Rosie. Losing a job would not be the end of the world. In the larger scheme of things, this was nothing for me to be afraid of. I knocked on her door energetically.

"Come!" Her husky voice beckoned me in.

I opened the door and walked in. "Hi, Phoebe," I said. Her eyebrows shot up. This was probably the first time I had ever addressed her by her name, having usually avoided calling her by any name.

Her eyes narrowed and she surveyed me up and down. "You're looking rested. Come sit down." She pointed at the stiff-backed chair across her desk and I complied. I looked at her ramrod straight back with new admiration. I would never like her, but I had fresh appreciation for the job she was doing. It couldn't have been easy to have attained her position in the medical field, which in her day was occupied mostly by men.

One corner of her mouth went up, her version of a smile. "Do you know what yellow chrysanthemums symbolize?" She went on without waiting for an answer. "Friendship, as well as energy, joy, and intelligence."

My mouth opened wide. "*You* got me the flowers?"

"Don't look so surprised. I decided that you—we—needed a fresh start."

"I … I so appreciate you giving me this second chance," I said, humbled. "I am feeling energized to tackle my job. And really, the whole pot thing, I hardly know—"

She waved her hand in the air. "I may not have always shown you all the support you needed, although I did recognize your abilities, even if you didn't exactly exude confidence and optimism." A little chuckle escaped her lips. "I thought you would have understood that I held you in high regard, having promoted you at such a young age. My goodness, I was in my forties before I had my first managerial position. What I didn't realize was that you needed more direction, mentoring, rather than just directives. My mistake."

194

I was at a loss for words. I blinked back tears and ran my fingers through my curly mop. "Thank you, Phoebe. I … I think I've had some maturing to do, but I won't let you down."

"Good. That settles that. Now, as you know, we've got a major inspection coming up next month. Let's meet next week and discuss your plans for tackling all that needs to be done. It has come to my attention that there are some problems with more than a few of the charts," she said in her usual manner, but I thought I detected a sly grin on her face.

After reassuring her that while we did have a lot of work ahead in the coming weeks, I was up for the task, I left. Here was a side of Phoebe I hadn't seen before. My fault. I felt gratified at being needed. I wanted to tell Derrick about my meeting, but again his office door was shut. Theresa had finished medicating for the day and was busy closing the book and locking up. I went back to my office, rummaging in my mind for ideas on how to tackle the preparation for the upcoming inspection. I started by drawing up a graphic worksheet with chart names and necessary data to serve as a checklist for progress, and was so immersed in what I was doing that I hadn't noticed it was lunchtime. I picked up the phone to dial Theresa to ask if she wanted to go out for lunch, but she didn't answer. Then my intercom buzzed. It was Derrick asking me to come to his office. I took a quick scan of my face in my compact mirror. Nothing had changed. I still had the same cheekbones, pale skin, blue eyes. No make-up, but what difference did it make? Derrick had seen me snot-nosed and all.

His door was still uncharacteristically closed when I got to his office, and I knocked before entering. The entire staff was there, but the first thing I saw was a chocolate cake on his desk, decorated with lettering in rainbow colors. Last time I'd seen a rainbow decorated cake was as a child; Mom had loved making rainbow-colored frosting. Before I could process the whole scene, everyone trilled in unison, "Welcome back."

I felt myself blush profusely. "You're a couple of weeks early for my birthday."

"Relax. We all know how superstitious you are about celebrating before your birthday. This is a welcome back cake," Theresa said, wielding a huge knife in the air. "We've been waiting for this all morning. But first, speech!"

"Speech?"

"You must tell us how you are feeling," Dinesh said, a bright smile showing his white teeth. "You look very good. Healthy."

"Tell us what was wrong with you," Kumar chimed in.

It was the moment I'd been expecting, for God alone knew what sort of unfounded rumors had surfaced about the reasons for my prolonged absence.

"Later everybody," Derrick said with his smooth voice. "Let's eat cake!"

I felt the tightness leave my body and I took the huge slice of cake Theresa offered me.

"I want to see you finish this," she chortled.

"Thank you all for being so ... welcoming," I said, a lump forming in my throat. "I'm sorry if I haven't always been a very ... supportive or understanding supervisor."

"But you were very right about the patients and the charts," Dinesh said.

"Most always," Kumar corrected, the corners of his eyes crinkling.

"Oh, yes, we're going to have lots of fun with those charts in the next few weeks," I said, rolling my eyes mischievously.

"And she's back," Theresa said. That was followed by laughter all around, including myself.

Yes, I was back. Still the same Marika, yet hopefully an improved version.

# ~EPILOGUE~

It is Sunday, my thirtieth birthday. I am sitting in Washington Square Park. Around me are students from the nearby university, walking in pairs or alone, talking, laughing, but mostly hurrying to their destinations. It is a gorgeous, brilliantly sunny late fall day; the tree limbs are bare and the air is crisp. The fallen leaves cover the ground in yellow, red, and orange hues; they make crunching sounds as kids jump and people trod on them. This may be one of the last days of the season when it is still warm enough to sit outside comfortably without bundling up. How I love New York. What a delight it is to look around and relish the life around me. A man passing by smiles at me and I think that I must make a nice picture, a young woman sitting on a bench, her face to the sun, her face ringed by wild curls.

I'm waiting for Derrick, who's taking me out for my birthday lunch. There will be no engagement ring for my birthday, but I have a proper date.

I see him in the distance as he walks towards me. He moves smoothly, as if his limbs are made of liquid. He's all wrong for me — on paper. Or that's what Mom would have said. He's the wrong religion, the wrong color, and even the wrong nationality. Perhaps she would have approved of his profession. I chuckled inwardly. Still, I'm inclined to think that he may be very right for me, at least right now. I've given up trying to visualize the future. He's dropped hints at planning a vacation together, to Jamaica.

"Been waiting long?" he asks. The dimple his smile conjures is still outrageous.

I shake my head. "If you only knew how long I've been waiting," I say enigmatically and smile.

# About the Author

 Judy was born and raised in Israel. When she was a teenager, she moved to the U.S with her family. She graduated from Columbia University with a Master's in Clinical Social Work and worked as a psychotherapist for many years before turning her life-long passion for and love of books into writing.

Her experiences as a therapist in a methadone program became the background for *Marika's Best Laid Plan*. Judy infuses her novels with the therapist's keen observation of human nature. She loves to write about people and all their foibles, which make them relatable and loveable.

Her career also included a stint in Jamaica where she taught at the University of the West Indies. She now lives in San Diego with her Jamaican-born husband. She spends her spare time writing, painting, walking the local beaches and trails, and cooking Israeli food with a Jamaican twist. She's also trying very hard to keep the flowers in her garden alive.

www.judystanigar.com
https://www.facebook.com/JudyStanigarTheAuthor
https://twitter.com/JvStanigar

Made in the USA
Middletown, DE
22 December 2021

56746676R00116